A
Reckoning

A novel by

MAY SARTON

W · W · NORTON & COMPANY · INC ·
New York

Copyright © 1978 by May Sarton
Published simultaneously in Canada by George J. McLeod Limited, Toronto.
Printed in the United States of America.
All Rights Reserved
First Edition
Library of Congress Cataloging in Publication Data
Sarton, May, 1912–
    A reckoning.

    I. Title.
PZ3.S249Re 1978 [PS3537.A832] 813'.5'2 78–9691
ISBN 0–393–08828–6

1 2 3 4 5 6 7 8 9 0

Chapter I

Walking down Marlboro Street in Boston, Laura Spelman saw the low brick houses, the strong blue sky, the delicate shape of the leafless trees, even the dirty lumps of snow along the curb as so piercing in their beauty that she felt a little drunk. She now knew that she was panting not because she was overweight, but because her lungs had been attacked. "I shan't need to diet, after all." The two blocks she had to walk from Jim Goodwin's office seemed long. She stopped twice to catch her breath before she reached her little car. Safely inside, she sat there for a few moments sorting out the jumble of feelings her interview with Dr. Goodwin had set whirling. The overwhelming one was a strange excitement, as though she were more than usually alive, awake, and in command: I am to have my own death. I can play it my own way. He said two years, but they always give you an outside figure, and my guess is at most a year. A year, one more spring, one more summer. . . . I've got to do it well. I've got to *think*.

She needed to get home as fast as possible. She started off, swinging out into the street so quickly a passing taxi nearly hit her. "In your own way, Laura, you idiot!" she said aloud. "Sudden death on Marlboro Street would never do!"

A half hour later she was standing at her own front door in Lincoln, fumbling for the key, and greeted by excited barks from inside. For the first time since Dr. Goodwin's verdict she froze, immobilized by a sharp pain in her chest, but the barking was hysterical now and she finally found the keyhole, opened the door, and knelt down to hug Grindle, the old sheltie, and to accept his moist tongue licking her face, licking the tears away as he had done when Charles died.

"Oh, Grindle, what are we going to do? What are we going to do?" Leaving Grindle and Sasha, the cat, was going to be the worst.

"Grindle," she said severely, "I've got to get over this right now. Stop licking, and I'll stop crying."

Sensing the change of tone, Grindle went and curled up in his bed, the pricked ears following her movements as she stumbled to her feet.

She went to the kitchen, poured herself a glass of claret, and took it into the library where she put a Mozart flute concerto on the player. She lay down on the sofa with her hands behind her head and reasoned it out. Grindle would go to Brooks and Ann, her son and daughter-in-law. Their children loved him. Sasha, shy and intense—what about her?

There were going to be some things so awful she must begin now to learn how to set them aside. One part of her being was going to have to live only in the present, as she did when Sasha jumped up and began to knead her chest. Laura pushed her off to one side where loud purrs vibrated all along her thigh. She felt herself sinking down, down into the music, the flute calling like a celestial bird with a thousand songs instead of only one in its silver throat. While she listened, she absorbed the brilliance of the light, light reflected from snow outside so that the room itself was bathed in a cool fire. Grindle gave a long sigh as he fell asleep in his corner, and Laura felt joy rising, filling her to the brim, yet not overflowing. What had become almost uncontrollable grief at the door seemed now a blessed state. It was not a state she could easily define in words. But it felt like some extraordinary dance, the dance of life itself, of atoms and molecules, that had never been as beautiful or as poignant as at this instant, a dance that must be danced more carefully and with greater fervor to the very end.

Poor Mamma, she thought, sitting up. She has been deprived of this. She is stumbling to her death, only half-conscious, if conscious at all, of what is going on. Her attachments now are only to those who serve her, Mary whom she hates and Annabelle whom she loves—ambivalent to the end.

Laura pulled herself back from those thoughts of her mother, so terribly grand—and so terrible, thoughts that always had mixed her up, made her feel uncentered, at a loss. Lay them aside now, Laura, you'll never solve that mystery before you die.

I shall have to tell Jo—and Daphne, of course. But Jo, the eldest of the three sisters, was the stumbling block: powerful, blunt Jo, wrapped up in her job; she had late in her life taken over the presidency of a small women's college. She repeated these facts about Jo, turning them over in her mind. No, she wouldn't tell Jo for a while. Besides, was there a real connection?

Here the record stopped. Without music, the house, the room where she sat became suddenly empty. I'm not scared exactly, but if there is no real connection with my sister, who is there? What is there? Only now did the full impact of Dr. Goodwin's verdict reach Laura, and she began to shake. Her hands were ice-cold. Fear had replaced the strange elation she had felt at first, and she rose and paced up and down, then leaned her forehead against the icy window for a moment. I'm not ready, she thought, I can't do it alone. But I want to do it alone, something deep down answered. And even deeper down she knew that she would have to do it alone. Dying—no one talked about it. We are not prepared. We come to it in absolute ignorance. But even as the tears splashed down on her hands, or perhaps because their flow had dissolved the awful tension of fear, Laura felt relief. After all, she told herself, we meet every great experience in ignorance ... being born, falling in love, bearing a first child. . . . always there is terror first.

In the few seconds of silence it had become clear that she was going to have to reckon with almost everything in a new way. "It is then to be a reckoning." And Laura realized that at this moment she felt closer to Mozart and Chekov than she did to her own sister. "I shall not pretend that this is not so. There isn't time. The time I have left is for the real connections."

The real connections? The question aroused such strange answers, all beating their wings in her mind, that she lay back again and waited for all this to quiet down or sort itself out.

Tell the children? No, not yet. Ben, so far away in California, struggling with his painting; Brooks still taking his father's death hard, that sudden death only three years ago; Daisy in New York with her lover, working long hours. But Laura knew she would have to tell Brooks and Ann pretty soon—they lived only a mile away. The children—the last thing she wanted or needed was to think about them, though she was leaving them in the lurch, of course. But I just can't cope with all that today, she thought. Family. I'm not asked to cope with it today.

Disposing of the house, things, money, lawyers—oh, dear, she had thought only of dying with grace, of making a good death, but not of all the affairs involved, the decisions! Tomorrow—not today.

Today, "the real connections."

Chapter II

What were the real connections? It was startling to see suddenly that in a strange way they had dropped out after her marriage because there appeared to have been no time and little energy for the kind of exploration in depth that she had found in the intense friendships of her youth—especially with Ella, the incomparable Ella of the year in Paris at the Sorbonne. But was it only that Ella was extraordinary, a kind of spiritual twin, or was it that adult life consumes the wide margins of time in which such relationships flourish? For they demand endless hours of talk, and when is there time later on?

When the children were small and she and Charles could snatch a moment together late at night, they had talked about how family life absorbs everything for years. Certain phrases came back to haunt: "We hardly ever see anyone anymore." "I never have time to write a letter even." "It's rather like being on a desert island with three wildly energetic lunatics." They had laughed about it, sitting by the fire with the ritual night cap before they fell into bed and curled round each other, too tired for another word.

It is the whole inner world, Laura thought, that gets

absorbed as life itself pulls us away from contemplation into action. As Laura considered all this she felt deprived. Yet when the children had left home, she had not chosen to read and think, nor had she even gone to England for a long visit with Ella as she had imagined she might. She had instead gotten herself a job at Houghton Mifflin, first to write jacket material and do odd jobs, then as copy editor, and finally in the last few years as one of the fiction editors. It had been a rewarding job, stretching her mind and her heart, and there had been real connections with her authors, intense while they lasted, while a book was being worked on, but not lasting, not to be built on in a permanent sense. There had, really, been little time for friends. Charles worked hard at the bank and was often away for meetings in New York and Washington. So, even though they were asked out to dinner two or three times a week and had people in, "real connections" in the way she saw them now had been few.

In the last few years Charles had been the only person with whom she shared her life on the deepest level, and—equally important—on the most trivial; but because he was a man there were areas of her being that she could not share with him. He was not good about discussing feelings, for instance.

Only with Ella, when they were young, had Laura been able to discuss why it was so hard to be a woman, their fears and resentments at being caught up in a web of sensuality they didn't want or understand. Sex at that time in their lives had been too frightening, too much of a muddle—Ella's word, "muddle"—and the cause sometimes of gusts of laughter when they talked about their fumbling, embarrassed response to any overtures from the men who took them dancing. They had been fighting, Laura supposed, to achieve some sense of identity before being swept up into someone else's needs and desires. "Why does Ed want to kiss me when he doesn't even know me as a person?" Ella had cried out. And why did these memories of that painful land of innocence come back now with such force? For they had been almost incredibly innocent, prepared in no way to take pleasure in their own bodies. All bodily functions were treated as faintly disagreeable by Sybille, of course. Anything below the waist one pretended not to notice! But even as Laura smiled, she recognized the aura of sensuality, of passion even, that had surrounded her and Ella, although it was never played out except in those ravishing kisses they pretended were "quite all right." About that they did not talk. It might have been dangerous.

The sensuality had remained a buried treasure, a secret world, for soon enough Ella had married, and Laura had spent two years in bed in Switzerland with TB. And after that, Charles, dear Charles who had taken her finally out of Sybille's power, had set her free, given her a body to rejoice in, lifted her out into real life at last.

When Charles died Laura realized—and it had been painful—that a good marriage shuts out a very great deal; she became for months simply what was left of another person, what was left of "two together." It had been painful to discover that invitations to dinner parties became fewer and fewer, and she herself, without Charles, no longer wanted to make the effort. For months she had been stranded in a limbo of grief and loss, making a desperate struggle to come to terms with what was left of her self. Without the children it would have been absolute desolation—without her sister, Daphne, who came and stayed for a month, without Aunt Minna to whom she could run for shelter whenever she felt the tide of grief rising too high.

At that time Grindle began to sleep on Laura's bed. He was quite hard to lift, but he was huggable and gave her the physical warmth she needed most of all. Those were the nights she ached in every bone of her body for Charles, tossed and turned in her bed, as though she would never rest again, and patient Grindle got up, turned around, and flopped down again with a groan of pleasure beside her. Sometimes Sasha leaped in through the open window and lay down on the other side. Sometimes then they all three slept till dawn, when Laura woke with lead in her limbs, wondering how to meet another day, turned on the light, and read whatever manuscript Houghton Mifflin had given her to work on.

"What am I going to tell *them?*" Since Charles's death Laura found she talked aloud to herself or to Grindle. She was working now on a rather interesting book, a novel by a young woman who was wrestling with a difficult subject, clearly autobiographical, about a young Lesbian facing the problem of how to deal with her parents and their violent opposition to her life-style. Laura had really wished to help this author, to make the book as good as it might be. Harriet Moors was not going to be easy to help, she surmised. There was too much pain, too much conflict, here. And would there be time?

"Do I want to go on working?" Laura asked herself. "How can I know? How can I know what it's going to be like?"

She supposed she must either withdraw into dying or live her life as well as she could until she had to give up. "Dying is living, and living is dying, Grindle." Yes, the point was to give up the nonessential, but to hold fast to the essential—and Laura felt sure she could go her way for a few weeks without anyone's knowing. She had taken a few days off with the excuse that she had some sort of virus, and in fact that was how she had explained to herself the lassitude and strange, stifled feeling in her chest. Next week she would go back to the office.

That decision came easy; on the strength of it she got up and made herself a sandwich and a cup of tea. "It's all in God's hands, Grindle," she said, taking a cheese biscuit out of the box for the dog who had followed her into the kitchen. It's because our relations with animals are so simple that they are such a comfort, she thought. No neurotic hostilities and angers in Grindle's eyes; for him cheese biscuits were the be-all and end-all for the moment.

This, Laura decided, was to be a day of just such simple being. After lunch she took Grindle for a walk, delighted as always by the intensity with which he followed his nose, emitting sharp barks as he discovered the scent of a skunk or raccoon and went tearing off, up and down through snowdrifts, and back to her to bark his news.

When they returned it was nearly three, and the light was already fading as the sun dipped behind tall pines at the end of the field. Inside, the house was dark, the winter chill creeping in. Laura lit the fire before going to her desk and pulling out Harriet Moors' novel.

She had forgotten everything in her absorption in the text before her and was startled when the phone rang. It was Aunt Minna, asking what the doctor had said. Taken by surprise, Laura was unable to answer coherently.

"May I come over, Aunt Minna?" she managed to ask after bumbling along about "nothing serious."

"Of course, dear. I'll have tea ready by the time you get here. Dress warmly, won't you? It's cold out."

There was no one else in the world who would remind her to dress warmly, no one else who had known her as a child, Laura thought, as she wrapped a scarf round her throat and put on her duffle. And there was no house now that had remained as it always was except Aunt Minna's white cottage behind its picket fence. It looked very much like the other houses on the street, and its unpretentious faded velvet Victorian sofas and chairs, its sepia photographs of olive groves in Italy, were probably not unlike those in the other houses; but the spirit that inhabited this house was unique. Minna Hornaday, Laura's father's sister, had always been a maverick, the odd one in a solid, conservative family, her brother, a foreign service officer in the State Department, and she a *sui generis* political force without official position—"a persuasive lunatic" her brother called her when she fought for the League of Nations and later helped organize the League of Women Voters. She ended up as a radical pacifist and antiwar agitator during Vietnam.

But Aunt Minna was more than her activities, more interesting. She had a genius for friendship, for touching people of all ages, for being able to communicate vividly and instantly across the barriers of age, language, class with anyone and everyone. She had a freshness, a zest for life, an expectant innocence that is the province of old maids of authentic genius.

Only since her eightieth birthday had there been the slightest diminution of energy. She wore a hearing aid now, but her gray eyes were as penetrating as ever. She still walked to town on good days, carrying a cane which she waved at oncoming cars, delighted to stop the traffic all by herself. She still resisted the idea of any live-in help. An elderly cleaning woman came twice a week and did some laundry as well as dusting around, but Minna declared that the very idea of someone's lurking about the house all day and fussing at her·when she did risky things, like climbing the ladder to get a book from the top shelf of her study, "would induce nervous breakdown or murder in a week."

Laura had opened the gate and run up the porch steps many times with some problem only Aunt Minna could possibly understand, but this time was different. She stood inside the gate for several moments, totally at sea as to how to tell Aunt Minna, or whether to tell her at all. But then the door opened, and Aunt Minna called out, "Hurry up, Laura, don't just stand there. You'll catch your death!"

Laura smiled at the irony of this and closed the gate behind her. Then there was the bustle of getting off coat and boots, admiring the pink cyclamen—"from an admirer," Aunt Minna said with a twinkle, "that boy who comes to shovel the path. He's quite a dear, borrows books, and loves to discuss things"—and settling down on the sofa with a cup of hot tea and a cookie beside her on the little table.

"You're out of breath," Aunt Minna observed, giving her a sharp look. "What did that young Dr. Goodwin say? He really seems awfully young to me. Do you think he knows his business?"

"Yes," Laura said, glad to embark on a subject other than her own state of health, "I think he's a good doctor, and humane."

"These viruses are devilish. Nothing seems to help but rest and patience. But who can rest these days? Still, you are a lot more patient than I am!"

But Laura could not respond. She felt frozen before the enormity of her news, locked into it, unable to extricate herself. Why had she ever come?

"It's not a virus?" Aunt Minna asked, putting her own cup down.

"No, it's cancer of both lungs and it's too far along for an operation to be of any use. Cobalt treatments, the maximum, might hold things up for a few months. I said no to that." Laura spoke these words without lifting her eyes, spoke them rapidly and loudly.

"My dear girl—"

"Well, it's a very strange feeling."

"You're not going to let yourself die without a fight, are you? Cobalt can work miracles. Why did you say no to it?"

The sharp attack was unexpected, and Laura reacted with anger. "It's my death, Aunt Minna, and I shall have it my way, God damn it." Then she added, "I should have said, God bless it. I believe that people should be allowed their real deaths."

" 'Do not go gentle into that good night.' " Aunt Minna had flushed with emotion, and her voice cracked a little as she repeated the famous line.

"It's too big—too important for romantic bluster."

"Yes, I suppose it is." There was a long pause. Aunt Minna took a swallow of tea, then, "You shouldn't be mortally ill. I should be. It's all wrong. It's a mistake. You're only sixty, Laura!"

"Yes, but . . ."

"But what?"

"I don't know how to tell you, but when Dr. Goodwin explained things—he did it very well, by the way, I admired his courage and tact—I had a moment of extraordinary excitement. Death must be the other great adventure, the way through somewhere just as birth is. I felt terribly excited, and when I walked down Marlboro Street to my car, every brick and tree looked so beautiful, I could hardly bear it. The blue sky—"

But Aunt Minna had withdrawn. Her eyes were closed. Laura was not sure whether she had heard.

"The trouble is I can't put it into words."

"Go on," Aunt Minna murmured. But then she opened

her eyes, very bright. "You can't have experienced everything. I'm not ready to die. I don't want to, not a bit. Every day something happens I wouldn't have missed for anything."

Laura couldn't help laughing at the intensity with which these words were spoken. "You're marvelous, that's all. And we don't have to talk about it anymore."

"Oh, but we must. You appear to be on an express train into infinity—and there's a great deal I have to say."

"I'm not going to tell the children for a while. I expect to go on working for a month or two, but," Laura said quietly, "I also want just to *be*. Just to watch the light on the wall. Play music. Read the things I want to read. Cut out the nonessential."

"You're talking about living, not dying."

"Am I?" Laura was startled. "Yes, I suppose I am."

"I feel the need for a strong drink," Aunt Minna announced. "You might fetch the bottle of brandy on the second shelf in the pantry and bring two small glasses."

While Laura was in the kitchen, she became aware of having been the bearer of evil tidings to a very old woman. She had been thinking of herself, not of Aunt Minna, of the shock for *her*, and now she felt dismayed by what she had done. It was all very well to talk about having one's own death, but the truth was that this was not possible, for one's own death is inevitably a burden and a problem for everyone else. We can't die alone.

"Thanks, dear. Let's sip a little brandy and talk sensibly. Of course you are absolutely heroically brave."

"No, no, I'm not. I just have to think of it as a journey, but out there in the kitchen I realized that it's not a journey anyone can make alone—other people are involved. And that *is* awful."

"The first thing is to find someone who can live in, cook and so forth. Do it right away so she gets to know you before you are really ill."

"I don't want anybody living in. Hovering about." The very idea brought on panic.

"If you're going to do it your way, you've got to plan *now.*"

"Oh, Aunt Minna, that's just what you said when I decided to spend a winter in Paris . . . do you remember? That was forty years ago. You made me see I had to go to the Sorbonne, not just drift around in bookstores. You were right, of course."

"I don't think Sybille ever quite got over my intervention."

"I've always wondered—was that what brought on the cool?"

"Maybe. I went right to your father and persuaded him that you were intelligent enough to be trusted with your own life. Nowadays children run all over Europe with knapsacks, but forty years ago, trips to Europe by young girls were chaperoned. Really, it was quite astonishing that Dwight agreed."

"Mamma was terribly upset. We were on the brink of coming home from all those years of wandering about. She was afraid we would never settle down into tame old Boston. And really only Jo wanted to. She plunged into Radcliffe like a duck into water." Laura sipped her brandy and looked into the fire. "What was it really about, you and Mamma?"

"I don't know."

"There is so much I still have to try to understand. Shall I *ever* understand Mamma?"

"Mothers and daughters—it's not really a very easy relationship, is it?"

[21

"What was your mother like?"

"Adorable, witty, neurotic I suppose ... the most wholly alive person I've ever known."

"Then why do you say it wasn't an easy relationship?"

"I cared too much. Our father—whom you never knew—was a rigid, rather stupid man, and when I was a child I saw my mother as a caged bird. I felt the wings beating against the bars in *myself*—I overempathized. That is one of the hazards of being a daughter."

"Why a hazard?"

"The child knows too much in some ways and too little in others—children really have an awfully hard time. You, Jo, and Daphne were no exception."

"We were lucky to have an aunt." Laura began to feel very tired, but she couldn't bear the idea of going home, not just yet. Here was warmth, the safe enclosure, love. She felt Aunt Minna's presence to be as much a cordial as the brandy.

"Sybille might have been a great actress," Aunt Minna ruminated. "She had the carriage, the beauty—oh, yes, the glamour! The way she wore her clothes, the theatrical lilt of her voice. But people who act offstage are troubling, troubled people, I fear."

"Do you really think so?"

"I know so." Aunt Minna was nothing if not definite.

"She was so beautiful," Laura said in a faint voice.

"You all three have it, too—those blue eyes. But luckily for you your good looks did not have the fatal glamour, the something larger than life, unattainable, like a goddess. You could be human."

"Yet I wonder whether we ever really were—or are. So much rage, so much energy went into revolt. It took us so long to grow up—and maybe Daphne never will." Laura got up and went to the window. It was dark now, and what she saw was the roof reflected, and herself, looking as white and exhausted as she felt. "Here I am sixty and I still haven't solved the riddle of Sybille, nor shall I ever." She went and kissed Aunt Minna lightly. "And it's time I drove home."

"We haven't settled anything," Aunt Minna said, sighing deeply. But she wasn't going to give up. "Laura, you simply must look for a housekeeper. Promise?"

"I'll think about it."

At the gate she turned back to wave and saw Aunt Minna peer out, unsmiling, give a brief wave, then turn away. It was bad to think of her alone now heating up some soup, having to bear the weight of what Laura had had to tell her. It was cold in the car, and Laura shivered. Home seemed eons away across the snow, but in the little cocoon, simply on her way, with nothing to do, nothing in her power to do, in the grip of a process over which she could have no control, except to let it take its course, Laura felt herself slipping down into some great current—and relaxed. Will could have no part to play here.

Life had lately sometimes felt interminable, an interminable struggle—the excitement, even relief, she had experienced when Dr. Goodwin told her the truth of her condition stemmed perhaps from the fact that setting a limit gave her a sudden sense of freedom. She did not have to try so hard any longer. In a way she realized this was what she had felt during her pregnancies, that she could let life do it, for a change—and now she could let death do it. She was carrying death inside her as she had once carried life, as the little car she was driving was carrying her—home.

Chapter III

Laura was wakened out of a dream by Grindle's soft, wet tongue licking her hand. It had been such a beautiful dream, she and Charles lying under pine trees somewhere, such a dream of warmth and communion, that she hated having to come back to the chilly morning. But Grindle was wide-awake and wanted to go out, so Laura got up, staggering, her eyes glued together, put on a wrapper, and went downstairs, the dog thumping down ahead of her.

"Out you go, impatient animal!"

The freezing air hit her like a blow. That pressure in her chest seemed to be settling in. I must get used to it and pay no attention, she thought, and no doubt hot coffee would help. She went back to bed then with a cup and let the day flow in. The gray light was gradually turning to amber on the walls as the sun rose above the trees. Because for the first time she sensed a touch of panic, Laura decided to go into the office and if possible see Harriet Moors. At present she felt strongly that she must be active, do whatever she could, keep the panic away. Not death but dying brought on the panic, the process now beginning its inexorable course inside her lungs. How did one deal with that? Was the whole of her being dying or only one part of it? And could she hold that part of her insulated against all the rest? Mind, heart, whatever she, the person, might be?

For a time she imagined that she could. She went down to her desk, found Harriet Moors' number, and called, for she seemed to remember that Miss Moors had a job, and she had better get to her before eight if so. Harriet Moors sounded rather frail and frightened at first but seemed delighted to accept a half-past eleven appointment at Houghton Mifflin.

"What about your job?"

"I can take an early lunch hour."

"I can have a sandwich sent in if that would help."

Laura did not have the courage to walk Grindle before she left. She was afraid that her little provision of energy would simply melt away in that cold air. After all, she had gone to see Jim Goodwin because she felt very queer and had been losing weight. The diagnosis certainly didn't make her feel any better, physically, and she had to admit this morning that it was going to be difficult even to pretend to lead her own life pretty soon. So why take in a perfect stranger, why insist on seeing Harriet Moors? Laura thought about it as she drove into Boston, but why analyze? She had felt that this was an interesting novel with an important theme, one not touched on before. And she had felt involved, she didn't know quite why—Ben, of course, and the fact that he had never discussed his private life with either her or Charles—they had all managed to avoid admitting the truth to one another.

She felt quite strange when she finally reached the office and sat down in her chair by a window looking out on the Common. Had it been only four days since she had called Dr. Goodwin from here? She felt she was returning from a long journey; the familiar Common was suddenly a magic scene, one she had dreamed of—children skating on the frog pond, the elegant outlines of the elms against snow, one old man feeding pigeons from a bench even in this bitter cold.

"How are you?" Dinah, the secretary she shared with Alan Price, looked in, her arms full of the day's mail. She dumped a pile on the desk.

"Rotten, I feel absurdly weak. You know these viruses, how they hang on."

"What did the doctor say?"

"To take it easy for several weeks. So I'll work at home as much as I can." Laura found it simple to conceal the truth. It had not been a decision, but the casual tone felt right. Time enough to throw a monkey wrench into the works.

"I'd be grateful if you would run through the mail, Dinah. I'm expecting that Harriet Moors in a few minutes. It will be a longish interview, I expect, and I'll go home after it."

"You shouldn't have come in, Laura. For heaven's sake!"

"Oh, well, that girl is nervous as a witch about her book."

Dinah shook her head. "And that's 'taking it easy'? Let me get you a cup of coffee, anyway."

Laura found even this modicum of attentive kindness hard to bear. She turned away quickly and took Harriet Moors' novel out of her briefcase, along with the notes she had jotted down yesterday, some of which she found as usual quite illegible. But this should not, anyway, be a working interview. Laura had learned from experience that a young writer was far too nervous to take in very much at this stage. Later on she must arrange a luncheon with Alan or Sally, whoever could be asked to take over, if . . .

There was a knock at the door, and Dinah came in with two cups of coffee and a young woman in a round fur hat, a thin, short coat, jeans, and high workman's boots.

"Miss Moors," Dinah said.

"Of course, come in. Sit down, Miss Moors." During the amenities—Harriet Moors refused a cup of coffee—Laura observed the visitor closely. She had a round, pink face, wore glasses, and partly because of her Dutch-cut black hair, looked awfully young. Their eyes met; Laura too was being observed, she realized.

"Well," Laura smiled. "How old are you, Harriet? May I call you Harriet?"

"I'm twenty-six."

Laura smiled again. "You look about sixteen, that's why I asked. And this is, I take it, your first try at a novel?"

"Yes."

"It's going to be a good book," Laura took a quick swallow of coffee and set the cup down. Nothing tasted right today.

"I can't believe it." Harriet flushed dark red, took out a kleenex, and wiped her glasses. "It's been such a struggle, for two years nearly. Do you think it's bad to be writing about something one is living at the same time? That was the hardest thing—it kept changing, because I changed."

"Here and there I was troubled by small inconsistencies, but they are easy to fix."

"If it ever comes out, it will have to be under an assumed name," Harriet said, frowning now, for she was suddenly confronted, Laura sensed, by having given so much of herself away.

Laura glanced out at the Common, fiddled with a pencil. "That's something you will have to decide." Why pull any punches? "But if you are going to be a serious writer, I think you have to accept that you must be absolutely honest—hiding behind another name seems like an evasion."

"But my parents—they would never forgive me."

"I know. That's every writer's problem. It can be excruciating."

"I'm not sure I have the courage to come out, Mrs. Spelman." Harriet was sweating profusely and again wiped off her glasses.

"Maybe you underrate your readers."

"You weren't shocked?" Harriet asked intensely.

"Why should I be?"

"I mean, after all—"

"After all, I'm a hundred years old?" At this they both laughed.

"No, but—well, how would you feel if one of your children—"

"My oldest son, a painter, is a homosexual." It occurred to Laura as she spoke the word that she had never said this outright to anyone before.

"Did he tell you so?"

"We've never talked about it, but from the time he was in prep school he always wrote me about great friends he had, lyrical letters about the meaning of love, philosophical letters about passion not lasting."

"Amazing."

"That he wrote like that to me, or that we have left it unanalyzed between us?"

"I don't know." Harriet looked confused.

"Well, one of the things that troubles me a little about your book is that the parents seem rather too obtuse, like caricatures."

"But my parents are like that!"

"Are they really? I felt sometimes, as I read, that you had overdone their reaction. Now and then I rebelled. Come, come, I wanted to say, can't you try to see their dilemma, and their pain, give them a break? For fictional purposes at least, it would make your book more convincing, less of a battle simply between generations—and after all, your parents must be quite young by my standards, in their late forties?"

"My mother is forty-eight and my father fifty-two. They're not intellectuals, Mrs. Spelman. My father has a grocery business, my mother never went to college, and they just don't know anything about all this. I might as well have told them I had leprosy!"

"Yes—I see it is going to take a lot of courage to publish this book. But why did you tell them, then? Do you mind my asking you that?" For Harriet blushed and shook her head at the question.

"Let's get back to the book as fiction. As I said before, I feel it's an important theme and that it will be publishable, but I also feel that it still needs some work, some thinking about. The parents don't come through as complex enough human beings to be quite believable. Perhaps there could be more tension between them?"

"Yes," Harriet nodded. "How do you know all this anyway?"

"I've lived a long time, and I'm part of a large family, a large, eccentric family, I suppose one might say. My elder sister, for instance, has never fallen in love with a man and can't admit even to herself that she has many times been infatuated by women. My mother is responsible for that—she broke up an early love affair rather brutally."

"A love affair with a woman?"

"Yes."

"So she *was* like my parents!"

"Not at all. My mother always understood—or so she imagined. She persuaded Jo that the person involved was an exploiter, that was all."

"And Jo let herself be persuaded?"

"Jo was thoroughly frightened. It was all long ago, in Europe."

"My book is *now,* and in the U.S.A.," Harriet said quite aggressively. "I'm not sure I want to make changes."

"Of course you must think about it, and with your permission I would like one of the young men on the staff to read it, and then perhaps we could have a joint meeting and talk about it again."

Harriet frowned. "I'm not ready for that yet."

"I didn't mean to push you. Perhaps I've said too much."

"No, please tell me the other thing. You said just now, 'one of the things that troubles me.' "

"It's that you simply must make the reader appreciate that this relationship between the two young women is real and deep. You walk all around it, give us all the periphery, but never take us to the center."

"I can't write about sex."

"I don't mean sex. In fact that might not work at all, even if you could. What we need is to believe that this is a possible long-term relationship, important enough so that Perry and Joan have to talk about it with Joan's parents and with Perry's mother."

"Of course. I thought I had made that clear."

"Young writers are so afraid of being obvious that rather often they simply don't tell the reader enough."

"I thought I had . . . that scene on the beach . . ."

"Well, would your own parents, for instance, understand what was really happening there, if they read it and it was not your book?"

Harriet laughed. "I guess not!"

Dinah now looked in, protectively.

"It's all right, Dinah."

When the door had closed again, Laura explained,

"I've got one of those low-grade viruses that hangs on. Dinah is afraid I'll collapse."

"I'd better go," said Harriet—with relief, Laura thought, watching her swing her pouch over her shoulder as she got up.

"It's my first day back, and I do feel rather shaky. I hope you don't feel depressed? Have I said too much? That's always a danger, the danger of trying to write someone else's book."

"I've got to think," Harriet said. "I guess I had hoped the work was done—it's rather awful to have to go back."

"Why don't we let Alan read it and see what he says? Maybe I'm all wrong."

"Alan scares me."

"He's really a dear as well as a perspicacious and kind reader. And he's much younger than I. I have an idea he can help."

"All right," Harriet said reluctantly.

The phone on Laura's desk rang, and she picked up the receiver while Harriet stood rather awkwardly at the door. "Yes, this is Laura Spelman . . . I'm very sorry, but I've been out of the office for a week. I'll get back to you as soon as I can . . . a month, you say? I'm terribly sorry, but I'm sure the manuscript only reached my desk ten days ago. . . . No, I'm not giving you the runaround. Good-by, Mr. Winter." Laura banged the receiver down. "What a rude young man!"

"I was luckier," Harriet smiled.

"Yours is not a seven-hundred-page historical romance!" Harriet, obviously cheered by the downing of Winter, said, "Good-by then . . . and you'll let me know what Alan says."

"Good-by, and don't worry. Let it simmer."

The door closed. Laura sat there, looking out the window. She did feel tired, but in a not unpleasant way, as

[31]

though she were floating, suspended above the public gardens in a dream. Would she be able to see Harriet through before—well, that was not her option. She had liked the girl. Harriet Moors had really listened and taken the criticism with grace. None of the screaming and howling about the Great Untouchable Work that Laura had suffered from more than one beginner. Harriet clearly did not think of herself as a genius, and that was a good sign. Too bad I forgot all about ordering sandwiches, Laura thought . . . but she let that fall, too.

Everything except to sit here for a while seemed too great an effort. And so she floated, unable to fend off the memories of Jo that summer in Genoa, shutting herself up in her room for hours to play jazz records, and their mother, flaming sword of righteousness cutting a life in two—so it had seemed to Jo—without a qualm. Why hadn't their father intervened? For the simple reason, Laura imagined, that he too had been persuaded by Sybille that the wild Alicia was a "bad influence" that had to be removed for all their sakes. Did she never have any doubt, Laura asked herself, did Sybille ever wonder years later whether she had not really murdered Jo rather than the fatal Alicia? For Alicia, tempestuous, beautiful Alicia, had gone on her way, weeping gallons of tears for weeks, and then no doubt falling in love with someone else. She had finally married after all, married into the Roman aristocracy. Laura had come across a photograph of her years later, looking as seductive as ever at some charity ball, Jo by then one of how many brief episodes in her life? But for Jo it had been like a long illness about which she confided in no one; and when it was over she had apparently decided that passionate love was simply too painful and that she would never allow herself to feel as much again for anyone.

Sybille called her "my little owl" and shipped her off

to Radcliffe where she graduated *summa cum laude* and went on to get a doctorate, plunged into the academic world with no doubts that it was where she belonged. She took to work like an alcoholic to the bottle, brilliant, effective—and cold. Power had appeared to be a satisfactory substitute for love, in her case. Did Sybille never see that? She seemed so proud of Jo, even to the point of subtly denigrating Laura and her all-too-ordinary marriage and life in the suburbs.

Mothers and daughters, not the easiest of relationships, Laura reminded herself. For after all, she too had a daughter, single-minded, uncontrollable Daisy! And now in her floating state she set them side by side— Sybille, Laura, Daisy—a puzzling sequence. At least she could say that she had never forced Daisy to give up a love affair, go to college, or do anything except what Daisy wished to do.

Daisy simply didn't want to be part of the family at all, had left home with a knapsack in the mid-sixties intending, as she announced, to discover America. She had worked as a waitress in Montana, then found her way to Seattle, and finally back to New York. In ten years she had come home three times, full of marvelous tales of her adventures, her always brief love affairs, and her determination to be free of any commitment. She had come home to be argued with, to be spoiled a little, to be given boots and jeans and a clean jacket, and then she had left again.

"What is she?" Charles said, "a tramp! Our daughter is a tramp!"

Laura had always said and believed that Daisy would settle down eventually, and in a way she had done so. She was living now with a man whom she was helping to support through medical school by being a secretary for an architectural firm. It was not exactly Sybille's idea of a life-style, but curiously enough Sybille and Daisy had some kind of intuitive understanding and acceptance of each other. Daisy had been outraged when the family decided together that Sybille must be in a nursing home. She had come back for a weekend to fight it out with Laura and her sisters and had made a terribly painful scene. "Why can't you have her here? It's a big house!" she had shouted. "Why can't Aunt Jo have her? Aunt Jo isn't even married!"

"She doesn't know where she is," Jo had answered quietly. "You don't understand. Your grandmother is no longer sane or herself. What she needs is hospital care." Would Daisy come home now for her own mother? Of course not, Laura said to herself. I wouldn't want it.

It had not been wise to allow herself to float into this particular configuration—Sybille, Laura, Daisy—it was too complicated, too unresolved altogether. If dying was to be a reliving of her entire life, Laura wondered for the first time whether she had the courage.

"It's just that I'm tired," she thought, "and I'd better go home to Grindle and Sasha"—those two creatures, outside memory and outside time, who brought her back to the eternal present, the present of saints and animals. Yes, she would take that young man's huge tome with her and not move for the rest of the day.

She stopped at Dinah's office, her briefcase packed. "Dinah, I'm going home."

"For heaven's sake, get some rest, Laura. You look awfully pale."

"Everything takes it out of me. It's so stupid."

"Maybe you should have some help, someone to take care of you for a week or so."

"Oh, no." Laura said passionately, like a child begging to be allowed to stay downstairs for another hour. "I couldn't bear that."

"Well, let me at least carry that heavy briefcase to your car."

"Thanks." To her surprise Laura was grateful for the offer, and it occurred to her that this was the beginning of something she was going to have to learn, little by little—to accept help, to be dependent.

Chapter IV

Laura made herself an eggnog with a teaspoon of brandy in it—shades of Aunt Minna!—and lay down, so tired suddenly that she found it hard to lift the glass. Grindle was outdoors, disappointed that she had not suggested a walk as she would normally have done. He will have to get used to fewer walks, she thought, and then none. If only it were not the dead of winter, she might have asked Laurie, her granddaughter, to bicycle over after school and walk him, but the roads were too dangerous now. Anyway, she had not even told Brooks and Ann that she was ill. Now she would lie here quietly and perhaps later on get at that manuscript.

Sasha jumped up and woke Laura out of a doze. She was determined to knead thoroughly and then lie on Laura's chest, but the weight was stifling, so Laura pushed her gently down, took a swallow of eggnog, and looked around at this familiar room, at the bookcases lined with vermilion, at the corner cupboard Charles had given her as a birthday present soon after they moved to Lincoln, where various treasures were stored: blue beads from Greece, a miniature copy of the Swiss chalet Sybille had rented for Christmas holidays when they were in Genoa, some beautiful Chinese plates that had fallen to Laura when the three daughters broke up their mother's house on Beacon Hill, as had the opulent dark blue Oriental rug. Laura let her eyes rest gratefully on all this beauty and order. Then Grindle barked to be let in; Sasha jumped down, not liking to be disturbed. As she opened the door and Grindle ran in, his tail wagging, his ears bent down in their tender way, she got the full blast of cold air. That, or something else, changed the mood radically.

For the first time since her visit to Jim Goodwin, she was invaded by panic; she knelt down to hug the dog, torn by the parting—when? How much time did she have? And how could she be ready?

"Oh, Grindle," she said, getting up now, "it's a lonely business, dying." Dying—the word brought on a flood of tears. "How am I ever going to do it, Grindle?"

And what if cobalt or chemotherapy could give her a few months' respite? Laura stood at the windows looking out at tree shadows on the blue snow and shook her head. No—no—no—she admonished herself. It was not death she was afraid of, not death that caused that tremor in her bones, but dying.

On an impulse she went to the bookcase and looked for George Herbert's poems. It was years since she had looked at them, years since poetry had been a living part of her life. She opened the battered book she had bought in London long before her marriage.

> I will complain, yet praise;
> I will bewail, approve:
> And all my sour-sweet days
> I will lament, and love.

The sweetness of it, like pure water from a well! And the pang, too, for Herbert had had such an intimate relation with his God, could carry on these loving arguments, this praise in absolute assurance that someone heard.

> Invention rest;
> Comparisons go play; wit use thy will:
> Less than the least
> Of all God's mercies, is my posy still.

Laura lay down with the book open on her lap, reading here and there the familiar poems, familiar and strange. When they were children, their mother had loved to read them poems, had also every evening come to say a prayer with each child. But had Sybille herself really *believed?* Or was even that intimate prayer a scene she played?

People of my generation, Laura throught, lived in an empty universe, more and more frightening as it became more huge and the concept of a personal God next to impossible to accept. What took its place, she supposed, was some vague idea that the cosmos was rational, every part of creation from ameoba to man part of a design far beyond our knowledge or imagination. One could believe one was an organic part of the universe, and that was why she felt so strongly that man, attempting to change the flow, to alter the design for his own purposes, missed the point. This, she suddenly saw clearly, was why she had said so passionately to Dr. Goodwin that she wanted her own death. She wanted to be part of a natural process, unimpeded. But was a cancer *natural?* If only Charles were alive, and we could talk about it! Charles had a way of getting right to the center of things; none of that intellectual embroidery Sybille indulged in. "Your mother is a siren," he sometimes had said, "a highly imaginative, undisciplined siren . . . and perhaps rather dangerous, for she believes in her own song while she is singing it." Charles had treated Sybille with a slightly amused deference, and they had got on very well.

Laura pulled herself out of these thoughts by opening her briefcase. She took one look at the heavy manuscript and laid it on a chair. In that second of dread and dismay before an effort that she did not want to make, she decided that she would not read it at all. She would make some excuse. For whatever dying of cancer may mean, she thought, it does not mean that I have to do anything now that is done merely for duty's sake. Lying and looking at the light marbling the white walls had meaning. The talk with Harriet had had meaning—and Laura was glad she had been able to manage it. It had meaning because deep in her own life as well as Jo's loving a woman had had its part.

Harriet's honesty, her troubled, troubling way of dealing with all this in a novel, *was* relevant. It had brought back vivid memories, so much that must be sorted out. Laura went to her desk and hauled out three big bundles of Ella's letters, tied up in string; then she sat with them before her and did not untie them. It had to be done, sooner or later, but for today she pushed them aside, just glancing at the lightning hand that wrote as though the pen could never move fast enough for the racing thoughts and feelings. Ella's slim figure in a pale blue coat her mother had had made for her at Redfern in Paris—how Laura had admired Ella's style!—was so vividly before her, there was no need to open a single letter. Ella was a born scholar, and that surely I never was, Laura remembered. While Ella worked furiously hard, her light often on after midnight, Laura came back to the pension from the theater or a concert, walking great distances alone through the Paris streets, then running up the strairs to knock at Ella's door. They poked up the fire. They sat on cushions on the floor and talked sometimes till dawn, talked about their parents, their sisters or brothers (Ella had two brothers at Oxford at that time), about Dostoevsky whom they were just discovering, and Shakespeare versus Racine, about Proust whom Laura was reading with the passion of a drug addict for his drug, about the theater, which was rich in those years of Dullin, Maguérite Jamois, Pierre Renoir, Lugné-Poë at the Oeuvre—and above all talked about what they wanted to be and to do with their lives. "I'll never marry," Ella had announced, but it was she who married first after all!—and believed years later that it had been a mistake, that she had been so jealous of her brothers and the secret joys of their lives that she had married one of their friends, partly to get inside a man's world, to be accepted as a person in her own right, and instead had felt she was merely and forever Hugh's wife, the wife of an Oxford don.

Laura still remembered how forlorn she had felt as bridesmaid at the wedding, and how much an outsider in the little church at Fernwall, the family estate in Kent. I'll never get over it, she had thought, it will never be the same again, now Ella is married. "Has gone and gotten married" was her phrase, as though Ella had left for the moon! Then, standing with the others, watching the car drive off and having perhaps drunk a little too much champagne, Laura had fled to her room and wept, wishing passionately that she could have taken Ella into her arms and held her as her husband now would, and keep her forever.

The phone rang, the imperious present summoning her back, and she heard Aunt Minna's voice.

"Oh, Aunt Minna, dear—"

"You sound very far away."

"Well," Laura laughed, "I was in what used to be called a brown study—why 'brown' I cannot imagine."

"And that means what?"

"Means I was sitting here at my desk thinking about Ella Worthington. I want her to know what is happening to me—you and she, and no one else for the time being."

"I tried to reach you this morning. There was no answer."

"I went to the office and had a long talk with a young woman who has written rather a good novel."

"I feel depressed," Aunt Minna announced quite crossly.

"I upset you, didn't I? I'm awfully sorry."

"Upset me? It was an earthquake. I didn't sleep a wink."

"O, dear! Would you rather I hadn't told you?"

"Of course not. I just can't accept it and I never will."

Laura felt incapable of arguing about anything at this point, and, rather cruelly, cut the conversation short by saying that she wanted to write Ella and would call back before supper. Other people were going to be the hardest part of all this, but at least Aunt Minna would come right out with whatever she felt, no holds barred. Laura smiled. "I tell her I'm dying of cancer, and she takes it as a personal affront."

But it was healthy. Laura had sometimes felt that the only thing life asks of us is to know what we feel and to come out with it. Exaggerated? Perhaps, but she had come to believe that Sybille's destructiveness as well as her power had come from not knowing what her real feelings were. When she had been so brutal about Alicia, was it not that she feared the same attraction to a woman in her own past? For Sybille had had passionate friendships all her life, with both men and women—passionate in the *mind*. The faithful wife personified who nonetheless played dangerous games with "friends," that series of glamorous, famous men and women whom she attracted, who were, each of them for a year or two, *the* great person, to be feted, and entertained, and invited for long private talks—quite unaware, too, of the cynical and perhaps jealous eyes of her three daughters, who observed these infatuations and could never be entirely persuaded of the "greatness" thrust upon them.

The room had become a dark cave while Laura sat at her desk in the fading light. Now she turned on the lamp and pulled out a sheet of paper, determined to accomplish something before she went to bed. She wrote intently, stopping to think, then scribbling fast. There had always been this élan when she and Ella communicated, as though there would never be time to say it all.

"Darling Snab," she wrote, "it's a cold winter here and I have strange news. You are the only person I am telling except Aunt Minna—and it may have been a mistake to tell her. I have cancer in both lungs, too advanced, the doctor thinks, to be operable. And in a way I am glad because it means, perhaps, that I can have my own death in my own way, not artifically prolonged by all the medical horrors. So far Dr. Goodwin has agreed not to try cobalt or chemotherapy.

"Do you remember in Paris how impressed we were with Rilke's feeling that death must be allowed to have its way, as an important part of a life? I feel that now with my whole being, and I know you will understand. This time I'm not going to be 'taken over' as mother took me over in Davos. I pray I'll have the courage to stick to this to the end.

"It's good that Charles is not here to agonize. The children are. Can you understand, Snab, that I don't want them around? Oh, how good it is to be able to write to you, say even what sounds awful, and know that it will be understood! Maybe only when one is young, without responsibilities except to oneself, or when one is dying, is one allowed to be ruthless? But is 'ruthless' the right word? What I mean is that only then is one allowed to shut out the nonessential. At the times when one is growing at great intensity and speed, one is allowed to look inward, one must look inward. Later on, life and all the web of human relations intangle the authentic inner person, don't they? Entangle and nourish at the same time. We can't live alone. But later on so much that 'has to be done,' gets in the way.

"All this has made me go back to you, to what we experienced together in that miraculous year. I have been living over those Paris days all afternoon with a package of your letters before me, yet not able to read them. I don't need to, it is all so vivid.

"Would you like me to send them back? I can't bring myself to destroy them. They are the record of an intensely satisfying experience, the record of growth. For years after Paris we wrote often, as though we could only fully understand what was happening—my illness, your marriage—in the light of each other's eyes. And what was it really all about? In some strange way our friendship seems the most important thing that ever happened to me. Don't laugh, dear Snab, when I say that the other most important thing seems to be dying. I want to do it well. It sounds crazy, but when I first heard I was lifted up on a wave of wild excitement, of joy.

"I wish I could explain it, but I must lie down now for a while. I am not in pain, but I have awfully little energy, and my chest feels as though a huge pillow were on it, and stifling me. The hardest thing so far is to know that death is there alive inside me. I have had a few moments of bad panic partly because I have no idea how long dying will take, when I shall have to have help here, a thing I dread.

"This is hard to say, Snab, darling Snab, but please don't think of coming over. I feel too naked in a queer way to be able to take emotion. But I remember *everything*."

Laura stopped there, for she felt rather ill, and took a cup of soup up to bed, after letting Grindle out and Sasha in. She woke at nine, suddenly remembering that she had promised to call Aunt Minna back, turned on the light, and picked up the phone from the bed table.

"I'm so sorry, dear, I went to sleep, just woke up and knew there was something I had forgotten. Please forgive."

Aunt Minna laughed. "I've been listening to the symphony, Mahler's Fifth. Ozawa is transcendent, I must say. It's taken me a lifetime to get to Mahler, but now I'm really with it." She laughed again, at herself, for the slang expression. Evidently her mood had changed.

"Go right back," Laura said, "sorry I interrupted."

"And you, sleep well. Is Grindle there?"

"Right here beside me."

"Good night, dear."

"Good night."

Infinitely comforting, that "good night." And sleep among all the joys of life came to Laura like a walk through a gentle field, as she gave Grindle a last rub on his tummy and turned over. "The dead are not asleep" was her last conscious thought, "for sleep is in the domain of the living."

Chapter V

The next day Laura felt better. She imagined that for some time there might be good days now and then. Drinking her coffee in bed, with Grindle's eyes fixed on each mouthful, she said, "We might even have a walk, Grindle, who knows?" and gave him a corner of toast.

What else would she do with a precious day? Not waste a drop of energy, enjoy every moment. Just now it was the rising sun, touching her bureau and turning the soft wood a deep rose, then making a cut-glass paperweight sparkle. She did not feel like reading nor like getting up, and she lay there for a good half-hour before she got dressed. In the night she had dreamed of their summer house in Maine—the grassy field that ran down from the terrace to rocky shore; she had dreamed that they were all floating in the old rowboat, becalmed under a hot sun—the shimmer of the water, her father's contented look under his floppy white duck hat, were still with her. Summers—the endless happy summers in Maine. Even when her father was hard at work in various consulates, they had always managed to come "home" for a month, except during the two years when Laura had been flat on her back with TB in Switzerland.

Maine rather than the various houses all over Europe and, after Dwight Homaday's retirement, on Beacon Hill in Boston, had meant home. If only I can live till spring, Laura thought, I'll go down for a week. I'll open the house. Maybe Daphne would come? Maybe we could have a family party, Brooks and Ann and the children. Who knows, maybe Ben could fly back, and Daisy be summoned—but even as Laura vaguely planned all this, she let it drop. It would not be possible; the very thought of the energy required made her quail. No, she would settle for going down herself alone, as soon as it got a little warmer. But what if? What if by that time she couldn't? No plans were going to be possible at any given point in the future. And that was that. She must consider only the day before her. Not tomorrow; today.

"Only the real connections—" it seemed years ago that she had determined to concentrate on these at the expense of all others.

She dressed carefully in her best tweed suit, high black boots, for she had known somewhere deep down inside, ever since she had waked in the middle of her dream of a grassy field, that today she would go and see her mother in the nursing home. This had become harder and harder to do in the past year—was it lack of love, true love that overcomes all debilities and decay? Or was it that the contemplation of the ruin of such beauty and power as had been Sybille's well into her eighties, seemed a betrayal? She had felt the last time that she should not see her mother like this, spilling tea on her housecoat, plucking at her clothes, that coming into the room was an invasion of privacy. Had her mother recognized her? In old age those sapphire eyes had paled, the magnificent throat was wrinkled as a turtle's—had she imagined a quick, angry look when she first came in? Was this really the best way to use a "good day"? Laura asked herself on the hour's drive to the "home" in Milton. Asking it, she realized that the decision had not been an act of will but simply the tug of the flesh itself—she *had* to go. This time at least, with a mortal illness taking possession, her mother could not exert, as she had in Switzerland, that absolute control, so imaginative, glowing, masterly, and terrible that Laura had imagined sometimes that she had been frozen like a flower in a glacier, entombed. And but for Charles and his warmth and conviction, would she ever have come to life, her own life (not her mother's idea of her life) again?

Arrived, after what had seemed a long journey, at the fourth floor, Laura greeted the head nurse.

"How is my mother, Mrs. Neal?"

"She has stopped talking lately. It's hard to tell."

"I haven't been in for ages because I have had a low-grade virus and was afraid it might be contagious." This time the lie was a real evasion, but Laura's ambivalence toward her mother was certainly not Mrs. Neal's business.

"Does she ever mention me or my sisters?"

"Not to my knowledge," Mrs. Neal said. "She's not really conscious most of the time. Sings to herself—"

"I'll just go in, shall I?"

Sybille was sitting in a wheelchair, her back to the door, when Laura walked in, after knocking to no audible response.

"It's Laura, Mother."

Very gently she turned the wheelchair to face the only other chair in the room and sat down, taking her mother's two hands in hers. They were ice-cold. Laura noted that her mother had on a ruffled pale blue wrapper and blue bedroom slippers, and her hair had been carefully combed and done up with a blue ribbon round it. They did take good care of her. That was something to be grateful for.

"Your hands are so cold, Mamma. Are you warm enough? Would you like a shawl round your shoulders? A hot-water bottle?"

Sybille Hornaday had not lifted her head. She was looking down—Laura could not see her eyes—humming something like a long, made-up song. There was no answer to her questions, but Laura held the old hands in hers, hoping to transfuse at least a little physical warmth.

"Why am I here?" The voice, even to the slight roughness in it, was so much like Sybille's real self that Laura dropped her mother's hands and wondered for a moment whether she had imagined the question, for already the humming had resumed.

"Darling, you're here because you need care. I'm at my job all day. You need nursing care." But it was clear that the door that had opened a crack in anger had closed again. Sybille was no longer there but was somewhere deep down where the strange song went on and on, shutting out Laura and everything else in her incongruous surroundings.

"I wanted to tell you that I'm dying, Mother." She was not aware of her own tears till she felt one fall, cold and wet on her hand. "I wanted you to know."

Even a year or two ago such a statement would have elicited an immediate, even an overwhelming response—suggestions that she see another doctor, that she go to the Lahey clinic for a thorough testing, and, after these practical matters had been taken care of, a long, intimate talk about life and death and God and love. How much she had resented this power to move and persuade, "to take the heart out of the body," as Daphne said bitterly. Yet today the absence of any response whatever came as a shock. She might as well have been a newborn babe howling at the chill air.

"I may not be able to come back," she heard herself say quite coldly and loudly. Then she got up and kissed Sybille on the cheek that was still soft as a rose petal, remembering how often as a child she had wanted to kiss her mother, glorious in evening dress with stars in her hair, and had not dared.

"Thanks so much, dear," her mother said, thinking no doubt that Laura was a nurse. Whatever the "tug of the flesh" had meant an hour ago—that old longing going back to infancy—Laura had to admit as she closed the door that there was no real connection, none at all. It had been absurd to imagine that what had never been said in sixty years could by some miracle be said now, because Laura was dying. She made appropriate remarks to the nurse standing at the door with a tray of medicines and fled to the elevator. At least for a few seconds she was safe in it, and she blew her nose.

Then the door slid open silently, and she heard her name called.

"Laura! Oh, I am glad to catch you!"

"Cousin Hope!"

There was no possible escape. Hope Fraser, dear old Hope, who had adored Sybille all her life, had already launched into speech. "Yes, I come twice a week to visit with your mother. I'm *so* glad to see you here, Laura. There's so much to talk about. Couldn't we go somewhere and have a cup of coffee? I know how busy you are. I haven't wanted to call you, but . . ."

"Where could we go?" Laura asked, feeling hunted. The nursing home was in a residential section.

"Mrs. Fraser," the girl at the desk called out to them, "you could sit in the waiting room. There's no one there. I'll ask one of the staff to bring you some coffee."

[49

"Oh, that *is* kind of you. That would be so easy and comfortable, wouldn't it, Laura?"

Clearly Hope was well known here.

Laura felt pinned down like a butterfly in a box. What could she possibly say to justify herself beside Cousin Hope's devotion?

"Dear Laura, do sit down. You look quite pale. I expect it was a shock to see your mother this time."

"You think there has been a change?"

"She does seem to be getting farther and farther away from us, do you agree?"

"You are awfully good to come so often."

"I don't have a job. Adrian is working harder than ever now he has retired, don't you know? He is writing a huge book. And of course we live nearby—it's a long way for you to come."

Pure goodness shone out from Cousin Hope, and Laura felt more and more ashamed. Hope had always been one of those people who saw everyone in the best possible light, who seemed to live unaware that there were such things in human nature as bitterness, ambivalence, hatred, and above all self-hatred. "Hope is simply a natural-born, dyed-in-the-wool saint," Sybille had once said. "I wonder why we find that irritating." "Because it isn't *real*," Daphne had answered, "She's too good to be true." Laura, lost in these thoughts, realized that there was a hiatus in the rush of good feeling, and that she was expected to respond.

"Oh, no—no, it's not far, not really."

"I wish you could have a talk with the doctor about the drugs they are giving your mother."

"Drugs?"

"I feel sure she is sedated. Couldn't they allow her to be herself, Laura? I mean, even if she does get angry sometimes?"

"Does she?"

"At first she was very angry. She wouldn't speak to me. I knew that meant she was very angry."

"I know," Laura said almost inaudibly.

"Of course it's terribly hard for you to see your mother like this."

"Yes, I suppose it is," Laura said absent-mindedly, as though she were speaking of someone else. The pinned-down butterfly felt completely detached.

Mercifully, a nurse came in with two cups of coffee on a tray and interrupted this excruciating conversation for a moment. After she had left and Laura had taken a sip of the lukewarm coffee (Is this how it tastes on the fourth floor? she wondered. Her mother liked coffee hot and strong.), Cousin Hope said, "You are not feeling well, are you, Laura? Is anything the matter?"

Startled back into full consciousness, Laura assured Hope that she was suffering from a low-grade virus and felt rather tired. Where to go from there? Take the plunge and talk about Sybille? It might be her last chance, and Hope deserved a little better than what Laura had been able to manage so far.

"I wish we could talk a little about Mamma. I sometimes feel I never knew her really. You, perhaps, did."

"I did," Cousin Hope's eyes shone. "I think I knew Sybille very well."

"Warts and all?" Laura smiled for the first time.

"No warts, dear Laura!" Hope visibly blushed. "What an idea! She was simply as far as I know a glorious woman, beautiful, brilliant, *everything!* She was so brave, you know—when you were ill—heroic I always thought, to shut herself up like that in that tiny village for two years, taking care of you." Hope, totally unaware of Laura's reaction, leaned forward confidentially. "I'll tell you something. It's really nothing, but it made a great impression on me. I've never forgotten it. Adrian and I were in London then, at the School of Economics, if you remember. I went to Harrod's and bought your mother a beautiful camel's-hair dressing gown for Christmas."

"That was dear of you."

"No, as a matter of fact, it was all wrong. You see, it was brown, and Sybille returned it and explained that for your sake she must never look dreary. Brown is a dreary color. It had to be blue, she said. Of course, I saw at once how right she was—after all, there you were flat on your back. Your mother had to look beautiful for *you*. It never occurred to me that that beauty was a kind of gift, you see? That's just a tiny episode—" (Yet, Laura knew, it must have hurt).

"I can't tell you how much Sybille taught me! Why, without her, I should never have known anything really about how to live—her taste, so absolutely *perfect!*"

"Yes, she made critics of us all and destroyed any impulse to create." Why had she said it aloud? Laura saw the stricken look.

"Go on, Cousin Hope. I didn't mean to interrupt. I was in a black mood, and you are doing me good. Please go on."

"She was so passionate about everything!"

"Like what?"

"Politics, my dear! I was totally ignorant about politics—your mother put me right about the Spanish civil war, I can tell you! And long before anyone I knew was very much concerned, she was warning us about Hitler."

"My father may have had something to do with that," Laura murmured. "After all, he was in a position to know."

"Your father had to be discreet, I presume. But he never seemed to care quite as deeply. Sybille threw herself into everything. Even as an old woman (it *is* remark-able!) she became involved in getting blacks bused out to the suburbs! But you know all this, dear Laura. What you cannot know, perhaps, is what an extraodinary ca-pacity she had for friendship. When Tommy . . . when we had to face the fact that Tommy would never grow up to be quite normal, Sybille used to come once or twice a week and read aloud to him. He loved that. She had such a beautiful voice! Who but Sybille would have found time? Laura, dear Laura, you mustn't let what is happen-ing now depress you. She was a great woman!"

What then turned her three daughters into cynics? Laura wondered. Why couldn't we ourselves ever quite believe in the golden legend? What turned us off?

"I'm so glad you remember all that—it's awfully good of you to come here now, so often, *dear* Cousin Hope." Laura was appalled to hear in her own voice an exact replica of her mother's intonation, just slightly conde-scending.

No, not condescending; the tone of someone *acting* the appropriate response.

"Well, I must go up now for a little visit. I hope I haven't worn you out."

The butterfly was released, but the pin had pene-trated. All Laura could think of was to get home to Grin-dle as quickly as possible, take him for a walk if she had the strength—and even if she hadn't—get back to some-thing simple, uncomplicated, that did not make her bones ache.

Was it really much harder to be a woman than to be a man, Laura asked herself on the drive home, not for the first time. Neither her father nor Charles had ever caused the kind of emotional conflict that her mother had. Daphne would say, she supposed, that they were "real" and Sybille was not. What if she had been allowed to go on the stage? Was she simply born to a career that she had been denied? That hunger for greatness, for the heroic, for the beautiful gesture—the theater would have used all that to great effect—and Sybille herself off stage might then have allowed herself to be simpler and more human. Who knows?

Of course she should have had three sons instead of three daughters. Laura had to admit that she herself had not found Daisy half as easy to bring up as Ben and Brooks—and why was that? What was the tension between daughters and mothers? Daisy had said it often enough, though without hostility: "I don't want to be like you, mother, buried alive in suburbia. I want a chance to discover who I am *first*, then settle down somewhere if I have to. I don't want to be caught."

At that Laura had smiled and said gently, "I was escaping from mother's high-powered expectations and life. I wanted what you think of as an "ordinary life"— that was what I *wanted*, craved. I had a huge hunger and thirst for the everyday, for the normal if you like. And on the whole," she remembered saying, "I have been happy."

She remembered saying it because Daisy had reacted unexpectedly with a flood of tears. "I don't want to be happy," she sobbed.

"That's good," Laura said dryly, "for the chances are you won't be!"

Ever since she had seen Dr. Goodwin, Laura had been flooded with remembered conversations, and once such a flood began it was next to impossible to turn it off. But it was tiring. She drove the last miles too fast, concentrating on the car to shut out the dialogue. And there at last was the house—peace, safety.

"Yes," she said to Grindle, who was barking frantically and looking up at her with questioning ears, "yes,

we'll go for a walk!" She took her cane out of the um-
brella stand and went out without even changing into
warmer boots. The air felt unexpectedly mild. After days
when the thermometer never climbed over twenty,
thirty felt positively springlike. "Where's your cat?" she
asked Grindle. But he had rushed off to roll in the snow.
Laura opened the front door and called, "Come, cat,
we're going for a walk!" Sasha trundled downstairs, then
sat, washing her face for several seconds. "Maddening
animal, come!" And at last she was at the open door,
shaking her paws in anticipation of the icy path. Finally
she came out and followed Laura twenty paces or so
behind. Grindle trotted on ahead, full of his pleasures,
darting into the drifts after a scent only he could possibly
catch in this weather, humping himself back onto the
road.

"Look out, Grindle, or you'll drown in the snow!"

When they got back a half-hour later, Laura was tired,
hungry, and aware that she had spent whatever vital energy she could expect to call on today. But she was able
to swallow a peanut butter sandwich and to drink a glass
of milk without feeling sick. That was better than yesterday. It was pure bliss to stretch out on the sofa then with
a Haydn quartet pouring its vitality into her like wine.

Pure life is what I want, she thought—trees, snow, sky,
the animals, a glass of milk, and music—these together
amounted to a taste of heaven on earth. It's all I need
now, she thought, smiling as she drifted off to sleep.

Chapter VI

Laura did not relish having to see Dr. Goodwin, but his secretary had insisted on the telephone that there were things he felt it necessary to discuss. "There will be time enough for doctors later on," Laura thought, "but of course he has me over a barrel because he knows so much that I don't know." Suddenly she remembered her father's saying in his dry way, "Of course, when you see a doctor, you take your life into your hands." But the awful thing was that one simply *had* to trust. Doubting Jim Goodwin would be like walking into quicksand. There had to be somebody to care for her crumbling body.

She was tense, when she sat down opposite Jim Goodwin and saw that he was looking at a sheet of X-rays.

"Well?" she asked, "what's all this about?" She couldn't keep the hostility out of her voice.

Jim coughed. "I want you to arrange for someone to be in the house. It's not a good idea to wait till you are feeling too weak to cope."

"Will that be soon? I feel remarkably well. Only, when I lie down, there is a sensation of stifling, but quite bearable so far. I hate the idea of a stranger hovering about."

"The alternative is the hospital, Mrs. Spelman."

Laura swallowed.

"I'm sorry to be brutal about this, but you must understand that I am your physician."

"Meaning that I have given my life into your power—what is left of it."

"Meaning," he said gently, "that I have some experience about such things. I want to help you all I can."

"Very well, I'll try to find a housekeeper."

"We may be able to help. Miss Albright has a list of possible people—of course they may all be employed at the moment. What you need is a practical nurse. Then, I would be glad if you would agree to a few days in the hospital. I would like to have a consultation with a surgeon, to be quite sure, frankly, that surgery is impossible, as I believe it to be from the X-rays."

"No," Laura said quietly. "I don't want to be interrupted."

"Interrupted?"

"Well," she sat up straight, "I'm living just now. I'm learning in a queer way how to live, what is important, and what isn't. I don't want to be interrupted."

"You're just like your mother," Jim Goodwin said with a smile.

"God forbid!"

"She was a great woman, a great personality."

"Yes, she was." For the first time Laura was close to tears. "I'm not a personality. I'm just trying to be human."

"Mrs. Spelman, would you like me to have a talk with your son Brooks?"

Laura was startled. "Why Brooks?"

[57

"Someone in the family has to be alerted."

"Oh, not yet, please! I must have a little time. You're making it all seem so near, so close—I'm not ready!" She was unashamedly weeping now. "All right, tell him, if you must." She got up and blew her nose. "Tell him I want to die at home." But then she sat down again and recovered herself. "On second thought, don't tell Brooks. Aunt Minna knows. I went over there just after you told me what was what last week. You'll be glad to hear that she too insisted I get someone to be with me in the house."

"Very well—but there will be decisions—"

"I'll tell Brooks myself when I feel the time has come when . . ." there was a pause. Then she smiled. "You see, I don't want to abdicate until I have to. If you tell Brooks, it's as though . . ."

"It would have been only to spare you."

"I realize that. Thank you. But the real thing is this sense I have that I need a little time just to live, as long as I am able, not to be impinged on by other people's feelings. Yes," she said, looking him straight in the eye, "that's it. That's the point—to be free of other people's sense of doom, *their* fears, if you will."

"Very well, I won't insist. There's one other thing, however. Your lungs are filling up, and the time will come fairly soon, I fear, when we shall have to drain out the fluid, at regular intervals, so you can breathe more easily."

"Oh," Laura said in a dull voice.

"I'll be glad to come and do it for you—after all, I live nearby."

"That's awfully kind of you."

For the second time Laura's eye filled with tears.

"I'll do everything I can, Mrs. Spelman."

"There's really no hope, is there?"

"There's always hope," he said, leaning back in his chair. "There are remissions, very mysterious because we really don't know why. There are sometimes remissions of a month or more, although with a malignancy in the lung—in your case in both lungs—well, as I say, it would be foolish to be too sure of anything. I'll tell you something. It's surprising that you feel as well as you say that you do, so, you see, one never knows."

Before Laura left the office Miss Albright called several possible practical nurses. One was willing to come in ten days. Laura had begged for that interval so passionately that Jim Goodwin had agreed to it. Mary O'Brien was to come and see her in Concord the next day, and they would talk things over.

"She's a very sweet woman," Miss Albright said, "a widow whose children are grown up. I'm sure you'll like her."

Laura sighed, then said, "I'll do my best." She hurried away then, compelled by some inner need so urgent that she hardly took time to button her coat.

Chapter VII

Laura felt caged at the very idea of Mrs. O'Brien, who was supposed to arrive at eleven. She had decided to stay in bed as late as possible. Comforting as Grindle and Sasha were, it was pleasant to be able to stretch her legs, now they were both out. She let herself float, sitting up with three pillows behind her so she could breathe, for she had wakened with a terrible fit of coughing and had thrown up some blood. All she could think of, of course, was Keats—Keats deprived of so much of his life. I have had my life, she reminded herself—for the sight of blood had been rather a shock—all of it, except old age. And though old age might be like Aunt Minna's, rich and passionate and angry, it could just as well be her mother's, a dwindling of intellect and spirit until there was nothing left but the needs of an infant. I'll be well out of it, she thought, looking around her room: the Graves sea bird she and Charles had bought together for their twentieth wedding present to each other; the shelf of special books, poetry mostly, to the left of the mantel; the birch logs in the fireplace—one of these days I'll have a fire up here, she thought. The last time she had done that was during an attack of flu years before. Charles had lit the fire then and had brought logs up. Would it be easier if he were here at her side during this last journey? And she reacted at once, no, no, thank God he isn't! Charles could never deal with real illness. It made him cross and overprotective, which made Laura feel guilty.

The phone interrupted these ruminations. Laura was sure it would be Aunt Minna and for a second could not identify this rather strained and muffled voice. Then she got it. "Oh, it's you, Harriet."

Harriet Moors sounded as though she had been crying. She apologized for calling Laura at home, "but could I come and see you? I . . ."

"I'm still under the weather, still in bed as a matter of fact. Is it that important?"

The silence at the other end of the line was eloquent. "Could you come out late this afternoon?"

Laura had another fit of coughing as she was giving Harriet the directions. It was horrible to have this day already committed—she had planned to go over some papers and throw things away. But she felt suddenly so weak, she didn't have the strength to dress and was only able to drag herself up because Grindle was barking to be let in. A spoonful of brandy in a second cup of coffee helped, and by the time Mrs. O'Brien arrived, Laura was lying on the sofa downstairs, dressed in slacks and a shirt and sweater.

The idea of Mrs. O'Brien had been repellent, but Laura found the actual person sitting opposite her in a wing chair quite endearing. Mary O'Brien was a tall, gaunt woman with a rather stern face that lit up when she smiled. She was very direct. Laura appreciated that.

"I shall have to have my weekends," she said. "I have

[61

two still at home and I must keep things going for them, although Rose Marie is a good cook now and Jack does a lot of odd jobs round the house."

"Of course," Laura said, thinking with relief, I'll have some solitude, after all. It seemed like a reprieve.

"How long do you expect you'll need me?"

"I don't know how long I have to live," Laura said, looking Mrs. O'Brien straight in the eye. "It might be six months."

"You're very ill, Mrs. Spelman?"

"Not yet," said Laura dryly "But Dr. Goodwin was very insistent that I have some help as soon as possible."

Mrs. O'Brien nodded. "Don't worry. I'll take good care of you. Of course I'm not a nurse, but I don't mind carrying trays. Do you have a washing machine?"

And after that Laura showed Mary O'Brien her room and bath and the kitchen and where things were in general.

"It's a big house for you all alone, isn't it?"

"I suppose so. My husband died three years ago, you see, and the children are married or away. I've lived here so long I never think about it one way or another." Because Laura liked Mary O'Brien, who appeared to take difficult things for granted, it was all settled with no fuss. In fact she felt quite euphoric when Mrs. O'Brien drove off, and went at once to the telephone to tell Aunt Minna the good news.

Of course the truth would come out when Mary O'Brien was around all day and all night, but at least it had become very clear to Laura that someone impersonal was what she needed, someone who would not be too involved. A strange relationship at best, it would require tact on both sides. But Laura to her own amazement trusted Mary O'Brien. She would, she sensed, be *practical*, and she had not winced or withdrawn when Laura made it quite clear what was involved, though she had not told Mrs. O'Brien what her illness was—that would come later—and she was grateful that Mrs. O'Brien had not asked.

Laura decided not to push herself, partly to be prepared for Harriet Moors, and partly because she wanted to listen to music—two Schubert quartets and a wonderful Octet in F Minor that she had not listened to for years. Everything important from now on would be going on inside her and would have, she realized, very little to do with other people or with anything she might feel she must "do." Her sense of haste even a few days ago about sorting out papers, about things she should arrange about before she felt too ill, was rapidly sliding away. The only reality for the moment was in these transparent voices of two violins, a cello, a viola. By half-past five, after a long nap, Laura felt honed down to essentials. What would it be like to have to summon herself when Harriet Moors arrived? She was really in no way responsible for this girl, after all. Take it easy, Laura admonished herself, and let her talk. Then the doorbell rang.

"Be an angel and put another log on the fire, will you?" Laura asked when she had helped Harriet off with her sheepskin jacket. "I'll get us a drink. What would you like? A martini perhaps?"

"A glass of wine if you have one."

Of course! Laura had forgotten that martinis were out-of-date. Nevertheless she mixed one for herself, feeling rather jaunty as she did so. Her usual drink was scotch.

Looking across from the wing chair to Harriet on the sofa, Laura noted that her visitor's hand shook as she took a sip of white wine.

"Well, Harriet, what's on your mind?"

"Just . . ." Harriet swallowed. "I've decided that I can't publish that novel."

"You've got cold feet? I can understand that."

"It's going to make too many people unhappy—my friend is terrified now. She thinks she might lose her job if people knew."

Laura deliberately looked into the fire, sorting things out in her own mind.

"You hadn't really faced it, had you? I wonder then why you made the immense effort that must have gone into writing this novel."

"I know. Why did I? I must be crazy!" There she sat, so young, so charming really, a very young person who had taken on the whole complex responsibility of public revelation without having measured the cost.

"But you believe in your work?"

"I don't know anymore." Harriet gave a strange little sigh. "Maybe writing it was just therapy."

"That doesn't sound like you."

"That's what my friend says. She's a teacher, and she's older than I am." Harriet clasped her hands to her chest and rocked with the pain of it. "If I publish this book it's the end of us—that's it: That's why . . ."

"That's tough."

"I feel awfully confused. That's why I wanted to see you. It's very kind of you to let me come." The round, troubled face broke into a smile. Laura could sense how much better Harriet felt at the moment because she had been able to come out with the matter. All very well, but what was Laura to say now?

"You seemed to understand. I mean, you talked about your son. And you felt my parents had been too harshly drawn. I thought maybe you could help. Is it just cowardice not to go ahead? Maybe if I destroy my book, I'm really destroying myself. I think of all these images, that one can't close the door against life, and having a first novel accepted is certainly the opening of a door. If one closes that door, isn't it fatal? But on the other hand if I close the door between Fern and me," Harriet fixed her eyes solemnly on Laura, "what am I doing to her, and to myself?"

"I'm an editor, not a psychiatrist. You are asking me questions I can't possibly answer." Then Laura, seeing the dismay she had caused, added quickly, "But that doesn't mean that I don't understand. I think you're in a horribly painful dilemma. I don't know what to say about it. I can understand better, though, why you thought of an assumed name. Maybe that is the solution, after all."

"Now it seems to me cowardly. Sooner or later I've got to face myself and not be ashamed. Besides, people find out." And she murmured half to herself, "Even if I did use another name, Fern would be terrified."

"It sounds to me as though Fern has some problems of her own. People pay a high price, I think, for leading a life they are not willing to live publicly."

"But it hasn't been possible. I mean, you lose your job. You are treated as a pariah. What I can't stand is the whole sexual bit, the way people look at you. And you know all they are interested in is what you do in bed. It's *horrible!*"

"You are very good about that in your novel. The reader is aware that the relation between the two women is real, not a matter of experimenting or of mere sexual adventure, or whatever. One reason I felt that we would want to publish is that the time has come for works of art that will deal with all this naturally and without sensationalism. If I may say so, the classics in the field—I am thinking of *Nightwood*—make the homosexual unsavory to put it mildly."

[65

"So you really believe my book has *value*."

"Yes, I do."

"Oh, dear . . ." Harriet sighed again. She took off her glasses and rubbed her eyes, then took a swallow of wine.

Laura laughed. "Maybe it would have been more helpful to say the book was not very good, after all!"

"Then I could throw it away?" Harriet frowned. "I guess I couldn't whatever you said or thought. I don't think I'm a genius, but I know I have to write the way a fish has to swim."

"I think you are a real writer. I've been in rather a crisis myself lately, but your book has stayed with me. I go back to it in my mind. That's one test for me of whether a work of art is truly alive. Does it take on a life of its own in the reader's imagination? The atmosphere—you are very good at creating psychological atmosphere. The choking reality of the parents' house, you do that very well."

"Oh, God, my parents!"

At that *cri de coeur*, Laura and Harriet burst into laughter. It was a shared laughter, and it had to do with how ludicrous and horrible life could be, at times beyond coping with.

Then Harriet got up and stood by the fireplace, obviously feeling at ease. "How lucky your son is to have you!"

"And his father," Laura said. "My husband was amazingly wise in dealing with Ben—of course it helped that Brooks, our eldest, was all a father could wish."

"Can't people just be people? You say 'dealing with'?"—

"Yes—well, it's going to take a long time to get over our ideas of what ought to be. It's the same thing with women. I was happily married, but when Charles died

I became aware that other people really had thought of me as Charles's wife. That's why the job at Houghton Mifflin was such a help. There, at least, I was Laura Spelman, a person in my own right."

"Was it hard—at first, I mean—hard to be a person all by yourself?"

"I felt cut in two. For months I really had no identity. Getting a meal was next to impossible, I lived on eggnogs." What am I doing, talking to this girl like this? Laura thought. Is that what one martini does now?

"Please go on . . ."

"Well, frankly, I think I'd better call it a day, Harriet."

"Yes, of course. I know you've been ill—I shouldn't have stayed so long."

"It's just, I do get rather weak in the knees."

Grindle now emerged from the kitchen where Laura feared he had eaten the cat's dinner, but at least he, eager to be caressed, barking his welcome to Harriet, made her departure easier than it might have been.

"We haven't settled anything," Laura said, helping Harriet on with her coat.

"No, but it's been a great help to talk to you. I'll have to go home now and think about it."

"Don't hesitate to call if you get into a tizzy."

Laura nodded her head reassuringly.

"Good-by, Harriet, and good luck."

Laura watched the girl walk slowly down the path. She waved, but Harriet started the engine and drove off without looking back.

"Where's your cat?" Laura asked Grindle, who barked and wanted to go out. "Very well, out you go—and bring Sasha back with you if you can."

She went back to her chair and the empty glass. It would not be a bad idea to put another log on the fire, but she did not have quite the energy to do it. She sat for a while looking into the crimson, dying flame. She sat there until the fire died and the chill forced her to do something about dinner. The aftereffect of Harriet's visit was a huge emptiness that she did not know how to fill.

Chapter VIII

Next morning Laura woke at six out of a bad dream. She was being smothered under a quilt and couldn't extricate herself. "Oh, Grindle," she murmured, reaching out to find his soft ears, "oh . . ." She was afraid if she moved quickly she would have a coughing spell, but she had to sit up to breathe. And Grindle, whom she had waked out of a sound sleep, now of course wanted to go out. Sasha was sitting on the window sill. God knows the animals asked little enough, yet how long would she be able to take care of them? Then she remembered Mary O'Brien. It was a relief to know there would be someone soon. Meanwhile she got up, struggled into a dressing gown, and stumbled downstairs with Grindle trying to get past her.

"There," she said, "out you go!"

So far, no coughing spell. She got some juice and went back to bed, sitting up now, with three pillows behind her. It was a gray dawn and the air had smelled of snow when she opened the door. She would just lie here for a while, she thought, and do what came most easily these days, drift off down the long, winding rivers of consciousness that always seemed to bring her finally to the house of their childhood summers by the sea. "I must go down once more," she thought. But alone? The very image of the icy-cold, closed house made her shiver. Why isn't it spring? This winter had been interminable, with unrelenting cold to sap energy and numb the senses. Would she be given one more spring? It would be good to live to see the leaves once more.

When the phone rang, she hesitated a second. Not answer? No, it might be Aunt Minna.

"Hello."

"It's Ann. Are you all right?"

"Why?"

"Your voice sounded so far away. Maybe I woke you."

"I was awake. Good heavens, it's after eight!"

"We want you to come over for supper tonight if you can. It's Laurie's birthday, you know."

"I really am in a bad way . . . I'd clean forgotten. Of course I'll come. What time?"

"Six? Are you feeling better, Laura? Did the doctor give you an antibiotic? I've been meaning to call, but we've all had colds. You know what that's like— everyone home. Chaos!"

"Grindle is barking to get in—I forgot all about him. See you at six." At least she hadn't had to answer about her health, and in the happy confusion of a birthday supper for Laurie no one would notice. But what to give Laurie? Laura got out her jewel case and laid it on the bed. There was the diamond star, Charles's present on their twenty-fifth anniversary, and the lapis lazuli necklace her mother had given her when she was twenty-one. Laura took it out, feeling the smooth stones slip through her fingers. There was an exquisite necklace of crystal balls, strung on a thin silver chain that Ella had given her as a wedding present. There was her grandmother's engagement ring, a sapphire circled in brilliants— The thought of giving any of these away, even to Laurie, caused her a brief but acute pang. So she left the jewels there on her bed and went downstairs, for Grindle's barks had become quite cross. She had left him out in the cold far too long.

"Come in, doggo, I'm sorry I forgot you. You shall have a cheese biscuit, and I shall have some breakfast."

While the coffee perked, she considered what precious little thing she might give Laurie—Laurie just ten years old today. It seemed a great blessing that she had known this wild little granddaughter at least for ten years, and the pang she had felt for a moment had been subtly translated now into a special kind of joy, quite new to Laura, the joy of divesting herself of a treasure. It had to be her mother's lapis necklace, passed on to her great-granddaughter. Sybille would like that. But would Laurie? She never wore a dress if she could help it and would probably much prefer a pair of cross-country skis! Nevertheless Laura ended by wrapping the necklace and wrote a card to accompany it: "a treasure for my treasure on her 10th birthday." It was, she suddenly realized, exactly what her mother had written forty years before except that Sybille's card had read, "for my treasure on her 21st birthday."

Was I her treasure, Laura asked herself? And she knew that the answer was yes. Sybille had exalted her children in a special pantheon reserved for them. We were not exactly told, but we somehow got the idea that we were more beautiful, more intelligent, and gooder than any other children. But what barriers that idea had set up between them and their contemporaries!

Still, it had been intoxicating, Laura had to admit. The family temperature ran so high, they lived on the edge of a perpetual drama, the great and famous coming and going, and those wonderful balls in Genoa when they danced all night with Italian officers and young men on the staff, or leaned over the banisters to see their mother's newest conquest taking off his coat in the hall, and deciding that whoever it was was far too ugly, not tall enough, or just plain too queer to be really the "great man" their mother searched for all her life as though for the holy grail.

Poor Pa, Laura thought, but had he suffered? Sybille's marriage had been wrapped in such a gauze of illusions and self-deception on her part that it was impossible to extricate the truth from the play. There was the privately published book of passionate love poems that Sybille had written Dwight when he was in the air force in World War I and they had been separated for two years. There was really no doubt in anyone's mind that they loved each other. They flirted outrageously across the dinner table, walked up and down the terrace before dinner talking so intently that the gong had sometimes to be sounded twice before they heard it, and wrote immense letters when they were apart. Yet Sybille had left her husband for two years to nurse Laura, an act that appeared to Cousin Hope and to their friends in general one of absolute, self-immolating heroism, and to Laura herself an imprisonment not only by illness but by something she dreaded even to think about, a kind of complete possession by her mother, as though she were a small infant. And what had Pa really thought about this? He drove to Davos whenever he could get away for a day or two, bringing them every luxury he could imagine— elegant bed jackets for Laura, gold slippers for Sybille, marrons glacés, a case of champagne once. But he never seemed quite at ease in their intensely feminine world, or for that matter, in the concentrated atmosphere of illness, the gossip about doctors, the implacable routines. Laura suspected that however much he had looked forward to seeing them, he was rather glad to get away again and to go back to his own world of diplomats and economic crises, and the sub rosa attempts to help the intellectuals and radicals whom Mussolini was relentlessly imprisoning when they could not be silenced. Laura suspected that her father, with her mother's complete accord, took some risks.

But why had Sybille insisted on changing her whole life around this illness? That remained a mystery. Guilt, perhaps. Did she think she had neglected a beloved child? Or after the painful episode of Jo's infatuation with Alicia, had she experienced a surge of overprotectiveness? Must I always be critical of Sybille? Laura asked herself. If she turned to George Herbert now, it was because Sybille had read so much poetry aloud to her in those years, as well as Virginia Woolf, and, curiously enough, Trollope. She could hear at this instant her mother's husky yet musical laugh. How they had laughed sometimes, laughed till tears streamed down their cheeks!

Her mother's taste and acuity, passions and dreams were stamped on her consciousness. There was no denying that. A great "personality" as Jim Goodwin had called her did this to her children. Laura's own children, at least, had not had to fit themselves into a heroic mold.

What she hoped she and Charles had done, what they had tried to do, was to create a safe, warm world in which their children could grow rather freely—but what parent ever succeeds? The very safety and usualness had created revolt.

Laura, invaded as she was these days by memory and a need to reckon with everything before it was too late, found these ruminations tiring. It was really a good idea to be pulled out of them into the immediate present of little Laurie and a tenth birthday.

She drove up to the brightly lit house that evening full of joy and expectation.

Ann opened the door. "Come in, come in, dear Laura," she said and kissed her. "It's ages since we've seen you!"

Laurie flung her arms around Laura's waist and hugged her so hard Laura nearly lost her balance.

"Happy birthday, my treasure! This is a happy day!"

"Guess what?" Laurie said, pulling her into the living room where they were attacked by the two golden retrievers. Laura, to escape their attentions, sat down quickly. "I got a real goose-down jacket—and snowshoes—and look, Grammie, a parakeet! His name is Aucassin." The parakeet was in a cage on a small table. "Daddy's going to make me a hanger in my room, right at the window."

"May I interrupt?" Brooks said, coming in from the kitchen. "What will you have to drink, Mother? How about a glass of champagne? I have some good and cold."

"Darling, that would be lovely."

"Someone gave it to us for Christmas," Ann explained.

"How does it feel to be ten, Laurie?"

Laurie had sat down on the floor with the two dogs. She was looking into the fire and stroking one big doghead with her right hand.

"It's all right," she said. "I guess."

"You don't sound overenthusiastic."

"I'm still not allowed to do anything I really want to do."

"Where's Charley?" Laura asked.

"I sent him up to put on a clean shirt," Ann said.

"He got very dirty painting my birthday present. See!" Laurie pointed to the mantel, where a large red and blue whale—was it a whale?—on a large piece of paper had been tacked up.

"It's the story of Jonah only you can't tell very well because Jonah is inside the whale."

"He seems to have decided on a present rather late in the day." Laura smiled.

"He didn't want to give me anything. He only did it because I told him I wouldn't give him anything for his birthday unless he did."

There was a loud pop from the kitchen, and Laurie sprang to her feet. "What's that? A gun?"

"Just your father," Brooks's voice called from the kitchen, "opening a bottle of champagne. Come and watch it fizz."

"I'm going to sit down for five minutes even if dinner is late," Ann announced, and dropped down beside Laura on the tattered sofa. "Charley's been a handful. He really doesn't feel well. He's had an awful cold."

And there was Charley, flushed and bright-eyed under his shock of fair hair, floundering about with one arm in the air, his shirt half on and half off. "Help me, Mummy. I'm all mixed up in this shirt."

"There, darling." Ann thrust the lost arm into the sleeve where it belonged and buttoned up the shirt. "Now say good evening to Grammie."

Brooks came in with a tray of glasses. "Here you are, Mother."

"May I have one? It's my birthday," Laurie begged.

"Of course, this one is just for you." And Brooks bowed gravely to his daughter as he handed her a half-filled glass. They really did look amazingly alike, each with the very dark eyes and straight black eye brows they had inherited from Charles. It occurred to Laura, and she was entertained by the idea, that Laurie in her tight jeans and turtle neck might as well have been a boy, whereas fair little Charley sitting on the floor with his teddy bear might have been a girl. Of course, as the eldest, Laurie had always done things with her father:

skied with him since she was eight, always insisted on shoveling snow when Brooks shoveled.

"Where's mine?" Charley demanded, frowning.

"As soon as I've given your mother hers I'll get yours—we must have a toast!"

"There," said Brooks, handing his son a juice glass with, Laura presumed, ginger ale in it. "And now, ladies and gentlemen, I want to propose a toast to Laurie. May it be a very good year in every way, lots of snow to ski on, 100 on her math papers every time, no quarrels with her brother, and—what else?" he looked down smiling at Laurie, who was drinking in every word.

"That's impossible. The last is impossible," she said. "You could say, an improved brother, I suppose. I'm awfully tired of Charley," she told Laura.

"I'm tired of you," said Charley, not to be outdone.

"Quiet, children. Grammie has a present for Laurie. Let's call a truce and open it."

Laurie sat down on the floor at Laura's feet and turned the little box in her hands, listening to what might be inside. "I can't think what it is," she said. Then she tore off the paper and gold string and opened it.

"Oh, it's a necklace—" for a moment she held it in her hands, feeling the smooth blue stones. "It's blue." She looked up at her father, as though for help.

"Your great-grandmother gave it to me for my twenty-first birthday," Laura said. "It's lapis lazuli."

"It's beautiful," Ann said, "let me see. You shouldn't have parted with it, Laura—you're too generous."

"Thank you, Gramma," Laurie said solemnly.

"It doesn't exactly go with jeans, but maybe you could wear it for dinner." Ann suggested.

"No," said Laurie, "I'll just keep it in my secret drawer, and I'll take it out sometimes and feel it."

"I want to wear it," said Charley. "I love it," and he

reached out to take it from his mother. "It's a jewel." He lay on his stomach reaching up toward his mother, full of mischievous avidity and delight.

"No," Laurie shouted. "He can't wear it, Mummy, it's mine!"

"Listen, creeps, go into the study and look at TV for a half-hour while I get supper onto the table, then Brooks and Laura can have a few moments' peace."

"Come on, Charley!" Laura pulled him up. And, surprisingly enough, they disappeared into the study together.

"What do parents do who don't allow TV?" Ann asked as she put the necklace back into its box and laid it on the mantelpiece.

"They go quietly out of their minds," Brooks answered, coming back with the bottle to refill their glasses.

"I won't be long," Ann said, at the kitchen door. "Enjoy yourselves."

Alone with her son, who was standing at the mantelpiece, looking down at her with smiling approval, Laura felt suddenly shy.

"It wasn't the right present," she said. "Laurie is too young, but I won't live forever and maybe it's time to . . ."

"Nonsense, she loves it. Didn't you see the way she handled it?" Then he came and sat down beside her on the sofa. Laura felt his eyes on her face though she was looking down. "You look fairly beat up by that bug you had. You've lost weight."

"And a very good thing, I was much too fat."

"What did Goodwin have to say? He's a nice man, but I always have the feeling that he relies on God rather than on medicine. You look to me as though you needed some shots of B-12."

"I'm all right, Brooks, don't badger me."

"Badgering, am I?"

"A glass of champagne and being with you and Ann and the children is far better medicine than B-12 could possibly be," Laura said. "Now tell me all the news."

"Well, I'm deep in local politics, you know. We're meeting a lot of opposition to putting up a really good disposal unit like the one in Wellesley. It recycles cans, even glass, paper of course. But it's expensive and taxes will go up. You can't imagine how fierce people are when their pocketbooks are involved."

Laura sighed. Since Dr. Goodwin's verdict she found it difficult to concentrate on future plans about almost anything. "You're marvelous, Brooks. How do you ever find time?"

"Conservation just seems to me the single most important thing I can do, I guess. I want there still to be an earth to support Laurie and Charley, and sometimes I really worry. I mean, time is running out. The ocean is polluted right out to the middle of the Atlantic."

Laura drank a swallow of champagne, and then out of nowhere had a terrible attack of coughing.

"Get me a kleenex, Brooks," she managed to whisper.

He came back in a second with a box and laid it beside her, then put his arm around her and held her fast. She was simply torn to pieces by the cough.

"This is no joke," Brooks said. "That's blood you just threw up."

"It's nothing, just an infection."

"Jim Goodwin had better put his mind on this," said Brooks. "Did he take X-rays?"

At last the spasm stopped. Sweat was pouring down Laura's face. She made a gesture with her hand that Brooks interpreted as a wish to be left alone, and he went in to Ann. She could hear them talking in low voices. Tell them now? It couldn't be a worse time, but what would be a good time? Laura wished she could just go home to Grindle and Sasha and be left alone. And maybe that was the thing to do.

Then Ann and Brooks came back together.

"Dear, there's plenty of time. The potatoes aren't quite done. The children are watching a basketball game, glory be. So just take it easy, will you?" Ann sat down beside her this time and gently squeezed her hand. Laura did not want to be touched. She was afraid of weeping.

"I'm working on quite an interesting first novel," she managed to say, sitting up straight, though it was an effort.

"No, Mother," Brooks said with quiet authority. "We want to know what this is all about, and you're not going to put us off."

"I won't be any trouble," Laura said. "A very kind woman is coming next week to help me out. I do feel curiously frail."

"That's good news," Brooks said, exchanging a look with Ann.

"Good news that I feel frail?" Laura managed a smile.

"Good news that you admit it. You're not going to pull one of your mother's heroic acts on us, are you? You've told me time and again what a strain that could be."

"Yes."

There was a long silence. In it Laura relinquished her right to die in her own way, and alone. It had been, she realized, a romantic impulse. Her children had some rights, she was beginning to see. Ann, especially, had been a very real comfort when Charles died. She owed them the truth.

"It's simply that I haven't very long to live," she said. "It's cancer of both lungs, too far along to be operable."

"Mother!" Brooks rose and paced up and down. Then the shock turned into anger. "You mean, Jim Goodwin just told you that outright? Why didn't he tell me?"

"Because I asked him not to, and as for telling me, I'm rather proud that he felt he could."

"But what if he's wrong?"

"The X-rays are all too clear."

Ann was sitting very still, her hands clasped. Laura felt that she must find a way to help them bridge the abyss, and get back to normal, if that were possible. "Something very strange happened that day in Jim's office. I felt exhilarated, as though I were entering some great mysterious adventure, and I wanted to have it all to myself, and not be taken over as Mamma took me over when I had TB. Can you understand?"

"We're here to do anything we can, mother. It's not going to be easy." Brooks looked bewildered, fumbling for the right thing to say.

"I've got this woman coming next week. She's experienced and seemed not at all afraid of the responsibility, and Jim is going to come and drain the lungs himself when the time comes when that will be necessary. He explained it all to me—and I want you two to back me up about dying at home." One look at Brook's face and Laura knew she must do something drastic right away. "The potatoes must be very well done. Let's have dinner."

"Are you sure you shouldn't go home? The coughing spell must have been exhausting," Ann said, taking Laura's hand in hers.

"No," Laura said, "I don't want to go home. I want to live all I can. How can I tell you? It's been an extraordinary time for me. I feel I can cut out all nonessentials without guilt. Laurie's birthday party is essential, and

I'm quite all right now. Go and get the children, Brooks, and I'll help Ann take things in."

"You're marvelous." Ann gave her hand a squeeze.

"No . . . oh no," Laura murmured. "It's not that." Then breaking the spell in the only possible way, she got up and offered to ladle out the creamed chicken (Laurie's favorite) but was sent instead to light the candles in the dining room. It's a lovely room, she thought—the window greenhouse lit up to show cyclamen and geraniums and one white azalea in flower. Ann had put a brilliant scarlet primrose in a pot in the center of the table, which had been set with red napkins at each place on a damask cloth.

"Sit down, Charley and Laurie," Brooks said quietly.

"I'm starving," Charley said, "can I have a roll right now?"

"No."

"Red is the color when it's so cold outside, isn't it Laurie? Here, you sit by me," and she reached out to touch Laurie's dark hair just as Ann came in with two plates. "That primrose! How did you ever do it?"

"Under lights in the cellar. You must take it home with you, Laura."

"Yum, creamed chicken. Don't you love it?" Laurie said, diving right in as soon as she got her plate. "I'm so happy I'm about to burst," she announced.

"So am I," Laura said. The candle flames were slightly blurred, and she saw the whole bright table, the flowers, in the way one sees through a window with raindrops streaming down, like an impressionist painting. After one of the fits of coughing, Laura had observed that the very weakness she felt made everything luminous and beautiful. Brooks had gray in his hair (unbelievable) but looked so handsome, so all there in his true self; Laura

[81

felt amazed that he was her son. When children finally grow up, they seem marvelous apparitions; how did one ever feel responsible for such a person? What had made Brooks was, finally, his passion for conservation, not his work, which was trivial by comparison. A real commitment, that is what had firmed him up, given him a new authority, she thought. And Ann, too, looked radiant in her ruffled white blouse, in spite of the dark circles round her gray eyes. Their marriage had come into its own at last, after some rough times when Ann had a full-time job teaching. She had given that up when Charley came, and Laura knew it had not been easy. But there would be time, she thought—though when children are small, it is hard to believe.

"What are you thinking, Gram?" She was suddenly aware that Charley had been watching her intently.

"Do you really want to know?"

"Yes," he said, giving her a huge smile.

"I was thinking how good life is in this house, and how beautiful you look, all four of you."

At this Brooks and Ann exchanged a look and burst into laughter. "You should have seen us almost any day last week," Ann said. "It's little short of a miracle that no one got murdered."

"More," said Charley, holding up his plate.

"More, *please*."

"Please," he added grudgingly.

"Tell me what's happening at school, darling," Laura said to Laurie.

"She's got a really good science teacher this year." Brooks answered.

"Let me tell, Daddy. Gram asked *me!*"

"Yes, I did, and I really want to know what you think."

Now that she had the attention of everyone, Laurie was overcome by shyness.

Laura tried to help her. "I seem to remember when I was about your age that we had Roman history. And that summer my father took us to see Hadrian's wall. What a sense one gets there that Rome was a civilization! Beyond it, the wild land and the barbarians."

"We're studying Indians," Laurie said.

"Awfully grim, isn't it?"

"Yes," said Laurie gravely. "It makes me sick. I mean, we broke our word—we massacred them. But the teacher is quite boring, so I don't do as well. In science I got an A. We're studying insects, bees and ants and beetles. You know there are *millions* of beetles, Gram? And we have ants in a glass thing in the window so we can watch them."

"It sounds fascinating."

Charley had got down from his chair and come to stand beside Laura, tugging at her hand.

"What is it, Charley? Something on your mind?"

"If you like, I'll say a poem."

"That would be lovely, after we've had our dessert, maybe."

"Now," said Charley

"Don't interrupt, Charley, it's rude," Laurie said rather smugly. After all, it was her day.

This was too much for Charley, and he ran around Laurie's chair screaming, "I hate you! You never let me do anything," and began to hit his sister.

Brooks quickly intervened and dragged Charley away into the kitchen where Ann was getting the cake ready, Laura supposed. Laurie began to cry.

"I wouldn't pay any attention to him," Laura said gently. "He's so little, and he wants some attention, that's all."

"But he hurt my arm," Laurie said. "It's not fair."

"At his age everything is now. It's very hard for him to

realize that some day it will be his birthday, and *he* will be cock-of-the-walk. Run and get a kleenex and then we can go on talking. There's lots more I want to hear."

So for a few moments Laura was alone at the table. For me, too, everything is now, she thought. She would never see these two children grown up. It felt so strange, as though she had been dropped down in a parachute into the center of life, shaken to the marrow by the sweetness, the intensity of it. This moment. "Are you all right, Mother?" Brooks laid a hand on her shoulder, and she looked up at him. "Perfectly all right. I'm having a wonderful time."

"What a lot of violence we learn to bury," he said, sitting down in his place again. "I'm simply amazed at how much sheer rage there is in Charley; in Laurie too for that matter. Were we as bad as that, Ben and Daisy and I?"

Now Ann signaled to blow out the table candles and when Brooks had done so, she came in with the cake with ten little candles lit and wavering as she crossed the room. "But where's Laurie?"

"I'm here," Laurie ran in. "Oh!"

Charley followed his mother, gave his grandmother a rather shy look, and sat in his chair. "It's chocolate," he said, "with white icing."

"Now darling, make your wish, take a deep breath, and blow."

"But I don't know what to wish!" Laurie said.

"Hurry," Ann whispered.

Laurie closed her eyes, then opened them, and blew, but she hadn't quite the breath for the last candle. It flickered on.

"You won't get your wish! You won't get it!" Charley shouted, filled with merriment at this pleasant thought.

"It doesn't matter," Laurie said. "It was a stupid wish."

"Brooks, be an angel, and dish out the ice cream, will you? The plates are on the counter."

When at last they had all been served, Brooks reminded Laura that they had been interrupted just when he had asked her whether he and Daisy and Ben had been as violent as his own children.

"Daisy used to have awful tantrums. I wonder whether it isn't just frustration at being the youngest, always being told you can't do this or that. My sister Daphne went through it, too. You and Ben didn't fight, did you?"

"Oh, yes, we did!" Brooks laughed. "We had the craziest fights. Sometimes Ben wouldn't speak to me for a week. That was when I got up one night and deliberately shuffled his whole battle up into total disorder—all those troops mixed up—it had taken him days to get them in place."

"That was mean of you, Daddy," Laurie said, delighted at this bad behavior.

"What did he do then?" Charley asked, fascinated by the possibilities.

"I told you, he wouldn't speak to me for a week."

"I wouldn't mind that," Charley said, "that's nothing."

"I felt awful—beyond the pale." But Brooks's mood had changed. He looked absently down at his plate, then took matches out of his pocket and lit the candles in their tall silver candlesticks again, did it very precisely.

"Mother," he said then, "would you like me to tell Daisy and Ben?"

"Not now," Ann warned.

Over their coffee in the living room, with the children off to have their baths, Laura explained that she had told Aunt Minna.

[85

"I felt she would understand, but instead," Laura laughed suddenly, "it made her very cross. I am doing something out of turn, I suppose."

"Aunt Minna reminds me of Charley," Brooks said, laughing too. "She is so absolutely direct she can't hide anything." Then he frowned. "But, Mother, I must tell Ben and Daisy. Don't you owe something to your children, after all?"

"I don't feel I do," Laura answered, suddenly upset and close to tears, because she felt isolated, too queer to be believable apparently.

"Can you deprive them? I mean, Ben will want to come home. I'm sure he will."

"That's just what I don't want. Damn it, Brooks, it's *my* death!"

The tone was so violent that even Laura burst into laughter, and the laughter broke the tension.

"Talk a little more about it," Ann said. "How can you accept it? You are really extraordinary—I mean, after all, you're not old."

Laura frowned. She really had not thought any of it out. She had been living on an instinct to be left alone that was as strong as an animal's.

"But I've had my life, I think. At any rate I would prefer not to follow Mamma's example."

"Yes, that's awful, of course," Ann assented quickly.

"But it's more than not wanting something—it's that I want to have this little space in which to reckon it all up. They say a drowning man sees his whole life go by in a flash—it's something like that."

It was time, Laura sensed, to go home. She was floating like a person in a high fever.

"Before I go home," she said, "there is something that would be a real help later on, if someone could walk Grindle for me."

"Of course," Ann said, clearly relieved to be given a function. "The children and I will love to do that."

Laura was on her feet now, a little shaky. She reached out to Brooks to find her balance.

"Want me to drive you home?"

"No, thanks. I'll just go and say good night to the children."

The children met her at the foot of the stairs, flushed and still damp after their baths and in their pajamas.

Laurie hugged Laura hard and said, "Thank you for my necklace, Gram!"

Charley jumped up and down, singing, "Good night, Gram, good night, Gram!"

And after all the good-bys, Laura was safe in her car and homeward bound.

Chapter IX

The next day Laura lay in bed all morning. She had to admit that she felt really ill for the first time. It had been a great effort to let the animals in and out, and she had climbed back into bed, quite glad to know that Mrs. O'Brien would be in the house in a few days, three days she counted off on the calendar. But for the moment it was good to lie still, watching the sunlight through the white curtains dapple the wall, taking a sip of coffee, and having a little think, as she put it to herself. Until now she had been so busy living and getting ready in her mind for whatever was to come that she had not felt fear. Now she was terribly afraid, not of death as much as of dying, of getting more and more ill, of pain. She could feel the beads of sweat on her forehead. But there was nothing to do but wait. Fear, she supposed, was as much a part of all this as a fit of coughing. It will pass, she told herself, look at the light, the blessed light, and dear Grindle on the rug by her bed licking the ice off his paws.

She closed her eyes then while images of Laurie's birthday swam up into her consciousness. She would not, perhaps, be able to go through a long family evening again. For the truth was that most of the time, she had been floating somewhere at a little remove from Ann and Brooks and the children. No "real connection" there, she realized. But how could that be? Her own children, her precious grandchildren, not real?

Or was it simply that the future no longer concerned her? What concerned her deeply, the images that floated up whenever she lay down and listened to music, had to do with childhood, early womanhood, before her marriage, had to do with the past. Perhaps that was because all the deepest questions were asked then. Whatever she was to become had made its irreversible imprint then. That was why Sybille haunted her these days, Sybille the most indelible, yet elusive, imprint of them all. And that was why Ella was so much in her mind, too, because only with Ella had she discussed what it was to be a woman. Only with Ella had she thought about feelings. Later on she was too busy living to think a great deal about what was really happening inside her.

Laura heard the letters slip through the door and land on the hall floor. Grindle was barking furiously, and Sasha might well be on the other side of the door, silently waiting for it to open. So Laura struggled out of bed and went down. And there was Ella's letter in a thin blue envelope among a pile of bills.

She took a glass of orange juice into the library with her while the coffee perked, and lay down on the sofa. Her hands were trembling as she tore open the blue envelope.

Ella's hand raced across the page, and for a few seconds Laura drank in the nervous, characteristic flow without deciphering the words. The image of Ella rose up before her vividly, the short, dark hair, the lined brown face and flashing dark eyes.

"Ella, my darling Snab," she murmured. And for a

moment she lay there with the letter in her hand like some magic substance, not even reading it beyond the salutation, "Dearest Snab . . ."

When had they started calling each other that, and why? She hadn't the slightest idea. The word "snab" was part of their secret language.

"When I had read your letter my first impulse was to fly over for a few days, though you commanded me not to. The pull was immense. Then I realized that was self-ish, and had to do with my frightful sense of coming loss—Oh, Snab!—and that I probably could be of no help, only something more you would have to deal with and respond to when what you need, as you say so well, is to make this tremendous journey alone. You sound incredibly brave, I must say—but then you always had stupendous courage, even in Davos where the odds against you were almost insurmountable and you were the prisoner of your mother. You did get well, how I have never understood, but you did. And now in the same way, you are determined to take mortal illness as some last great experience—it is so characteristic when you say, 'I want to do it well,' and also when you say that at last you can shut out everything that is not important. Ah, that's the true snab speaking!

"In Paris we used to say that was how we meant to live, cutting out the nonessential. Do you suppose growing up always means diluting that fierce purpose for the sake of others? Only someone with a daimon, a genius maybe, would feel justified in doing so later on, at least if the someone is a woman!

"But for a year we had the luck to be able to be angelic, anarchic beings. I did work very hard, as you remember, with a kind of passion, unlike you, my Snab, who per-haps wisely chose to enjoy. Thank goodness, for you led me into so many marvelous wild adventures. Do you remember spending a fortune to taxi to Chartres on Christmas Eve, then having to spend the night in the cheapest hotel where we were devoured by bedbugs? Remember the hours we spent with Cézanne at the Orangerie? And your infatuation with the nightclub singer Stroeva, in her tuxedo and diamond studs—a Russian? 'Tu sais les mots câlins et tendres'—of course you remember!

"And our long passionate arguments about religion, whether God was really the creation of man or not, whether one could manage to live without God. And how little we wanted to marry because marriage, we felt, implied surrendering—but that is not the word I want— losing our power to command our own lives?

"Yet we did marry, you more happily than I. I certainly felt after I married Hugh that I had ceased to exist, or almost, as a person in my own right, at least for all the years when the children were growing up. Interesting, isn't it, that, late in life, we have each come to enjoy a job, and to do it well? Oh, darling Snab, my pen runs across the page, running to meet you, in a kind of desperation to get it all said, to encompass what we experienced together, to come close, and the only way I can do it seems to be remembering our youth.

"I wish I could imagine just where you are and how you are feeling as you read all this nonsense. Under it you must divine how deeply I am with you as you embark on this last journey, how I shall long for some word when you can. But I also know and accept that writing will become difficult and then impossible. I'll send messages along the way. Let us stay together in spirit to the end, and beyond the end."

Laura let the page fall. Beyond the end? As long as Ella lived she, Laura, would have an existence—they had talked about it often, how little by little, we are more and more peopled by the dead, and how as Ella had put it the last time they met and were sitting under a great oak in her garden, drinking tea, "The dead help the living." Not in a mystical sense, they had decided, but simply by having existed and through a continuing influence that could at times seem almost uncanny, as some phrase or way of reacting came to the surface just when it was needed. Not distance or time had ever come between her and Ella, and now at this moment, alone in the house, Ella's presence was so vivid that Laura lay there on the sofa for an hour basking in it.

Someday soon she would answer the letter, but now she wanted music. She finished her coffee though it was stone-cold, let Sasha in, and put a Mozart concerto on the record player. It is beginning to be a timeless world, she thought, letting herself float on the current of the music. And that is what she must learn to keep, not let go—to be as often and as much as she could wholly alive in the eternal present.

So when the telephone rang, that brutal, imperious interruption, she did not know what time it was, and answered in a daze.

"Oh, dear Aunt Minna . . . yes, I was lying here listening to Mozart."

The anxiety in the old voice at the other end of the line was tangible. "I had a wonderful letter from Ella this morning, and last night at Ann and Brooks' I had to tell them because I had a fit of coughing. Ann will come and walk Grindle later on with Laurie."

"I have been thinking," Aunt Minna announced.

"That's no news." Laura smiled.

"I mean I have been thinking about what I can do for you, and I wonder whether you would like me to come and read to you for an hour in the afternoon or whenever convenient?"

For a second Laura hesitated. Was that what she might want or need? But then she realized that it was exactly what she needed. *The Wind in the Willows,* the old favorites from the *Oxford Book of Verse,* George Herbert, maybe Jane Austen, Gerard Manley Hopkins.

"But how would you get here, darling?"

"Take a taxi. Why not?" Aunt Minna lived so frugally that it was hard to remember that she had ample means.

"I'm already thinking of things we might read." Then she added quickly, "After this weekend. It's my last before Mrs. O'Brien comes. Why don't we say next Tuesday at four? You *are* an angel, you know."

"I don't know about that. It's really an underhanded way of being sure I'll see you without being a bore."

When Laura put the receiver down, she looked at her watch and realized that she had had no lunch. It was nearly two. So she made herself a sandwich and then couldn't eat it, but managed to swallow a glass of milk in small sips. Was it really a good idea to have Aunt Minna come regularly as suggested? How could she know? How could she tell? But God knows they had all been trained to arrange time in consistent ways, not to waste it, and Laura supposed that even for the mortally ill a routine might be a support. She had the absurd vision of herself walking out into a wilderness alone and having to decide right away what to take with her, without really knowing at all what it was going to be like. I can't make plans, she realized, and that is that.

Then, at long last, she made up her mind to write the chief editor at Houghton Mifflin and resign her job, with the one proviso that she go on editing for Harriet Moors as long as she could. Her hand holding the pen felt like lead; she said the essential as briefly as possible. It was, she knew, the beginning of the letting go, the letting go of her identity as a person in the world. The job had been a life raft after Charles died, but that was long ago "and in another country."

Now she was a listener to music, a watcher of light on the walls, a person who must be more and more concerned with the inner world.

She must have slept because she woke with a start at the ring of the doorbell and a crescendo of barks. The dark was closing in though it was, she saw, with a glance at her watch, only half-past three. "Be quiet, Grindle," she said quite crossly as she got up and went to the door. And there was Ann with a florist's wrapped package in her hands.

"Come in, come in!"

"I brought some spring flowers."

"Spring flowers?" Laura felt as excited as a child. "Spring now? What a marvelous idea!" and, as Ann stood hesitantly inside the door, "Take off your coat."

"Wouldn't you like me to take Grindle for a walk? That's really why I came."

"Well, it would make him happy. How thoughtful of you, Ann."

So while Ann went off wih Grindle, who was barking his joy, Laura went into the kitchen and unwrapped the flowers. She stood for a moment looking down at them, daffodils, blue iris, yellow tulips, two purple anemones, a few branches of freesia, and breathed in their cool sweetness. How crisp, how alive, they were. With the bitter cold outside, the frozen snow, it did seem a miracle that such freshness could appear and be *real*. Laura stood there in a state of pure joy, just looking and smelling.

Arranging them in a Venetian glass vase from Sybille's house proved to be quite difficult. They flopped or stood up too straight. The task was almost beyond her strength, and when Ann came back, Laura lay down on the sofa with the flowers on a low table beside her, and was glad to let Ann make them a cup of tea. Then they talked. No one had been in the house since Laura had her news, except Harriet and Mrs. O'Brien. And she had to admit, now, that she had been lonely, and it was a comfort to look across at Ann, lovely in a pale blue turtle-neck sweater, a corduroy skirt, and elegant high boots, her cheeks pink from the cold and her eyes so bright.

"The flowers—" Laura sighed her pleasure. "What a dream!"

"I wanted" Ann said shyly, "I was afraid—I mean, I didn't want to intrude, but . . ."

"It was a very good idea," Laura said. "I've been lonely but I didn't know it."

"It was wonderful of you to come to Laurie's birthday. The first thing she did this morning was to ask for her necklace. We had put it on the mantelpiece last night, you remember."

"It's much too grown-up, but I hope she'll wear it happily later on, and I wanted to give it to her myself." Having said the obvious, Laura felt marooned. She took a sip of tea and laid the cup down. She saw Ann alone so rarely that she didn't know where to begin. "Brooks seems in good form?"

"Very. He's a different person since he has become so involved in conservation. Sometimes I think it's because he has a legitimate outlet for anger!"

Laura smiled. For all her rather forced eagerness, Ann had a wry perception of things that often hit the mark.

"That is certainly a help."

"My problem is that I don't. I envy him."

"But you're not an angry sort of person, are you?" As soon as Laura had uttered the words, she realized how condescending they had sounded.

Ann laughed her ironic laugh. "I'm hardly a person

these days—you know all about it, Laura, two small children and no help. You can't imagine how exhilarating it was to go off alone, buy flowers, and come and see you! I felt like a tiger escaped from the zoo."

They exchanged a smile and then allowed themselves a small silence. Intimacy begins in silence, Laura was thinking. And it's true that I have almost never had a chance to talk with Ann alone. So I know something about her as a social being but almost nothing about what goes on inside. Shall I, can I make the effort? What I really want is to put on a Mozart record and look at the flowers.

"But I mustn't tire you, I'll be gone in a minute."

"Stay," Laura said gently. She had seen the shadow cross Ann's face. "I'm not ill, you know. It's just that I can't seem to cope with practical things. I'm way off somewhere in a daydream, but I'm very glad to be pulled back into life—Charles and I used to complain when the children were small that we never saw each other. It was very different in Mamma's day. She was our enchantress who did all the amusing things with us, like going to the opera or the zoo, or inventing plays, but there was always a nurse or a governess to drag us away when it was time for dinner. Someone else did the drudgery, and until those years when I had TB in Switzerland, she and Pa had all the time in the world for what they liked best, entertaining the charming and the great, and being with each other."

"They really did seem entranced with each other, at least so I felt the few times I saw them together before your father died. Of course I was terrified of your mother. She was so grand! I felt tongue-tied and at a total loss. She always seemed to be in on some tremendous secret that made her life glorious in ways I couldn't even imagine. Brooks adored her, and I always felt diminished in his eyes after we had gone there to lunch."

"Yes," Laura sighed, "I expect you did. Mamma was very good at that, though it was not a conscious thing at all."

"She didn't really like women. Am I right?"

"I don't know. No doubt she would have preferred three sons to three daughters, but she did have several adoring women friends, you know, long-lasting, real friendships."

"But for her—I'm guessing—a lasting friendship had to be based on someone adoring *her*."

"Yes . . . and no," Laura said, thinking of poor Cousin Hope. "Maggie Teyte, Edith Wharton were famous by the time mother knew them, and with each of them she wooed, if you will—she could be a marvelous listener. Maggie Teyte always said she never had an audience like Mamma, and Mamma was not acting when those French songs brought tears of something like rapture to her eyes, and no doubt a pang too because of course Mamma should have been an actress. That would have solved everything."

"What was it like to be her daughter?" The question had been in the air for some time, Laura sensed, yet it caught her off her guard.

"Heaven and hell," she answered. "That's true," she said, surprised at her own answer. "That's really it. It was heaven when we were quite small because Mamma did enclose us in a kind of magic charm, and we didn't mind then that she was acting the part of an adorable mother because she played it so well."

"Oh, dear," Ann laughed. "It does make our life now seem pretty dreary by comparison. Colds, tantrums, endless meals to be provided, no Edith Wharton coming to dinner—very little heaven around 4 Concord Place!"

"But it's real, you see. And somehow Mamma's life was never quite real."

"What was the hell?"

"The hell? Hard to say it in words, or even to know. I suppose the hell was never landing."

"Never landing?"

Laura laughed. "You see, it's too complicated—how can I say it?—never landing on earth, hard, dirty, ordinary earth. That's what we longed for."

"May I ask a pointed question?"

"Of course."

"Did you feel that you had landed when you married Charles, then?"

"Yes, I did." Laura lay back with a pillow behind her head. "It was a kind of miracle because under mother's aegis I might have overlooked Charles—he was neither very rich, nor very brilliant, and only got through law school by the skin of his teeth, but Charles was real, funny, loving, warm. I was literally starving for just that."

"You must miss him terribly."

"I did. Well, *you* know, dear Ann, you were such a help when Charles died, but now I am glad I can do this alone. It would have been doubly difficult with Charles agonizing at my side. I couldn't have borne that."

"You are an amazing person," Ann said, her eyes very bright.

"Am I?" Laura laughed. "Most of the time I feel too queer for words. We're all loons, really, my two sisters are quite impossible, each in her own inimitable way, impossible. And I? I suppose I am possible, which was a relief for my children, anyway." Here she suddenly sat up "But even so—and we did, I think, make a good open and loving world for our children—only Brooks has come through into happiness."

"The open world has its dangers, too."

Again Laura indulged in a silence. It was good to know that she and Ann could talk like this, talk and be silent. In the silence she was thinking about Daisy who appeared incapable of choosing a life, the rebel without a cause, wondering for the millionth time what had gone wrong. She was drawn back from these thoughts by Ann's getting up.

"I'm tiring you, and it's time I went. Thanks for the tea and telling me all you did." As Ann stooped down to kiss her, Laura reached out for her hand and held it tight, looking up into her face, for a second so close. "Dear Ann, I haven't heard a word about *you*. Sit down a minute. After all, there isn't infinite time."

"I really have played hooky long enough—and I'll come back."

"But I may not be here in the same way," Laura said quietly. "We have to face that fact." She felt it imperative to capitalize on this moment of intimacy. "Everything is now for me these days."

Ann was silent. She had sat down as bidden, but she looked withdrawn.

"I can guess that these are not the easiest years of your life. I remember at times feeling caught when the children were small, caught and so tired that getting through the day was all I could ask of myself. You seem so marvelously able to do it all, you create such an atmosphere of, how shall I say, ease and joy? Brooks is a lucky man, and I, dear Ann, am grateful."

But I am blundering about, Laura realized, talking too much, and she lay back and looked at the flowers. The anemones had opened wide, their dark, velvety hearts revealed. "Look at the anemones," she murmured.

"Yes." Ann gave a long sigh. "I suppose I'm scared because I feel Brooks is outgrowing me. I can't share in what interests him most because there simply isn't time or energy. When he comes home from those long meetings I'm in bed, half-asleep. I feel I've become a donkey and he is proving to be a race horse."

Laura laughed aloud at this. "I really can't see Brooks

as a race horse, A dear Morgan perhaps, docile and biddable."

"He's really changed. He's on fire about conservation. It's as though everything, his intelligence and heart, his sensitivity to everything natural—you know—as though it all pulled together." Ann frowned. "I feel mean because I can't match that fire, or catch it, for that matter. I feel so dull, Laura!"

What was there to answer to this, Laura wondered. The only answer was time—in a few years you will be in another place altogether. But when someone is in acute pain—and she could sense that Ann was close to tears—"time" is no answer at all.

"Our marriage has been a see-saw—" Ann went on. "Maybe all marriages are. Ten years ago I was absorbed in the school. I was coming into my own then, and perhaps Brooks sometimes felt I was not there for him, and maybe I wasn't. Our first child was to solve that and bring us together in a joint enterprise."

"But that wasn't what happened?"

"Laurie is a tremendously vital little girl. I must tell you something rather amusing," Ann interrupted herself, "Charley really wants to be a girl too, and he is very feminine, you know."

"And nobody is going to worry about that," Laura said. "Wonderful things are happening, Ann, and one, I think, don't you? is the acceptance of androgyny."

"Brooks worries."

"Nonsense. Charley wants to imitate his sister. That's natural enough, she is such a power."

"I sometimes think Brooks and I are more separate and have less of a real union since the children came, and that worries *me*." She got up and this time put on her coat. "I've stayed much too long. Tomorrow I'll bring the children—we'll walk Grindle, and we won't stay a minute. You've been an angel. I guess what I really think is it's damned hard to be a woman, Laura." She smiled.

"Yes."

Ella would agree with that statement, Laura thought later, lying in the dusk, unwilling to turn on a light. If a woman marries and has children, she is going to have to give up a large part of her life, perhaps a third, to child-rearing, to homemaking, and this is simply not true for a man, so all the emphasis today on "becoming oneself" only adds to the inescapable conflict.

"I don't want to settle down." She could hear Daisy's passionate outbursts. "I don't want to lock myself into the prison like you."

And it did no good to assure Daisy that she, Laura, had never felt like a prisoner, for Daisy simply did not believe it.

Sybille, Laura, Daisy. One extraordinary and destructive woman, one rather ordinary woman, and one maverick. What did it really add up to or mean?

I'm much too tired to find the answer to that, Laura thought. What I need is some music. "And where is Sasha?" she asked Grindle, who was asleep in his bed. "Where's your cat?"

Chapter X

Daphne had called and was on her way from New York, so Laura's precious last days before Mrs. O'Brien descended had been seized, preempted by Brooks's taking things into his own hands. Daphne had called at ten that night, waking Laura to a dreadful fit of coughing, and after the call she had been too angry to sleep. Now it was morning at long last; Grindle was out; she was drinking a cup of black coffee; and in a few hours Daphne would arrive. This was the day Laura had planned to read Ella's letters and pack them up to be mailed. She had planned the day for that, for music, for reading poetry, for assembling herself before the invasion. To be deprived of it made everything feel disorderly, chaotic, impossible to handle. The wastebaskets should be emptied; she should put on clean sheets and get the laundry ready to go—what would she find to give Daphne for dinner? Or should they simply stagger out in the rain, for of course it was raining, and in a few hours the roads would be soup as the dirty snow melted into mud!

Only Sasha, licking herself at the end of the bed, had her usual air of serenity.

"But I've got to move you, Sasha." Even cat tranquillity must now be disturbed to air the bed and get started.

Making the bed left Laura so weak that she went downstairs and, after opening a can for Sasha and letting her out and Grindle in, lay on the sofa in her wrapper, trembling with weakness and rage. What time was it, anyway? Half-past seven, too early to call Brooks.

"Oh, Grindle," she groaned. "I'm not fit for anything, not even to get up and fetch you a cheese biscuit. I'm a wreck, Grindle."

There were the flowers, the anemones still closed back into buds for the night. They had not changed. And for a moment Laura let her eyes rest on them, trying to shut out all the nagging thoughts, "the must-dos," for their silent beauty. But she felt nauseated, and it is hard to contemplate beauty when you are about to throw up. Laura closed her eyes. Tears slid out from under her lids. It's hard, she told herself, it's just plain hard that I am not to have my one last day before it is all taken from me. But somewhere deep down she knew that this kind of self-indulgence was something she could not afford. She must hold onto herself. "Hold onto oneself"; what an odd locution. It meant getting a grip again on that small core of defiant self-assertion that had kept her, so far, from self-pity, she supposed. It meant not giving in, not breaking into a million pieces. It meant forcing herself to get up, take a pill for nausea, and then slowly swallow down a bowl of cornflakes.

By eight o'clock the black mood was fading. She had not thrown up, but she was still angry enough to call Brooks.

"Hi, Mother."

"I asked you not to tell anyone, Brooks."

"I know," there was a slight hesitation, as well there might be. "But, Mother, you have to think of other people, for God's sake. I only told Daphne, your sister."

[103

"I told you I wanted my own death my own way, Brooks. What right have you to butt in like this? It simply means that you are not to be trusted. I'm very angry."

"I'm sorry, Mother. Listen, Ann wants to speak to you."

"Laura," Ann's voice came through, "I realize this is hard for you, but—"

"These were my last two days before Mrs. O'Brien comes. It's not fair."

Laura had the strange perception that Ann and Brooks were talking like parents and she like a recalcitrant child. ("It's not fair," the cry of childhood!)

"We should have thought of that, shouldn't we, Brooks?" Ann did seem to have a glimmer of understanding. "How can we help? Would you like us to ask Daphne over for supper?"

"Never mind. What's done is done. I'll manage."

Brooks came back on the phone. "Mother, I just felt it was too great a responsibility for me alone. I'm awfully sorry if I bungled things. Please try to understand."

"Maybe it's all right," Laura said grudgingly. "Daphne can tell Jo, Ben, and Daisy, when I feel it's time. Daphne, not you, Brooks. Is that clear?"

"Yes, Mother."

It was all right with Ann yesterday, Laura thought, but she is not family. Why was it that family seemed such a threat, a threat she simply couldn't handle? People at one remove—Harriet even, a perfect stranger—yes. Family tore the nerve. Yet even as she asked herself the question, Laura knew that she would be glad once Daphne was there. She had better get dressed now and be ready.

Putting on a soft pink shetland sweater and gray slacks and tying a Liberty scarf around her neck, Laura met herself in the mirror several times. Lately she had

avoided the mirror. Her appearance was perhaps important to other people—she must not allow herself to look
like an old rag bag—but in her own mind appearance
was becoming quite irrelevant. Still, it was a shock to see
that a veil of wrinkles was taking over her face. I'm becoming an old woman fast, she saw. She slipped a belt
around her slacks to hold them up, for she had lost
weight.

> "Hope lies to mortals
> And most believe her
> But man's deceiver
> Was never mine."

She murmured, and that sounded like Housman, but she
couldn't quite remember. Daphne would be shocked by
how she looked. Dear old Daff who had been given extraordinary beauty and couldn't have cared less, or
rather actively tried to protect herself against what she
believed was a curse, a kind of albatross around her
neck. "It's like being an empty bottle. No one cares
about what is *inside*, men don't care anyway." But the
fact was that young men had been terrified of Daphne.
Dear old Daff was, underneath a highly cultivated crusty
exterior, horribly sensitive to what was going on in other
people, and even more in animals. Daff would get a
shock.

But the meeting, when the doorbell rang an hour earlier than expected, was of course not at all what Laura
had imagined. She opened the door and was immediately struck by how awful Daphne looked, in a dirty
trench coat, her gray hair tousled and her intense blue
eyes surrounded with great dark circles.

"Laura darling!" Laura didn't have to say anything,
she was enfolded in Daphne's arms. "I couldn't wait—I
took an earlier plane, didn't sleep a wink."

"Where's your bag?" Laura asked, brushing the tears away with an impatient gesture.

"Oh, I left it on the step."

By the time the bag had been brought in and Daphne had taken off her trench coat, Laura was quite aware that the tears that had taken her by surprise like a fit of coughing had spurted out because she could not get used to Daphne being so old. When she thought of her sister, the person she thought of was twenty or thirty even, but never fifty-five!

"Are you all right, Daff? I must say you look awful. Let me make you some coffee."

"All right? How can I be all right when I hear from Brooks that you are dreadfully ill. All right? Laura, you are a monster not to have told me yourself."

They were leaning on the kitchen counter, waiting for the coffee to heat up. Daphne leaned over and laid her hand on Laura's shoulder, and looked so penetratingly at her sister that Laura felt her eyes as tangibly as her touch and turned away to look out the window at the sturdy row of pines at the end of the field.

"I didn't mean to tell Brooks, but I had a stupid fit of coughing after dinner, and they made me tell them. He broke a promise when he called you."

At this cold answer, Daphne suddenly laughed.

"I know I seem quite preposterous. For all I know cancer changes one's personality. I'm not secretive, but—oh, hell, don't ask me to explain. I can't. Let's drink our coffee in peace. You can light the fire, Daff, if you will. Put on another log. Stooping makes me cough."

"Anything to oblige, your majesty."

"You know, I've been thinking, one thing illness does is to make one humble. I have no illusions that I can handle this alone. There is a kind Irish woman coming to look after things the day after tomorrow."

Daphne received this news in silence and drank her coffee.

"You're thinking, why not family, aren't you?"

"It did cross my mind that after all I am your sister, and my job is not so important that I can't leave it. I did that when Charles died, you remember."

"Darling, you were wonderful."

"Thanks. My ego was about to disappear from view for good."

It was quite a help that Grindle made it known that he had been outdoors far too long, and Daphne had to be jumped at with a crescendo of delighted barks and thoroughly licked after she had let him in, Sasha gliding past without recognizing her presence. "Grindle at least is glad to see me," she called back from the hall. "Yes, adorable creature, you may lick my ears."

"How is the job?" Laura asked, when Daphne had come back to lie on the floor by the fire, and Grindle had quieted down and settled beside her to be scratched around his ears.

"I'm pretty fed up with the human race," Daphne said. "The horrible people who maltreat their animals and then bring them in sick or neurotic—a dog who is left alone for hours every day and gets no exercise for instance and so becomes vicious. You should hear Dr. Gordon tell those owners off. It's all part of the total wreck of civilization, I suppose. But animals are so *innocent*."

Watching the clever, sensitive hands stroking Grindle, Laura remembered the time when Daphne was about the most beautiful girl she had ever seen and had wanted so desperately to be a vet. It was treated as an adolescent whim, and she was packed off to Smith College.

"Do you think you should have been allowed to be a vet?" Laura asked.

"Whatever made you remember that?"

"I appear to spend most of the time remembering, trying to understand. Although there's so little time, in a
strange way I feel liberated of all that used to consume
the days, the endless papers that fill the wastebaskets
every day. I'm through with all that, you see. I'm trying
to reckon everything up. I don't 'do' much anymore, but
I think a lot." It was, after all, good to have Daff to talk
with, and Laura looked across and smiled. "Tell about
being a vet."

"It's so long ago." Daphne lit a cigarette and took a
long puff, then laid it down on the hearth. "Does smoke
bother you? I can put this filthy thing out."

"It doesn't bother me."

But it did bother Grindle, who gave Daphne a queer
little look and removed himself to his basket.

Laura watched her sister, sitting there smoking and
poking at the fire, a ravaged face, tragic in repose—but
then what mature face is not, Laura asked herself? An
unravaged face would mean an unlived life.

"What are you thinking, Laura, with that penetrating
look of yours?"

"I was thinking that you look like someone who has
really lived her life."

At this Daphne looked up, and they laughed together.

"Meaning that I look, as you said when I came in,
awful. Life is such a struggle. I almost envy you." But
shocked at her own statement, Daphne quickly withdrew it. "That's a sin."

"I don't see why. When I see Mamma I know I am lucky
not to end it like that. I went the other day and Cousin
Hope was there, faithful Hope who goes in every week
to worship at the shrine, even though the goddess is no
longer there."

"In your reckoning, what happens about Mamma?"

Daphne sat up now, quite straight, leaning one elbow on her crossed legs.

"She haunts."

"I suppose I have spent most of my life trying to be her opposite, and a lot of sense that made!" Daphne laughed her harsh laugh, so often directed against herself. "It's possible that I did have a vocation—after all here I am trudging over to the animal hospital every day, paid next to nothing. But how does one know? I allowed myself to be persuaded."

"You were very young, and then we were all so rootless. It was terribly wrong that you were forced to stay in Switzerland when I was ill."

"I wonder. I loved skiing passionately, and Mamma was so absorbed in you, I was comparatively free then. What I missed, I guess, was Pa. At sixteen I needed him, and he wasn't there." Then she looked across at her sister. "How you ever survived I can't imagine."

"Charles helped! I could have become quite unreal if I hadn't met Charles."

"Jo has simply fled into her ivory tower where she can run everything in sight and be accountable to no one, except the trustees, who of course think she is a genius. And what did I do? Spent my life trying to achieve independence, I suppose, falling consistently and foolishly in love with one inappropriate man after another."

"Dear Daff, you always did exaggerate—have there been so many? David surely is a more or less permanent part of your life and has been for twenty years."

"Good heavens, yes! What seemed impermanent has become permanent, almost in spite of me. I'm just an old cushion he can rest his head on. He's frightfully overworked, of course, and still has to cope with that archneurotic wife of his."

[109

"But you do love him?"

"Do I?" Daphne asked herself. "I suppose I must. He is the one man I have known whom I could accept wholly, as he is, the good with the bad. Maybe that is love. And then he needs me. He really does."

"How strange our lives have been."

Daphne got up. "Darling, I'm going to exhaust you. Let me buzz around, make your bed, do the dishes, empty the wastebaskets, whatever, and you put on a record, or have a little rest with Grindle."

"That sounds lovely."

"You're white as a sheet."

"I want to think about everything, but after a little while I feel too tired . . . too stupid."

It was, she realized, much easier to lie comfortably and think about Daphne than to carry on a conversation, for then the flow of memory was stopped and short-circuited. But first, music. Laura got up and found a Haydn cello concerto. The strength, the virility of Haydn was what she craved. And what had she meant when she said their lives had been strange? Strange, she supposed, because they had been insignificant. Was it cruel and obtuse to think of Daphne's as a failed life? Beauty, intelligence, superior sensitivity, finally put to use to work as a drudge in an animal hospital, and to support and bring aid and comfort to David who, it had to be admitted, was a great man in his way, one of the pioneers in heart surgery—but without any of the structure or social position of a marriage to support. The fact was that Daphne was still living the life of a young woman, not one nearing old age. And she had stayed amazingly young because she was still so vulnerable, so unprotected. If, as Yeats thought, "there's more enterprise in going naked," then one had to admire her.

Daisy did. Daisy felt that Daphne was a hero. "She hasn't compromised, you see," she had told Laura once. "She hasn't let herself be caught. She's absolutely authentic."

"But she's failed at everything!" Laura suddenly remembered the whole conversation and how astounded she had been by the passion in Daisy's voice.

"Except at being a great human being, Mother," Daisy had said with withering scorn.

"Jo's never compromised," Laura had gone on, and the scene had remained so vivid in her memory because that day she had persisted like a balky donkey in rousing her daughter's anger and contempt. "Jo has done exactly what she wanted to do."

"Aunt Jo may have done what she wanted, but—oh, can't you see? What she wanted was to be safe, safe from any really deep human relationships, and to feel justified in fending off anything that might disturb her self-immolation in that college. She's a workaholic if I ever saw one."

"Some people might say she's devoted and selfless."

"Oh, my God, Mother! Some people won't pay the price of being a woman, let's face it. Jo's just as limited in her way as a woman who lets herself be swallowed up by family life and becomes a drudge—except that that sort of woman is at least *human*. She is not."

Laura remembered that she had felt ruffled and cross by the time her intransigent daughter left.

What was it then to be a woman? More complex and far more difficult, she was beginning to realize, than it is to be a man.

Daphne must have heard her sigh, for she came in and sat down. "And what was that sigh all about?"

"Daisy." Laura waited a second, poised on the question whether it would be wise to open up that subject now. "I was remembering a wild argument we had not long ago about you and Jo. Daisy thinks you are a hero."

"I fit in with her anarchic views, that's all."

Suddenly Laura got up, lifted up by an irresistible idea.

"Daff, would you drive me down to the house in Maine? We could go tomorrow—take a picnic—"

"But, Laura, it's February! The driveway won't even have been plowed."

"Oh, yes, it's kept plowed because of the risk of fire. And Mrs. Eaton down the road has the key and would light fires for us."

"It's possible, of course, and you know I'd do anything for you, Laura. I just wonder whether it could be worth what is bound to be exhausting for you."

"I have to do what I can and not count the cost. It's the last chance. Could you stay till Tuesday possibly?" Laura did not know quite why she felt such urgency, but the pull was as strong as the undertow in the cove. "The smell of salt and iodine—the gulls—oh, Daff! The sound of the sea."

"Very well. But in that case you had better rest all afternoon and not say a word."

"Angel!"

"I'll stuff some eggs, and maybe there's a can of deviled ham somewhere."

"I think there may be. Look on the top shelf." Laura felt weak with excitement. "A thermos of consommé—remember the old picnics?"

"Of course. A thermos of consommé and a thermos of martinis. We'll do it, darling!"

"One last time."

"But February, Laura! I think it's an awful risk."

"I'll manage. Liquor helps."

"I didn't mean your health. I meant—"

"We'll have to risk that." And "that," Laura knew, meant whatever memory had in store for them in a cold February house.

Chapter XI

"Here we are," Laura murmured, as Daphne drew up in front of the long flight of steps to the front door. Here it was, the childhood fortress, the house of all the summers, green trim, weathered shingles, many-paned windows sparkling in the sun, standing there like an ark surrounded by its porches. "How the trees have grown, Daff!" For in the fifty or sixty years since they had been planted, Norway spruce and hemlock, arbor vitae had enclosed the space around it. By common accord they sat for a moment, after Daphne had turned off the ignition, just taking it in. The piles of snow made no difference. It all looked like itself.

Then Mrs. Eaton opened the door, hugging herself in an old gray sweater. "Well, you made it!"

Laura got out and went ahead. "We just had a yen to see the old place—and Daphne was up from New York. How are you? I'm afraid it was a nuisance shoveling the steps and all."

"Not a bit. Silas did the shoveling. Brought in wood enough to last you a week!"

"Where is Silas?" Daphne asked, as she arrived carrying the picnic in a basket. "I want to see that boy."

"Well, he had to go back to the store. The Rundletts are down in Florida, and Silas is tending the store for a while. It's a change from lobstering, and he takes to it. Seems like he'd rather stay on shore these days, and I don't blame him. Fishing's not what it used to be."

Laura had gone into the big living room and was sitting on the little bench, warming her hands at the fire and looking around at the Japanese prints on the wall, the white wicker furniture and its blue and white chintz cushions, the blue Chinese rug.

"Sit down, Mrs. Eaton," Daphne was saying.

"I'd like to, but I have to get back to heat up some chowder for Silas. I would have brought you some, but of course the water is turned off, and I thought it might be more trouble than it's worth."

"It's a lovely fire. Thank you," Laura said.

"And thank Silas, if we don't see him," Daphne added.

"Don't you worry about anything. I'll come back tomorrow, roll up the rug again, and put the cushions away."

Daphne went to the door with Mrs. Eaton and then pulled two chairs up close to the fire. "It's cold," she shivered. "We can't stay long."

They listened to the pick-up trundle down the road, and then Daphne opened the thermos and poured two martinis into paper cups.

"Listen," Laura said before she took a swallow, "the sea."

"Tide's rising," Daphne said. "You can hear it. Even on a calm day remember how there's a little roar as the tide pulls the waves in?"

For a long moment they listened to the immemorial sound.

"What did we used to do first?" Laura asked.

"Race down to the shore and take off our sneakers and go in wading. Remember how cold the water was and how the stones hurt, and how hard it was to keep one's footing!"

"Then we had to be sure everything was still there, the tree house, the old rowboat, the mossy dell, the lady slippers—in that small clearing among the firs. Oh, the smell of it all! The pine, the salt—"

"The wild roses. On some days when the wind came from the sea all you could smell was roses." Daphne looked ten years younger, her cheeks flushed in the firelight. She looked happy, Laura thought.

"Aren't you glad we came?"

"I am." Daphne got up and stood back to the fire. "And now we must think of a toast. Pa always liked toasts."

"And was very good at them."

"What shall it be?" Daphne threw her head back, thinking.

"There's only one possible toast today, in this house—to Sybille!"

But this brought Daphne sharply back from her dream.

"Why Sybille?" she asked, frowning and looking down at her drink. "Why Mamma?" she asked more gently.

"It's her house, after all. She said we had to have one permanent place. And you have to admit, Daff, that was a true piece of wisdom. She insisted that we have family summers, don't you remember?"

"I was too small. I don't remember the house ever not being here."

"I think I wanted so much to come back, because—" Laura hesitated to put so wild and deep an impulse into words, and suddenly she was crying.

"Laura, what's the matter?"

"Nothing— Mamma— I thought perhaps—"

"Yes, I see," Daphne broke in, as Laura blew her nose. "You thought perhaps if we came back here, we could solve the riddle once and for all."

"I suppose so."

"A beautiful mother and three beautiful daughters," Daphne said, "it shouldn't be a riddle at all."

"All human relations are riddles," Laura said. "And the same person may be a fury and an angel all at the same time. Here in this place we saw Mamma mostly as an angel, wouldn't you agree? Remember our reading Shaw and Ibsen around the fire?"

"And Shakespeare—how I loved being Ariel!" Daphne said, sitting down again. "Of course you are right, L., to recapture the magic world. We were, until we began to grow up, actors in a supremely interesting play." And she smiled one of her bittersweet smiles. "Family life was the soap opera in those days!"

The sisters exchanged a mischievous glance. "Summers," Laura murmured, "messing around in boats—"

"Falling in love with the local boys. Can you believe that Silas is fifty or more? Do you suppose his red hair has turned gray?"

"Pa getting so nervous and cross before our yearly picnic on bird island, packing baskets of food into the motorboat, and once forgetting the beer! What a disaster! We got so thirsty before the day was over we nearly pooped."

"I had lemonade. I was too young for beer."

"You were lucky!"

Daphne put another log on the fire, took one look at her sister, and pulled a sandwich and stuffed egg out of the bag. "Here, darling, you'd better eat something before you vanish behind the looking glass, like Alice."

"Thanks. I don't feel much like eating." It was quite

[117

impossible, Laura said to herself, to feel nauseated in these circumstances—no water. Was Brother Ass, her body, from now on going to intervene in any pleasure? "Give me a sip of coffee, Daff, will you?" She wiped the sweat off her face, and the hot coffee did go down. And for a moment she let herself sink into a kind of limbo, a state of nonbeing, shutting off the valves into feeling or thinking. She closed her eyes.

When she opened them, Daphne was standing in the big window looking out to sea.

"Daff?"

"Are you all right?"

"I had a little nap. I feel better."

"The sea is that extraordinary blue, Fra Angelico blue Mamma called it, and there's a paler line just at the horizon." Daphne came back and sat down, stretching out her hands to the fire. "I've been thinking."

"I've been not-thinking," said Laura. "I'm getting quite expert at that."

"You are kinder to Mamma than I am, I wonder why."

"I think of her as Sybille, not as Mamma. I think of her as herself, as she was when we were young—not now, of course. Maybe growing up is being able to think of one's parents as people in their own right."

"Perfect detachment? That's impossible!" Daphne said, with something of her old violence, that sudden flame that used to leap up when she was angry or upset.

"No, not that exactly. But Sybille was a truly grand person, a hero to Cousin Hope, Daphne. We have to remember that. She made immense demands on herself, never was self-indulgent, had real guts when it came to fighting for anything she believed in, and did it all with such style, *Noblesse oblige*. Don't you think she exemplified that?" Daphne did not answer, and Laura went on, possessed now by the quarry, not tired or ill, lifted up again on the stream of time, of life itself. "Grandeur is not perhaps something children want of their parents. Parents must be normal, comfortable, not extreme, so Sybille was disturbing as a mother, there's no doubt in my mind about that. But we adored her. Have you forgotten how she looked when she came to kiss us good night, wearing her jewels, in that flowery Liberty silk or a white linen dress I always loved because there was something grecian about it, so plain and elegant? Is not great beauty—and you have to admit she had that—not a gift to one's children, after all?"

"She certainly thought so."

"But didn't you?"

"No. It was like a shield between Mamma and me," said Daphne in a cold voice.

"Yet of the three of us, you alone inherited it."

"Like some enormous, very grand house in which I couldn't live, if you must know."

"You really hated being beautiful, didn't you?"

"I felt inadequate. And then—it put me always in a false position. Mamma loved adoration because she never wanted to be near anyone, you see. I hated it because I felt it made a wall between me and other people." She laughed. "It was like being perpetually overdressed. And what made it worse was that I didn't know what I wanted to do with my life. Oh, well, here we are, Laura, survivors of that great blaze—Mamma!" And Laura, as Daphne threw back her head and laughed, caught a faint glimpse of the beauty she had been at twenty.

"Yes, we were burned, but my children got the glow, and I'm glad of that. Daisy connected with Sybille, and Daisy is not apt to go overboard for anyone as you well know." Thinking of Daisy, Laura sighed. "I suppose I am kinder in my thoughts toward Sybille because I am more aware than you can be, Daff, how damned difficult the whole mother-daughter thing is."

"What is it that's so difficult? Talk about it," Daphne

again sat on the little bench, stretching her long legs out.

"I wish I could. I only know that somehow Ben, especially Ben, but Brooks too, could take criticism for instance. And Daisy simply flew into a rage if I made the slightest critical remark, and still does, for that matter."

"Of course that kind of thing was left to governesses in our day. I can't remember Mamma being critical—only I always felt snubbed by her praise. That was it!" Daphne said clapping her hands. "I used to write poems—do you remember that?—and Mamma was always so kind, but in a way that made me go and tear the poem up. And then she read some great poem, you know, and I just shriveled."

"Her standards were extremely high."

"Oh, I admit that. That's half the trouble. If you must know, it took me years to stop being an insufferable snob when it came to the arts. We were so damned superior."

"But Sybille really wasn't a snob. Look at the people she invited!"

"Yes, but they had to be special in some way. There was that rumpled poet at one time, but Mamma thought he was a genius. Genius was acceptable even if dirty and rude."

"The odd thing is that although she had such taste, she really often 'took up,' if that is the phrase, with terrible duds. There was that philosopher with some crazy theory of the universe." Laura smiled. "Yet there were real stars, too, Maggie Teyte, Edith Wharton, and after we moved back to Boston, the Whiteheads."

Daphne lit a cigarette and smoked for a moment while Laura, suddenly hungry, ate a sandwich. The fire was dying down, and the room felt suddenly terribly cold.

"We are going to have to leave, Laura. It's just too cold."

"Put another log on the fire. I don't care if I freeze.

What does it matter? I want to stay just a little longer, Daff." For Laura was still in pursuit of her quarry, still carried on the current of a strange excitement.

"Of course, darling, whatever you want. I'm glad we came," she said, lifting another big log and throwing it onto the embers in a shower of sparks. "Aren't you? It was a good idea of yours."

"Yet coming here, back into the good years, back into what was, after all, a marvelous childhood, has not made you less relentless, has it?"

"Somehow, L., you had your real life—"

"And you have not had yours?" Laura frowned. She did not really want to contemplate her sister's failure, if it had been that.

"Of course not. I was so busy trying not to be like Mamma that I suppose I have ended up being nothing at all."

"But that's not true. Your measure is still Mamma's, that only some extraordinary gift, some heroic act, some larger-than-life-size accomplishment is what matters."

Daphne gave her sister a frightened look.

"Since I've known that I haven't long to live, it's strange, but I think I've come to understand better what it's all about, why we're on earth."

"Lucky woman!"

"Isn't it simply to grow, to become more human—not achievement, not fame, nothing like that—and Daphne, you are such a great human being. You're such a loving, warm person, and you had to break down a lot of walls to become that. I think you're splendid," Laura said.

"A splendid failure," Daphne answered, but she looked shy, confused, exactly as she had as a child when someone praised her. "I guess it takes a long time to grow up."

"Yes, and in a queer way Sybille never did. Because

growing up means being able to look at oneself, and to understand oneself. She never did—and that, in the end," said Laura with a kind of triumph, for she had perhaps reached the quarry at last, "is what made Sybille so destructive."

"If only I could see her just once not in a noble role!" Daphne said, holding her head in her hands.

"Well, Jo," Laura said quickly. "She was anything but noble in that role."

"You mean about Alicia?"

"I think Sybille behaved really badly there, ruthlessly, and I think she did it because she couldn't face the same thing in herself. There was a powerful undertow from the subconscious. Passionate love for a woman! That terrified her, so much that she acted ignobly for once—does that make you feel any better?" Laura asked with a smile.

Daphne didn't answer. She was looking into the fire. The log she had put on was blazing now. But after a long moment, she stretched out her arms and yawned, then she got up and walked up and down, stopping for a moment to look out to sea again. "It's clouding over."

Laura waited. She felt that they were close to some ease, some opening out of the tight place where Sybille had loomed like a beautiful, malignant goddess. It was so terribly important that they do so, that she waited almost holding her breath for what Daphne would finally come to see and to utter—if anything.

"I have learned something in these last years, something I wish I had learned long ago."

"What is that? Dear beautiful Daff, what is that?"

"I've learned to like women. Mamma didn't like women, did she? I now have two or three real women friends. It's a tremendous blessing, Laura. It's opened up a whole new world for me. Do you suppose Jo has any real friends?"

"Oh, I don't know—maybe."

"Women have so much to give one another, and to learn from one another. I've never been active in the women's movement, but I have to admit that the whole idea of a sisterhood has come about, and is beginning to happen, women helping one another, women being able to talk to one another, not as rivals. That seems quite new."

"I hadn't thought of it like that. What I see at my job is people, especially women, being less afraid to be honest with one another and with themselves."

"It's a far more open world than when we were young, L. At this stage in my life I am more nourished by women friends than even by David. For, let's face it, with David I have really been for years a kind of psychiatric nurse, an ego-builder . . . it's exhausting."

"The balances are delicate, so delicate. In a way Papa played a feminine role in their marriage, didn't he? He was the admiring, consoling one, the fervent audience for Sybille's performances."

"He was a romantic, at least about women." Daphne looked across at Laura and suddenly laughed. "It's been awfully good to talk, Laura."

"I wanted this so much," Laura murmured. "To be here in this house where we were happiest, the house of childhood, to come to some kind of reckoning that could include Mamma without resentment and without guilt."

"We haven't quite made it," Daphne said. "But I have to admit that that when we walked in I felt as prickly as a porcupine. I didn't want to think about childhood. I didn't want to remember."

"And now?"

"Oh, I suppose I'm a little closer to accepting Sybille, as you call her, to imagine at least that had I not been her daughter, I might have liked her. Who knows?"

"Just one more thing before we go. Why did Uncle Root commit suicide?"

"Don't you remember?" Daphne asked, astonished. "Ma always said it had been a noble act. He was terribly in debt, and after his death his wife and children got life insurance."

"All I remember was the awful strain of nobody weeping, and how you and Jo and I went down into the cellar and howled with rage because it all seemed so inhuman and crazy. He was such a lovable man! Do you remember that summer when he taught us to ride and Pa hired polo ponies for us?"

"That was the summer when we used to sneak out and slide down haystacks in the salt marsh—strictly forbidden of course." Laura had gotten up now, and while they talked, Daphne scattered the logs and packed up the thermoses. Then she stood there for a moment, thinking. "Uncle Root threatened to shoot Mamma if she went on the stage—and he meant it. There was something awfully queer about all that."

"Well, you said it, Daff. Family life was soap opera when we were young."

All the way back in the car they were silent. Laura dozed.

Chapter XII

Lying in bed next morning, her breakfast tray pushed aside, and Mrs. O'Brien due in an hour, Laura realized that it was a blessing that Daphne had insisted on staying till afternoon, for then she could tell Mary O'Brien what to do, show her where things were, get her settled in. After an uncomfortable night, coughing, unable to find a position where she could breathe easily, Laura realized that all that would have been beyond her strength. Never mind, she thought, we got to Maine—we did it. And Daphne did seem to understand that for the present Laura needed to be alone in her own house, and as free as she could be, and had agreed to go back to New York at least for the present. She had also persuaded Laura that Daisy and Ben and Jo, too, must be told and that she, Daphne, would see to it.

It's all getting organized, Laura thought—in her moment of exhilaration on Marlboro Street, when she had first imagined some great new adventure opening out, the adventure of dying, she had not envisioned that. It was going to be little bits and pieces, after all. There wasn't any way, since a life nearing its end is so much a part of the human web, of abstracting herself from others completely. She felt agitated and restless because so many things were to happen today—Mrs. O'Brien first of all, Ann to walk Grindle, and finally Aunt Minna at four to read to her. Could it be that a routine might give her the space, the sense of living in eternal time that she had nearly lost in the last days? For the moment, Laura sank back onto her pillows and closed her eyes.

Downstairs she could hear Daphne talking to Grindle in her special voice for animals, and Grindle barking, immediately responsive to such attentions. Lovely not to worry—Daphne would let him out and Sasha in.

Laura must have slept, for she was suddenly aware of voices downstairs and looked at her watch. Just after eleven. Mary O'Brien must have arrived. In a moment Daphne was there in the room, sitting on the bed, taking her hand. "Do you feel like seeing Mrs. O'Brien? She's downstairs making a custard. She's all unpacked and settled in."

"Mmmm, custard sounds good." Laura pushed herself up on the pillows. "But I really must get dressed. It's awfully late."

"Why not have a little talk with her and then get dressed?"

"All right. I do feel a little tired."

"If I were you, I'd stay in bed all day. After all, we had quite an expedition yesterday."

But this was the siren's song. Laura felt she must not allow herself to lapse into invalidism until that was necessary.

"We'll see. Do send Mrs. O'Brien up." And she whispered, "Don't you think she's all right?"

Daphne nodded enthusiastically. "Great", she whispered.

Then she took the tray and disappeared. While Laura waited for Mrs. O'Brien, she had the strange perception that this woman whom she hardly knew was to be her nearest companion on the journey, Charon, and knew far more about where they were bound than she did—if not the destination, at least the hazards and pains of the journey would be familiar to her. Whereas for Laura it was all unknown.

Not the children, not Daphne, but Mary O'Brien and Aunt Minna would be her rod and her staff from now on. So when Mary O'Brien appeared at the door, enveloped in a large white apron, Laura felt a real tremor, not fear, but the unknown coming closer, the unknown that she must learn to befriend.

"Sit down," she said. "My sister told me you were all settled in—I must have dozed off after breakfast. I'm tired because we took a long ride yesterday to our old summer house in Maine."

"Yes, your sister said you did." Mary O'Brien smiled. When she smiled, her rather severe face, with deep lines around the mouth, was quite beautiful. "So it's a good idea to take a long rest today."

"I don't know," Laura answered. "I have the feeling that I must do all I can while it's possible." Then she gave Mary O'Brien a testing look. "I don't want to coddle myself—and I don't want to be coddled."

"You are to do what you want, Mrs. Spelman. I'm here to help you do just that, so," she said without smiling, "I think we understand each other."

"Thanks," Laura said.

"A cheese soufflé and salad for lunch?" Mary O'Brien asked. "I looked around and that was about all I could find. Miss Hornaday said she would show me the way to the market, and we could get in some things this afternoon."

"That's perfect. Give me my purse, will you be so kind? It's on the dresser. Let me give you twenty-five dollars, and you can use it as you need it. I don't expect it to go far these days!" Again Laura hesitated, but she might as well get it over, and she added, "I don't have much appetite, Mrs. O'Brien. You mustn't be hurt if I can't always eat a meal."

"We'll find things you can eat. Now don't you worry about that." Then she laughed a rather shy laugh. "The last place I was at, such a sweet old lady, all she wanted was custard and, of all things, boiled onions, sometimes a little meat if I chopped it finely." Mary O'Brien got up. "Now you just take it easy and don't worry about anything."

"I'm going to get up for lunch," Laura said.

"Very well." And Mrs. O'Brien withdrew. For such a tall woman her feet were light on the stairs. There was something soothing about her quietness, and Laura blessed the good fortune that seemed to have brought a benign presence into the house.

They had their lunch served on trays by the fire, feeling a little like schoolgirls having a special treat. After lunch, as Daphne smoked a cigarette with her coffee and the time of her departure drew near, the mood changed.

"You know," Daphne said, sitting now at one end of the sofa where Laura was lying with Sasha beside her, "I feel a lot better than when I came. You've done something rather strange and wonderful."

"In what way?"

"I feel that my life isn't a total waste, somehow—what you said about growing more human, that that is what it's all about."

"Darling, that's pretty obvious." Looking at her sister's lined face, where so much conflict and pain had written its legend, Laura was moved nearly to tears. That was one thing that she couldn't control, tears. She felt the strong clasp of Daphne's hand and for a second held it.

"I never have believed in myself, but you made me understand a little more about Mamma, too. Maybe it's all linked. Don't cry, darling."

"I'm not," Laura said, blowing her nose. Then she laughed. "Of course I am! It's ridiculous how much I cry—but about the good things—it's goodness that makes me cry, you see. You haven't had a fair deal, Daff."

"Oh, I expect I have." And there was that lift of her chin, the poise of the throat that brought back memories of the beauty she had been. "I must go and throw things into my bag, L."

"Yes, it's time," said Laura, glancing at her watch. "Did you call a taxi?"

"They'll be here in fifteen minutes."

Mrs. O'Brien came in to get the trays then. "Now don't you move. I'll be back for the other one."

"It was a delicious lunch. I ate every bit of mine."

"It's a pity your sister has to go."

"She'll come back if I need her. You see, I really want to be alone. I know it must seem queer."

"Takes courage to face things alone, but I guess I might feel like you. Family is just too close sometimes."

"A very old aunt of mine, Miss Hornaday, is coming for tea, and to read to me. She'll come every day. I think regular visits like that may be a help. It's just . . . I dread anything emotional. Oh, and I forgot to tell you, my daughter-in-law will come every afternoon to walk Grindle. I'm afraid I can't do that anymore."

"Walk the dog?" Mrs. O'Brien looked dismayed. "Why, I'd be glad to do that—good for me to get out."

"Would you really?"

"Of course."

"Where is Grindle anyway?"

"He's in the kitchen. He's a friendly little dog, isn't he?"

"Friendly and rather greedy, too. Don't you spoil him!"

Then the doorbell rang, and Daphne ran down the stairs with her little suitcase and called out, "Just a minute—I'll be right out."

Laura was standing beside her as she closed the door.

"Daff, thank you for coming, for taking me to Maine—for everything."

"A pleasure, dear," Daff said lightly, and then she was gone.

Long farewells were not in the family tradition, but Laura stopped halfway up the stairs, wishing she had taken Daff in her arms for a good hard hug. Was that kind of closeness something she could no longer afford?

"Is there anything you need, Mrs. Spelman?" Mrs. O'Brien asked, standing at the foot of the stairs.

"No, just a long rest. When Ann Spelman comes for Grindle, tell her I'm tired, will you? It's just marvelous that I have a shield."

"Very well. Now you lie down and have a sleep."

But lying on her bed, Laura realized that this visit, dear as it had been, had left her now strangely defenseless. Once her solitude was impinged upon, she lost ground. Or rather the deep current on which she had floated until Daphne came was closed off. Instead of floating she felt imprisoned in a sick body. She could almost feel the cancer, this mysterious thing inside her that could not be eradicated, that must be allowed to take over little by little. "How can I do it?" she breathed, tears streaming down her cheeks. "How can I accept this?" and then she remembered—what an angel memory can be!—their father's old friend Owen Paine, who had been crippled by arthritis and in the last years lived in a wheelchair. He used to say, "Sister Pain is very near and dear to me." At the time it had seemed just a little precious, a little literary perhaps—now she began to understand. I must try to think of everything on that plane, of death as a friend, coming closer, a mysterious friend to whom I am more intimately connected than with any human being. The real connection? Was it perhaps simply death itself? And if so whatever was going on in her body was only part of something else, like a rising tide, like the slow murmur of waves that could be perceived as relentless or as inevitable. As she dozed and dreamed these things, peace flowed in.

It is poor old Daff who still has to carry the burden of living, not I. Not I.

"That rest did you good," Mrs. O'Brien observed when Laura went down at four to find the tea tray there and the fire burning brightly.

"You've done everything, you wonderful woman," Laura sighed her pleasure.

"No trouble. I'll bring the teapot in when your aunt arrives."

"Did Ann come? I didn't hear the doorbell."

"She came, and Grindle had a good walk. And she brought that cake."

"Dear thing."

"I hope it's all right," Mrs. O'Brien said. "I told her I would walk Grindle, and she didn't need to come after today. I think she wants to look in on you Mrs. Spelman, and she didn't like it."

You can't keep people out, a voice inside her reminded Laura. Life was going to keep on impinging and breaking the current, and it was this that Laura did not know how to deal with. Now, Aunt Minna—she would call Ann later and explain—for the doorbell was ringing impatiently.

"Here I am, dear," said Aunt Minna, a green bag of books swinging from one arm.

"Come in, come in. Mrs. O'Brien will hang up your coat."

Aunt Minna had on a ruffly blouse and a blue tweed suit, and her eyes looked fiercely bright. Her presence itself was an electric charge as she obviously sized Mrs. O'Brien up and meanwhile talked a blue streak, out of shyness, Laura imagined. It occurred to her that this was the first time in years that she had seen Aunt Minna outside her own house. So, while they drank their tea, she learned that there was a leak in Aunt Minna's roof, that she had had a call from an old colleague, and that she had brought three books to choose from: a Trollope, *Pride and Prejudice,* and Dag Hammarskjöld's posthumously published *Markings.*

"Ah," Aunt Minna triumphed when Laura chose Hammerskjöld. "I knew you'd choose that one. I'm dying to read it again myself."

"I'm really quite well," Laura smiled. "I really don't have to be read to." Seeing Aunt Minna's dismay, she added quickly, "But if we can get into a routine, I have an idea it may be a godsend later on when I'm going downhill."

"Downhill? I would prefer to regard it as climbing, you know, some very high mountain with a name like X-5 so you will sometimes get very tired and be out of breath." The answer shot back, and Laura laughed.

"Very well. Let's start up X-5 with Hammarskjöld."

Chapter XIII

"I feel you're keeping us at bay, Laura." Ann's voice on
the telephone the next morning had a tinge of asperity.
"You know we want to help in any way we can."

"Dear Ann, the cake was wonderful. Aunt Minna ate
three pieces." Laura knew she couldn't leave it at that.
"Mrs. O'Brien really wants to walk Grindle, and I can
understand that she needs to get out of the house."

"Oh, yes, I see." But it was clear that Ann did not see.
"So Aunt Minna was there?" (Aunt Minna was allowed
in and I was not, was clearly what was meant.)

But how could Laura explain, possibly, to this dear,
young, vulnerable daughter-in-law, that Aunt Minna was
welcome partly at least because she was so old, and with
her Laura could be a little child being read to. More, that
Aunt Minna could be considered an intimate in a way
none of Laura's children was. How to explain anything
at all, for that matter?

"I'm not going to try to explain everything I do, Ann.
I'm feeling my way. Aunt Minna will come every other
day for a while and read aloud to me. That is why she
was there. She loves doing it—and honestly I just can't
have you interrupting your life every day to walk my

dog!" The silence at the other end of the line was eloquent. "Ann, you've got to understand!" Laura was so
angry suddenly that she blurted out more than she had
meant to, or even knew she felt. "This is the first time
ever that I can live my own life without thinking of other
people. I mean to do just that."

"You're amazing, Laura, absolutely amazing," said
Ann, then she chuckled, and the chuckle became a
laugh. "But you've made your point and 'I hear you,' as
they say."

"All right, dear. Now there is one thing you can do that
would be a real help, and that is to come over today or tomorrow, when convenient, and take Mrs. O'Brien to the
shops, show her where to get food, the farm for eggs and
an occasional chicken. After that, she says she can drive
herself."

"I'll come this afternoon," Ann said cheerfully.

And that was that. But the effort, Laura realized when
she put the receiver down, had been immense. Her
nightgown was soaking wet, and for the first time in several days she had a fit of coughing.

"Stifling—" she managed to say when Mrs. O'Brien,
silent as an Indian, was suddenly there by the bed.

"Let me lift you." Somehow Mrs. O'Brien managed to
get Laura into an upright position, then to stuff pillows
behind her.

"Thank you," Laura breathed. "That's better."

"Why don't you let me answer the phone from now on,
Mrs. Spelman? Then you can decide whether you want
to receive the call or not."

"Yes, please."

So it was that Laura dozed for a while and heard the
phone ring twice, thinking with great relief that she did
not have to answer. When Mrs. O'Brien came up with a
cup of tea at eleven, she said that one call had been from

the doctor, who planned to look in early the next morning, the other from Harriet Moors.

"She seemed rather upset when I told her you were ill, but I told her I would give you a message, and I think she was crying."

"I must get up," Laura said at once.

"Now take it easy. She left her phone number, and when you've had a little rest, you can call her if you want to. Here it is," and Mrs. O'Brien carefully unfolded a piece of paper from the pocket in her apron.

Laura lay back, breathing shallow breaths. Any deep breath made her cough. How had she managed to forget all about Harriet Moors? In fact it was as though that part of life that had been associated with Houghton Mifflin had already floated away down the stream. Yet from the beginning something in the girl had touched Laura deeply. She had to know what was happening to this almost complete stranger! How to fathom that?

Thinking about it for a few minutes before calling Harriet, Laura found herself wondering about her sister Jo. What would Jo say to this girl? It was perhaps that the unfinished haunts one, and for forty years the ghost of Alicia had haunted. Every deep relationship has pain in it, Laura reminded herself, but for the deviant the risks were higher, the courage demanded to go one's own way so much greater—Harriet's friend, older, and with a job perhaps at risk—well, it was understandable perhaps that she had taken an adamant position. And what then? It was an excruciating dilemma for poor Harriet, already strung up over her parents' reaction. I must call her right away, Laura said to herself, with a tremor of fear. What if she—

She dialed the number and waited while the phone rang and rang, but just before she was about to hang up, a blurred voice answered. Blurred by tears? By drugs?

"Harriet, this is Laura Spelman. I'm sorry I was asleep when you called."

"They said you were ill."

"I am, but I'm concerned about you. Are you all right? You don't sound like yourself."

"I'm not, I'm . . ." a sob prevented further speech.

"You're upset. Why don't you just come over right away?"

"But . . . but—"

"I'm not too ill for an hour's talk. So come right along. Blow your nose, and we'll see what we can do to help."

"Thanks."

Had Harriet taken on more than she could be expected to handle? Laura tried to remember the name of a psychiatrist, but here was someone very pure and honest, very young too. Tampering with Harriet, forcing a certain kind of analysis—was that what could help? Only, Laura decided, if she was depressed beyond the power to make decisions, only if she was suicidal. But how was one to know? Laura was suddenly so agitated that she put on her socks inside out, but what did that matter? At least she had managed to get dressed, while Sasha wound herself round her legs, getting in the way, in a sudden fit of passionate purrs.

"There, my cat, now we are going downstairs."

"Good heavens, Mrs. Spelman, I thought you were asleep!" Mrs. O'Brien looked startled.

"I've asked Harriet Moors to come over for an hour. She's in trouble."

Mrs. O'Brien did not comment; instead she put a match to the freshly laid fire, and when that was done, she said, "Well, you'll want to talk with her in peace. I'll go out and get in some food while she's here. Like that you won't be left alone."

"Fine," Laura said. "Let's have a tenderloin and some fresh peas."

"I've got some frozen fish chowder melting for your lunch."

"Perfect."

Laura put a Haydn concerto on the player—Haydn for strength—and indeed the music poured into her like a shot of strong liquor. She stood back to the fire, looking at Ann's flowers, still beautiful on the low table by the sofa where she had spent so many hours lately, reading and listening to music. There was her desk, piled high with mail she had not even opened. She really must get at it now Mrs. O'Brien was here. She would take it up to her bedroom and read letters in the morning before she got out of bed.

Harriet should be arriving any minute, and here was Mrs. O'Brien coming downstairs in her coat, ready to go. So it was opportune that at that second the doorbell rang.

"Come in. Mrs. Spelman is in the library," she heard, and then something whispered—no doubt a warning not to stay too long.

"Well," Laura said, as Harriet hesitated in the doorway, "come in to the fire. How is it outside?"

"It feels like rain."

There was a silence after the front door closed. Harriet dropped her bag from her shoulder to the floor and sat down on the sofa. Laura in the wing chair glanced once at the blotched face, behind dark glasses, and looked away. A glance was enough.

"You've had a hard blow, haven't you?"

"No," said Harriet in a low voice. "I just feel hopeless. I feel like an animal in a cage."

"That's bad," Laura said.

"Oh, Mrs. Spelman, I shouldn't have come. It's just . . ."

"I don't think what you're going through is the easiest thing in the world, and that's why I told you to feel free to call, so don't worry." Perhaps it would be a good idea to keep on talking for a while until Harriet pulled herself together. "One good thing about illness is that a lot of nonessentials get eliminated. I can't work, you see, and lying around gets boring"—a lie, but in a good cause. "So, let's just talk for a while. Mrs. O'Brien has gone out to do errands."

But now that she had arrived, Harriet Moors was clearly almost incapable of speech. She took out a kleenex and blew her nose.

Laura hazarded a guess. "You've made your decision? You've decided not to publish your novel?"

"No, oh, no!" Harriet got up, walked up and down for a bit, then stood at the window, her back to Laura. "That's the trouble—that's it. I can't see anything to do, any way out."

"Except to jump out the window?"

This brought Harriet back. "How did you know?"

"It doesn't take exceptional insight to gather that you feel you are at an excruciating impasse, Harriet. Everyone contemplates suicide at some time, just as little children all run away from home at some time."

Harriet managed a smile, then frowned. "Children run away when their parents won't let them do what they want to do—at least the only time I did was when my father wouldn't let me have a bike."

"Exactly. But what if circumstances are such that the child can't run away? I had TB of the spine when I was nineteen. For two years I lay flat on my back in a sanatorium."

"Wow! How did you handle it—the anger, the frustration?" For the first time Harriet sounded like herself.

"By thinking."

"I think myself round and round in circles, that's the trouble. How in hell can I break the circle?"

"Talk about it—"

"Well, if I let this book be published under my own name, it means the end of Fern and me. I guess I had accepted that it would make a rift between me and my parents, but that's already there—but Fern—we haven't slept for nights. We just wrangle and cry. She looks awful, and it's all my fault." Harriet was close to tears again.

"I wonder whether it is all your fault. She is older than you are, I seem to remember. She must have made some kind of decision when you first became lovers. She must have known the risk she was taking, didn't she?"

"Well, maybe—but she says now that when the book comes out, she might as well wear a placard round her neck with LESBIAN written out on it." Here Harriet broke down and sobbed. "She says she will lose her job. She says it will kill her."

"So what are you supposed to do? Tear up your book?"

"I suppose so."

"It's interesting that you talk about suicide but apparently not about destroying your work. Is that some sort of clue, maybe?"

Harriet sat down on the floor, and Laura saw that at last she was beginning to examine the problem rather than simply screaming with pain. Laura moved over to the sofa and stretched out.

"You mean it shows that I have sort of made the decision, only I can't face its consequences."

"Maybe."

"But how I can be sure that it's worth it? That it's good enough? Fern says I wrote it just to come to terms with my convictions about what we are, and that it's nobody else's business. She says maybe I wrote the book instead of going to a psychiatrist to handle my parents' attitude."

"If so, it was rather a respectable way of doing that."

[139

"Then why not tear it up? Oh, I'm so tired," Harriet groaned.

"What would happen if you did tear it up? Would you feel relieved? I wonder."

"Like an abortion?" Harriet said bitterly. "It's my work. It's myself—the best of me! I won't destroy it, God damn it!"

Laura wanted to shout "Bravo!" but restrained herself.

"If you did destroy it, wouldn't the ghost of the book haunt you and Fern? Could you hope to build a stable relationship on such a violent act?"

"I don't know."

"And neither do I, of course," Laura said quickly.

"It's awfully hard," Harriet murmured. "I mean, I love Fern."

Laura waited. It was not the moment to say that Harriet was young, and that there would be other people, eventually another person. Love is an absolute, after all, or seems so when one is in love. What she could talk about was the work.

"You asked me how you could tell that your book was worth such pain, how you can be sure—I never answered that question. I am not a writer, as you know, but I have worked with a lot of writers, and this question comes up often, not in just these particular circumstances. I think every writer sacrifices a good deal for his work. Families pay a high price when they have a writer in their midst! And no writer is ever sure that he is a genius and has a right to whatever he takes from life to do what he feels he must do. I think your book has value—I told you so when we first met—but that doesn't mean it will be a success. Most first novels sell a few thousand, and the author is lucky if he gets reviewed."

Harriet was listening intently, but she said nothing. Laura knew she had to go on now, go further on to some ultimate conclusion. "One simply gives what one can and hopes for the best." It sounded rather lame.

And now she felt an impulse to do something strange. "You know what?" she said, "I feel like listening to the Bach cello suites—so much like a voice, so much like the climbing of a mind." She got up and searched for the record, wondering as she knelt on the floor why she had had that impulse, for she had not listened to these records for years.

"Do you mind?"

"I'd like that," Harriet said. "If it's not too much for you."

"We'll listen to two or three of them anyway."

Harriet sat, leaning against a chair, looking into the fire. She had taken off her dark glasses and was, Laura noted, a great deal more composed than when she had arrived like some battered bird, wild and askew. Perhaps I have given her a respite, Laura thought, but she had no illusions. Harriet was going to suffer, and there was very little one could do to help. Some things have to be gone through. For some difficulties there is no good solution, and they are the agonizing ones.

Little by little such thoughts subsided, and the intricate, thrilling voice of the cello took over. After the first record, Harriet got up and turned it over without a word. And when that stopped, Laura sighed. "It does compose the mind, doesn't it?"

"Can words ever do that, I wonder?" Harriet asked, running a hand over her forehead as if to smooth out a frown.

"Oh, yes, poetry does—and sometimes novels may, over their long, extended pattern. Your novel may very well do it, although that seems strange. Many, many people are confused about the problem it deals with, and maybe a few will understand it all a little better. I feel proud of you that you will publish," Laura added and saw the blush of pleasure suffuse Harriet's round face.

"I have a sister who did not have your courage—I think I have mentioned her?—who did not stand up to our parents, who cut herself off from someone she loved, who would not face the consequences. It's a matter, after all, of being, isn't it? She has been immensely successful, but she has always seemed to be a half-person to me, and to my other sister. Maybe that is why I have found myself involved in your book and in your life. It's all very strange."

"It's awfully kind of you," Harriet said. "I know you haven't been well—and—oh, dear, I've probably stayed too long already!"

"No, no, it's all right. Bach has revived me!" Laura paused. She was trying to make up her mind whether to take the leap, tell Harriet the truth about herself, or whether to let her find out.

"I hope you feel better soon," Harriet said, looking uncomfortable. She reached for her bag and got to her feet.

"Stay a moment longer," Laura said, for it was clearly not possible to let Harriet leave and never see her again without warning. "You see," she went on as Harriet sat down beside her on the sofa, "I won't get better."

"You don't want to?"

"In a way, yes—the thing is, Harriet, that there is cancer in my lungs and they can't operate. So—" All she could do now was cover the huge hole she had torn in the space between them with words, Laura felt, let Harriet have time to recover from shock. "I guess we won't meet again. And that's why I felt I must tell you."

"You're so ill, and yet you read my book and let me come and talk. Why?"

"It's a question I have asked myself. When I was told what the matter was, all that day I kept thinking that now I could plan my life, maybe for the first time, and the phrase that kept coming back was 'the real connections.' I did not need to have anything to do with what was not a real connection. And—I think you'll understand this—I felt enormously relieved. I felt that the only thing I could do and must do was to try to come to a final reckoning with everything."

"But—" Harriet looked bewildered, as well she might. Laura smiled. "You appear to be a real connection, I don't know why myself. Perhaps I have been haunted by my sister Jo's decision so long ago to run away from her own deep need, and I told you, I think, that my second son, Ben, is a homosexual. So you see, for myself, not the editor, your novel had reverberations. But more than Jo and Ben, I had to face the fact that for me myself one of the real connections, one of the deepest and most nourishing, in some ways more than my marriage, good as that was, had been a passionate friendship with a woman. I still can't bring myself to reread her letters, but I must soon. Your book, and then our talks, have been part of something important, revelatory."

Harriet had covered her face with one hand. Now she reached over and took Laura's hand and clasped it hard.

"Women's feeling for one another has been a buried world for so long, a cause of fear and shame," Laura murmured, holding the warm young hand in hers. "Now at last we are beginning to understand the blessing."

"Oh, thank you" said Harriet. "Thank you for everything."

For a second Laura looked her straight in the eyes, then she asked the only question that really mattered: "You are going to be all right?"

Harriet nodded, got up, flung her bag round her shoulder, and gave Laura a dazzling smile. "If I could live the way you are dying!" she said unexpectedly.

" 'Down to hell and up to heaven in an hour'?" Laura laughed. "I must admit that so far—" but then she leaned over in a spasm of coughing, the cough she had managed to keep from happening for an hour. "You'd better go," she gasped.

Mrs. O'Brien, who at that instant opened the door with her key and came in loaded with packages, was not pleased. Harried fled. "You shouldn't have seen that girl."

Laura lay on the sofa, sweat pouring down her face.

"Oh, yes," she managed to say. "Oh, yes. It was important."

Chapter XIV

Laura pushed her breakfast tray down to the end of the bed. She had managed three swallows of coffee, but toast, a poached egg were out of the question this morning. Even sitting high up with three pillows behind her, it felt as though she had a balloon in her chest pressing, pressing.

"It's so hard to breathe," she whispered when Mary O'Brien came for the tray.

"Dr. Goodwin will be here in a few minutes. He'll know how to help you, dear." It was the first time Mary O'Brien had used an endearment, and Laura wasn't quite sure that was what she wanted, though in just a few days Mrs. O'Brien had become indispensable. She closed her eyes, but that didn't work because then she was even more enclosed in her body, so she picked up the pile of mail that had been accumulating and went through it listlessly, three-quarters of it being, as usual, requests for money from every conceivable organization from Defenders of Wild Life to Amnesty International. These Laura dropped on the floor. But there was a letter from Amy Preston, whom she considered a real friend, and just because she was a real friend, it seemed impossible to face. Finally Laura did open it. "Isn't it about time we met? What about lunch some time next week when you're in town at the office?" Laura let the note fall.

At first it had seemed the easiest thing in the world to shed relationships, as easy as taking off one's clothes before an operation. She had not even thought about Amy since she had begun this ultimate reckoning. And now she felt it quite impossible to see Amy, and next to impossible to tell her what had been happening. Some-one else—Ann perhaps—would have to begin letting people know. Laura had the sensation of lying in a thicket, unable to see the sky for the mass of little branches and twigs. It felt like years since she had seen Amy, so much had happened, and now she was far far away, and there would never be time to catch up.

How had she ever managed to talk to Harriet? Yester-day was eons away, and Laura realized that very possi-bly she would never again be able to engage in a real conversation with anyone. I'll just have to hobble along with Brother Ass and Mary O'Brien, she thought, manag-ing to make herself smile at the image. Then she half-dozed until the doorbell rang, and in a few seconds she heard Dr. Goodwin's quick, firm, step on the stair. Amaz-ing how much character one could sense in the way someone climbed stairs! Mrs. O'Brien's tread was so light, Laura often did not hear her coming.

"You sound like an army with banners," she managed to say, as Jim Goodwin came in.

"My goodness, I hope not!" he answered. "Can I just wash my hands?"

"Of course, that door."

He left the door open and talked as he opened the tap and washed and dried his hands. "Mrs. O'Brien says you didn't eat your breakfast. Pressure on your stomach builds up as the lungs fill. I think I can do something to ease that for you."

"Good."

When he came back, he sat on the bed, took her wrist, and looked away as he found the pulse.

Laura liked his face, the narrow gray eyes and taut mouth. She had always liked it, but now it occurred to her that she was absolutely in this man's hands, so it had become newly important that she trust him.

"Would you just sit up—slowly—and lift your nightgown up, so I can get an idea what's going on? That's it—that's good," he said, running the stethescope up and down her back and listening, listening.

"O.K. Mrs. Spelman, now lie back."

This she gladly did. Sitting up had been tiring.

"Since when have you found it hard to breathe?"

"Every day this week, but sometimes for an hour or so I feel better. Sometimes I can eat a little."

"It's probably worse in the morning, isn't it? Now I am going to drain some fluid out of your lungs. It won't hurt, and I'm sure you'll feel a lot better."

It took a little while to get everything ready, and while he got out his instruments and what looked like huge plastic bottles—could there be that much fluid?—Jim Goodwin talked reassuringly in just the way, Laura suddenly remembered, that her father had talked when he was totally absorbed in fastening a fly to his fishing line. "It looks like an early spring," Jim Goodwin said. "There are crocuses coming up in our garden—about two weeks early, I figure. The brooks are in flood. That's the sound of spring, all right, in New England at any rate, isn't it?" He gave a little cough. "Well, I guess we're ready. Let me help you sit up again. I'm first going to anesthetize a little place on your back so you won't feel the needle go in. O.K.?"

It didn't hurt, but it was nerve-racking and seemed to go on forever as Jim Goodwin asked, "O.K., Mrs. Spelman?" every few minutes. Laura couldn't see what was going on, but the tension of sitting up so long took its toll. Sweat poured down her face. And when at last he told her, "That's fine," and she could lie down, it took self-control not to cry.

"Would you like to see?" he asked, cheerfully holding up a bottle half-filled with dark-orange fluid. "I think you're going to feel a lot more comfortable today."

For a moment Laura waited for the shock of that dark-orange color to be absorbed. She felt like a whole world, a world of many countries, and in one country a frightful war was in progress although in another country, her mind, for example, everything was going on as usual— and she wondered how long it would be before the war spread and perhaps engulfed the world.

Dr. Goodwin was sitting now in a low armchair, jotting something down on a card.

"Did you expect—" she couldn't phrase it—"is this normal? I mean, am I worse than you thought?" Laura could hear the phone ringing far away as Jim Goodwin carefully put the cap on his pen and tucked the card into a note case. She was watching him closely and was surprised to see that his hands shook, as they certainly had not done during the small operation.

"You are not quite like any other patient I have had. From what Mrs. O'Brien, said, you have been about certain errands of mercy—in your condition, that is highly unusual and very brave, I must say."

"That young woman was suicidal—I mean I was afraid she might be—but," said Laura with a smile, "I think it's the last time. Besides," she added, "why not spend what I have?"

Jim Goodwin sighed and passed a hand over his forehead before giving her a penetrating look. "I would very much like to get you to hospital for about three days."

"I am worse then?" she was not going to let him off.

"Not worse than I expected," he answered slowly. "Both lungs are affected, and when I first saw you, as you know, we had to face that there was not very much we could do at that stage."

What Laura wanted to ask was, "How long?" But she couldn't quite bring herself to utter the question. She closed her eyes.

"Why the hospital?"

"I would like to get more X-rays and then confer with a colleague about possible cobalt treatment."

"No," Laura said unexpectedly loudly. Then she saw Mrs. O'Brien in the doorway. "What is it, Mrs. O'Brien?"

"Your daughter, Daisy, is on the telephone. She was quite insistent that she must talk to you."

"I can't," Laura murmured, even as she tried to sit up.

"Why don't I have a word with her?" Jim Goodwin had leapt to his feet. "Is there a phone downstairs?"

"Come with me," Mrs. O'Brien said. "It's long-distance."

Laura lay still. I just can't cope with everything at once, she thought. Her whole being at that moment of Mrs. O'Brien's appearance had been gathered up in fierce determination not to be carted off to the hospital. After a while she could hear low voices in the hall. Well, let them make the decisions, all except the hospital. For a little while still she was in command of her body, her dying body—dying in this strange war in one part of it. Laura lifted up one of her hands and looked at it. It was perfectly itself, even the liver spots and the slight swelling in the knuckle of her little finger were exactly as they had been two months ago. It had been a useful hand, she thought, good at holding a trowel, able to type very fast.

But the war in her lungs was draining the strength of all the rest of her, and if she couldn't eat? Somewhere she had read that patients with cancer of the lung die of starvation.

Her eyes were closed, and this time she did not hear Jim Goodwin's firm step. She heard his voice and found it wonderfully reassuring. He had taken her hand in his and was holding it in a firm clasp.

"I had a talk with Daisy," he said. "She wants to come this weekend, and since Mrs. O'Brien will be off for two days, I thought perhaps that would be a good idea."

"You took it right out of my hands, didn't you, Jim?" Laura had never called him Jim before. She opened her eyes then and caught his anxious look.

"No," he said, "I told her I would confer with you and call her back immediately if you didn't feel up to it. My thought was that you might prefer to have her here than our sending over a nurse."

Laura nodded. He was right, of course. He was trying to help her.

He released her hand now and got up. For a moment he walked up and down, then went to the window and stood there looking out. "As for the hospital, we can put that off for a couple of weeks anyway."

"I want to see the spring." It occurred to Laura as soon as she said it that this was the first time she had looked forward. She had been trying so deliberately to let go, but she had said, "I want to see the spring."

"I think you will," Jim Goodwin said gently. "I think I can promise you that." And that meant, Laura calculated, that she had a month.

She bit her lip, but that didn't stop the tears flowing.

"Rest all you can. I'll be back in a few days."

And he was gone.

It was not going to be as easy as she had imagined to let go.

Chapter XV

During the next few days Laura kept very quiet. Mrs. O'Brien persuaded her to stay in bed till teatime when Aunt Minna came to read aloud. Ann was commandeered for one morning, to help Laura decide what letters must be written to inform old friends that she would be *hors de combat* for a month or more, and under doctor's orders must lead a restricted life and not have visitors.

Draining the lung had certainly helped; she had slept better ever since Jim Goodwin's visit, but eating was getting harder every day. Even a cup of tea sometimes brought on nausea. The only thing she had been able to swallow was oysters, tried at Mrs. O'Brien's suggestion. But Laura was determined now to live till the spring, till the trees wore their gauzy early green, till the first daffodils. She wanted to see them, needed to see them more than any person, and that was strange. Or was it? Flowers, trees were silent presences and asked nothing. And perhaps the contemplation of beauty was the last resource. "Look thy last on all things lovely. Every hour. . . ." Yes, she would do that as long as she could.

Ben had telephoned, luckily in the late afternoon one day when Laura felt more energy then usual and could communicate something. "Darling Ben," she said, "I listen to records, especially Mozart and Haydn, and I look at things, and talk to Grindle and Sasha." Here she had laughed. "I expect I sound feeble-minded."

"Mother!"

"Don't sound anguished. I'm trying to tell you that all is well. I'm learning a lot."

"But I want to come—as soon as this big painting is finished."

He could not possibly know how relieved she was to learn that this visit at least could be put off.

"Of course you must finish it. What I wanted to tell you—" (but how to say it?)

"Is that people are no help. Is that it?" Trust Ben to catch her meaning even from three thousand miles away.

"Thanks for saying it for me. Oh, Ben, people drain me—it's that—can you understand? When I talk I get a fit of coughing. But Aunt Minna comes every afternoon and reads. We have finished Hammarskjöld and now we are reading Trollope—so soothing."

There was now a silence. A silence on the telephone with the interlocutor so far away opens up a huge hole.

"Are you all right?" Laura asked after a moment.

"I guess so."

"Come when you finish that painting."

Another silence, then a strangled voice unlike Ben's, "You're not dying, are you, Mother? You've got to tell me."

"Maybe I am, darling. Everyone must sooner or later."

"But—but you sound so casual about it—Christ, Mother, how can I stay here and paint? I'm coming back tomorrow."

"No," Laura said firmly. "You are not. Finish what you are doing. Please, Ben."

"Very well, I'll try."

"I guess I'd better say good-by for now."

"Good-by for now."

She set the receiver down and lay back on the sofa.

"Well, you shouldn't have talked to him," Mary O'Brien said after one look at her. "You're all tuckered out."

"No, I'm glad I could. Ben is a very understanding person, Mary, but he wouldn't have understood. I had to explain things myself."

For the past few days, Laura had found herself calling Mrs. O'Brien "Mary." It was the beginning of a new phase in their relationship. Nothing had to be explained, thank goodness, between Mary and herself, for Mary was the person who really knew about this illness, the one person Laura allowed to see her weakness, allowed to take over, without a protest. It had begun, this new phase, one morning when Mary had come for the breakfast tray, only tea and dry toast now and the toast rarely consumed, and Laura had asked her to sit down for a moment.

"No one wants to talk about death. It frightens people, doesn't it?"

"Well—" Mary hesitated, "yes."

"You have seen it, haven't you?"

"Yes."

"Mary, it would help me to know a little more about it, if you could tell me."

"I'll tell you a strange thing. It seems as though a person dies when he is ready, when he wants to go, and not before."

"Really? Is that true?"

Mary's eyes when she was moved became very dark blue, and now she looked at Laura with a strange little smile and said, "I've never told anybody this, they don't ask. But I can tell you, Laura Spelman, that the ones I've seen looked—" she clasped her hands in the struggle for the words, "They looked—"

"Not afraid?"

"Oh, no, they looked as though they could see things we can't see, and the kingdom of heaven was within them."

"It's hard to imagine."

"Old Mrs. Cotter, she was really a difficult woman, if I say so myself. Once she said to me, 'The trouble with me is I don't wear well'—she fought with all her friends, and her children for that matter. God was not with her that I ever saw," said Mary with a chuckle. "But when she died, that old woman looked beatified. I'll never forget her look at the end. Never."

Then they had changed the subject and talked about making a stew for the weekend so Daisy would have something easy to heat up for herself.

There was something ironic about Daisy's coming now that Laura was critically ill, and ironic, too, Laura thought, that she had to accept such a visitation because she needed the help over the weekend. Everyone took it for granted—even Mary O'Brien, who was sometimes so perspicacious—that Laura wanted Daisy to come. In a way, perhaps she did, though she had no illusions that they would at the eleventh hour reach some kind of accord, after so many years when whatever contact there had been had ended in recriminations. What do I hope for then? Laura wondered. A moment outside time, outside the past, when we might begin to be friends? And could it be that that might be possible only now because only now was Laura herself in a position of weakness? Perhaps.

These thoughts were interrupted by the arrival of flowers from Amy, a delightful glass bowl filled with bright pink roses and forget-me-nots. "Be good and get well soon," the card said in Amy's bold hand. Laura let it fall.

"Thanks, Mary. Pretty, aren't they?"

"Will it be all right if I take Grindle for a walk? It seems like a good time."

At the word "walk" Grindle, who had been asleep on the rug by her bed, leaped up and began to bark.

"Oh, Grindle, be quiet!" Laura said crossly. The barks fell on her ears like a blow.

"Come on," Mary said firmly. She turned at the door with a questioning look.

"By all means, Mary, take him out."

Strange, the relief, even excitement she felt knowing she would be all alone in the house for a half-hour. Mary's presence was discreet, and she managed to do the housekeeping with a minimum of noise or fuss, doing up Laura's bedroom when Aunt Minna came in the afternoon—but being quite alone was something entirely different, as if when anyone was around, Laura did not feel entirely free inside herself to think her own often outrageous thoughts, to float on that deep current again, to let things happen in the psyche without even the mild censorship of another presence. Every relationship pulled, even with a very slight thread such as that joining her and Mary. When the phone rang and rang, Laura did not answer it. It is not a moment when I wish to respond, she said to herself.

Instead she went back into the current and floated. She was remembering Charles's look of pure happiness when he came into her room at the hospital after Daisy was born. "Darling, it's a girl." He had so wanted a girl! And Daisy, from the beginning, had been an ultrafeminine person, though in her own ineffable way. She, the youngest, with two brothers, had wanted to do everything they did a little better than they, from climbing trees to playing baseball. Her hair cut like a boy's, wearing blue jeans and jerseys, she looked like an androgynous boy and crowed with delight when she succeeded in pinning Ben's shoulders to the ground, which was not difficult; he was always so gentle with her. Laura had to admit that she sometimes resented Daisy who appeared to have the best of both worlds, applauded as a wonder when she did well at boys' games, but demanding and getting the attention of Charles as his beloved daughter who flirted with him, Laura thought, outrageously, and with all the wiles of a woman. So she got a boy's bicycle when whe was twelve and her first lipstick when she was fifteen, both from her father. In return she taught her father to smoke pot when she was in college. But that was before she took off on her own with a knapsack to "see the country" after she graduated.

Daughters, Laura thought as she floated down the stream. So much harder than boys to bring up because . . . here a branch impeded the passage of flowing waters . . . it is much harder to be a woman than a man.

So after all that freedom and all the paths open to become whatever she wanted to be, Daisy had ended up living with a boy five years younger than she who was an intern. Laura had not been allowed to meet Saul; "he hates Wasps," she had been informed by Daisy in the aftermath of Charles's funeral. "But Charles met him and liked him a lot," Laura remembered answering, offering her neck to be guillotined. "I know, in New York," Daisy had answered, "It's just this whole rich atmosphere of the *goyim* he couldn't possibly take. Suburbia," she had said with her usual contempt.

And now this grown-up person called Daisy who had once had tantrums and had to be put in a tepid bath in her clothes, was due to arrive by her own wish at the bedside of her dying Wasp mother. At this point all Laura could think of was those slow-moving, hibernating wasps who made their appearance in March from somewhere in the attic and died hanging on to a wicker lampshade, as one had done the other day in her bedroom.

I do not have to pretend any longer, she told herself. I am permitted to die as I am, what I am. No one can try to change me. It's too late.

It was a comfort when Mary O'Brien called, "We're home!" and Grindle trundled up the stairs, his tail wagging, his pink tongue ready to lick her hand.

It had been Laura's experience that things waited for with dread rarely turned out as expected. Everybody looks so old, Laura thought—Daphne, now Daisy, whose face had tautened, whose reddish hair had a touch of gray in it. Daisy, lean and elegant still in tight jeans and a lavender suede jacket, was no longer the sharp, self-assured, brusque person with whom Laura had argued about nearly everything. She had become gentler, and from the first moment when she flung her knapsack down and ran to her mother without a second's hesitation and kissed her on the cheek, Laura realized that this encounter was not going to be what she had imagined; so that she herself, armed as she had been and prepared to be attacked, found herself newly attentive to this unknown daughter.

Now Laura was lying on the sofa listening to a Mozart piano concerto while Daisy was busy in the kitchen, heating up Mary O'Brien's stew for their supper. Laura had made a salad and set out a bottle of burgundy. We managed to get separated, she was thinking, very long ago when Daisy became her father's rather than her mother's daughter. Was it that? Or was it simply that Daisy had set her mother and her mother's life aside as irrelevant, as uninteresting, in her own hunger for life and determination to find out all about it on her very own. She had said as much, but thoughtfully this time, and without animosity. "Your life didn't seem to have anything to do with my life. That sounds crazy, doesn't it?" And she had gone on to talk about Sybille, who had nourished her need for the absolute and the heroic. "Granny seemed really to understand everything—and it was so marvelous that anyone as old as she could blaze away as she did about the war in Vietnam. That was the last time I saw her—she had gone to march in Washington!"

"I'd forgotten," Laura murmured. But now she did remember and how angry she had been, for it seemed an absurd risk to take. She had even called Jo, hoping Jo would back her up and make it impossible in some way for their mother to embark on such a crazy expedition. "I was hard on Sybille." For seeing it all freshly through Daisy's eyes, Laura winced at how mean-spirited she had been. By then she herself had washed her hands of Sybille and Sybille's extravagant passions for this or that, a person or a cause. "My sisters and I had learned to protect ourselves, I suppose."

"Should I go and see her, Mother—while I'm here?"

"She wouldn't recognize you. Why should you make a gesture that has no meaning? Far better keep your memory of that intensity and passion intact."

"Besides I'm here to take care of you, aren't I?"

"I don't need care," Laura had said, "as you can see."

Daisy had frowned and rocked back and forth, her arms clasped round her knees. "You haven't eaten anything except a mouthful of scrambled egg since I arrived. You're starving."

"Probably. Eating is the one thing that seems rather difficult—so I'm weak—I get tired. Otherwise ..." Seeing the strain on Daisy's face, Laura added quickly, "Jim Goodwin has promised me the spring."

"You sound so calm, Mother."

"The truth is that dying is the most interesting thing I've ever done."

"Wow!" Daisy sat up, her eyes very bright. "You've got guts, I must say."

"No. It's just that when there are limits, it's easier to handle some things. The irrelevant can get pushed away. That pile of mail on my desk, for instance. I never think about such things now. I live in the present, Daisy. It's quite a relief."

But the present had also unfortunately contained an exhausting fit of coughing later on in the evening. That could not be glossed over, and Daisy had been shocked. Ever since, she had been careful not to let her mother talk for very long. Now it was Saturday evening, their last evening, for Daisy would go the next day and was asked over to Sunday dinner with Brooks and Ann.

Laura was hoarding her energy. She had not even lit the fire. She was learning to let other people do things that might bring on sudden exhaustion. Stooping was one of them. She lay, floating on the music, reaching over to stroke Grindle's soft ears now and then.

"Now can I open the champagne?" Daisy called from the kitchen. She had brought a bottle of champagne at Saul's suggestion—apparently he had told her that champagne was good for Laura's condition.

"Splendid," Laura called back. "Oh, just light the fire would you? Then we'll pop that bubbly, as your father used to say."

"Daddy loved festive things, didn't he?" said Daisy, bending to light the fire. When that was done, she stood up and began what became quite a struggle, to get the champagne open. "Oh, dear, I wish I could do this like Daddy—there—now . . . now!"

"That was very satisfactory," Laura smiled, for the cork had hit the ceiling, making Grindle run away into the kitchen. "Even though Grindle thinks war has been declared."

For some reason Grindle's exit struck them both as very funny, and Daisy laughed so much she could hardly pour.

Laura lifted her glass, watching the bubbles rise to the surface.

"There's so much I want to say, to ask—but I'm so afraid of tiring you." Daisy, Laura noticed, was for once sitting in a chair rather than on the floor.

"You look prepared for some fatal interview," Laura teased. "And what if I do get tired? Does it matter? I want all of life I can have."

"All night I was thinking about you and me. Why is it that mothers and daughters appear to have a harder time than mothers and sons?"

"I've wondered, too." Then Laura plunged deliberately into the turbulent sea. "Did we have a hard time?"

"Oh, Mother, you were always criticizing me. I felt I could never do anything right! Don't you remember?"

But Laura did not remember. What she remembered was Daisy's stubborn refusal to do anything that was asked of her, from wearing a dress to dinner to not climbing tall trees to the very top. "As I remember," Laura finally answered, "you were always criticizing me," and then they laughed.

"Well," Daisy said thoughtfully, "when I was sixteen or seventeen, I must say you seemed to represent everything I despised, especially money."

"Money?" Laura was startled. "Money?" she repeated. "Daisy, we aren't rich and never have been. Mamma and Papa gave away huge amounts of money to all those causes—there wasn't that much left."

"But she wore dresses by French couturiers, Mother, for heaven's sake."

"Yes, she did, and they were often handed down from her really rich cousin in Philadelphia."

"Maybe, but the whole atmosphere I grew up in was somehow privileged—I guess that is the word. There were servants, for instance."

"Well, I paid for Sarah Page by working at Houghton Mifflin. I earned that, after all."

"I'm sorry, Mother. I guess I've never thought much about it. But I felt that you and Daddy really didn't know very much about real life. You've been so safe."

"If you've been brought up in the eye of the storm as I was (you can have no idea of the dramas we had to witness as children), maybe what you long for is something quite simple and normal, like family life in a comfortable suburb. But, if you must know, quite a lot of what you call 'real life' comes into a publisher's office. I'm not entirely beyond the pale."

Laura felt nettled and knew that this was not a good idea. Keep calm, she said to herself. "But that isn't the point, really, is it? About mothers and daughters—I can understand that a mother, these days, is rarely the exemplar a daughter needs."

"Because," Daisy said, "we really don't know what it is to be a woman, what we want of ourselves—I don't even know whether I want to marry or not, for instance."

"You'll have to decide pretty soon, if you want children."

"Don't, Mother."

"You talk about reality—you might as well face the fact."

"I wonder whether I'm capable of that kind of commitment." Daisy slid down to the floor. "Nothing seems
permanent or that solid to me. Maybe marriage asks
more than I can give. I'm not even sure Saul and I will
ever get married. It would be hard on his family if he
married a non-Jew.

"What sort of people are they? You've never told me."

"His father's a dentist; his mother appears to be a
rather neurotic, rather ambitious woman who flits in and
out of volunteer jobs looking for something she never
finds. They play golf on Saturdays and have a huge family Sunday dinner to which various aunts, cousins,
heaven knows who, come, and Saul has to go, willy-
nilly, so we never have a real weekend together. Saul is
the only child, which is hard on him." All this was
blurted out rather mechanically as though Daisy were
not really interested.

"Why didn't she have another child?"

"Oh, she always thinks she has some fatal disease—
and perhaps she did have an operation and can't. I've
never seen her alone, and I'm not exactly welcome at
these family gatherings, so . . ."

"It doesn't sound like a happy future from all you
say—what is it about Saul? It's gone on quite a while."

"Three years of my life," Daisy frowned. "My job is
o.k., but it isn't my real life. He is."

"But you love him?"

"Women get caught, that's the trouble. I seem to have
attached myself to Saul like a limpet to a rock, against all
reason." Daisy got up and refilled their glasses, but instead of sitting down again she wandered around for a
few moments, picking up various objects and setting
them down. Then she said, rather unexpectedly, "We
have a lot of fun together—and you have to remember
that Saul is at the hospital day and night, so I really can't

be with him very much. It's tantalizing, and then when
we do have a night and a day we just go wild. Sometimes
we make love for twenty-four hours and never get up. I
suppose that shocks you."

"Not at all. But that won't last. And then what?"

"Sometimes we spend a whole day at the zoo. Sometimes we see two movies. I can't explain it, mother, what
it is about him, except—" here Daisy turned back from
the window and sat down again. "He's so alive. He's so
full of life he's like a child let out of school and he pulls
me along with him because he charms me. He charms
me," she said again. Laura observed that she was close
to tears and wondered why. Daisy had not been a
weeper, except when she was in a rage.

"And if you do get married? It sounds as if maybe you
should?"

"I'd always be an outsider, Mother, wherever we
went—even far away from New York. I'd never be taken
in, you see, and for Saul being with me is betraying
something deep inside him. I know that. He talks about
going to Israel—I would love that. But he would be a
little uncomfortable, you see. He would always have to
be explaining me as though I were a black, and that's really how I feel, like a stranger."

"I just don't believe that. It seems so old-fashioned. I
mean, after all—" and suddenly Laura felt quite cross. It
seemed almost unbelievable, like something in a Victorian novel. "After all, love is always taking the stranger
in. When Charles died, I felt cut in two, but we were
never exactly one, you know."

"You mean Daddy was very simple and you were complicated?" At this Laura laughed, because Daisy had a
way of reducing things to the bare bones, and perhaps
she was right.

"I'm not complicated," Laura answered seriously.

"The complications came from Mamma, and from my being ill so long before I married. I suppose some part of me had been walled away so I could survive, and only because Charles was such a truly loving, giving person, did it work. I think we did have a good marriage," she added quickly.

"I used to envy the way you looked at each other across the table."

"Did you?" Laura felt suddenly shy, aware now as she had not been at the time, of Daisy's eyes observing, being envious. "If you must know I was a little envious of you and your father. When you were born, I knew I had given him what he wanted most in the world."

"I just think family life is impossible," Daisy said. "You can't win. It's so damned complicated. Nobody gets what he wants. Or if he does, then someone else in the family doesn't. And the awful thing is that women have had to be the ones to balance it all and keep it from falling apart! I just don't think I could do it, Mother."

"Since the women's movement has taken hold, perhaps we are able to be honest at last—so much is coming out into the open that had been buried. That's why Sybille felt so violently about it."

"Did she? She never said so to me."

"She felt the sacred was being violated. Things talked about lose their mystery, she felt—and perhaps rightly so. Also there was too much she couldn't face, it would have been too terrible."

"Like what?"

Laura lay back on the sofa, taking a kind of inward leap. Was this the moment to talk about Sybille? To break her long silence about all that to her children, and especially to Daisy who admired Sybille? "I think I'm a little too tired to try to say it. The great thing, dearie, is that you knew Sybille at her best, and at her best she could be rather wonderful."

"I feel you are putting me off. Oh, dear, of course, you're exhausted. I'm going to get us something to eat and leave you alone for a bit—only—" Daisy turned back at the door, with a look on her face, puzzled but determined, that brought her back vividly as a child, "I hope you'll talk about it later on."

The conversation had taken its toll, though all through it Laura had felt she was being borne on a rising tide, racing with it toward some understanding at last between herself and this subtly rejecting Daisy. I don't feel rejected now, Laura was thinking. The door has opened between us, and neither of us is quite as much on the defensive. That's good, she said to herself, even as she sank into a half-doze. "A house of gathering," someone, maybe Jung, had called death. But exhausted as she was, Laura wondered whether her mother would ever have a place in that house where all could be gathered, all accepted—except her. Would she have to die to be delivered of Sybille?

"Ella," she murmured.

"There," Daisy was saying, "I made you an eggnog and a tiny portion of Mrs. O'Brien's delicious stew in case you could taste it." She laid a small tray beside Laura.

Laura opened her eyes and made the long journey back from semiconsciousness. "Oh, thanks. Don't forget to have some salad. I made it for you."

They sat opposite each other in a companionable silence. Daisy put a new log on the fire. Laura took a sip of eggnog and managed to swallow it, and in a little while she had taken about a third. To swallow more would be

[165

to push her luck, for nausea now was increasingly the enemy. Daisy at least was ravenous. Laura, watching her dive into the stew, remembered Daisy's fiercely hungry mouth at her breast and how it sometimes hurt.

"I've been thinking about what Granny felt about the women's movement. In a way I suppose she had it all. I mean, she seems so fulfilled."

"Fulfilled?" Laura set her glass down in sheer amazement. It was actually the last word she would have used in regard to Sybille, who went on from height to height and never appeared to be satisfied, her head full of visions of glory.

"She was so much part of everything important in her time—the arts—all those writers and painters she knew and, through Grandpa, politics. Think of her marching in Washington for peace! She knew so many famous people, yet she talked to me as an absolute equal."

"I suppose you could say it was a great life," Laura said slowly. "But fulfillment . . ." she hesitated.

" 'Fulfillment' means being whole, is that it? And you feel she wasn't? She stayed hungry and terribly alive, and maybe that's better."

Laura bit back the words, "Not if one has been as destructive to others as Sybille was to us—and to all those people she picked up so fervently and then forgot about when the next hero appeared." Instead of uttering them she forced herself to get up, and hurried to the kitchen where she vomited the eggnog.

Daisy was there in an instant, to hold her forehead in a strong hand as the dry convulsions shook Laura.

"Oh . . ." she groaned.

"It's all right, Mother. I'm here."

Laura was weeping now, hot tears streaming down her cheeks, from weakness, she told herself. Something was cracking open inside her, and it was painful. She felt absolutely defenseless before her child, stripped down to this vomiting animal, waiting for the seizure to pass. But at the same time, she was leaning on Daisy's cool hand, grateful for the strength and the tenderness there.

"I think I'd better go to bed now," she said when she could turn around and lean her head on Daisy's shoulder, taking short, panting breaths, her face bathed in tears and sweat.

Very quietly, Daisy held her up, held her in her arms like a baby. Neither of them needed to say anything.

Chapter XVI

The dawn came now at half-past five, and Laura, who had been awake for hours trying to find a position in which she would not cough, welcomed the faint light bringing the room alive, little by little. The curtains breathed gently in a light breeze. She felt strangely at peace. When Daisy appeared at six to ask whether she would like a cup of tea, Laura held out her arms, and they hugged silently. She felt so serene she was surprised by Daisy's anxious face.

"You didn't sleep, Mother?" Daisy asked.

"Not much, but I am learning to float. I don't know how to describe it, like being carried on a current. I felt happy."

"Oh, Mother." Daisy fled to make the tea.

Later she put on the Mozart clarinet quintet and some Beethoven sonatas for Laura to listen to upstairs. They were in unspoken agreement that Laura would stay in bed, and when she went to the bathroom, she knew she had to, for she felt quite faint just making the small effort of walking across the room twice. Daisy took the animals for a walk later on, and Laura sank into a lovely sleep, bathed in sunlight. She felt it on her face like a gentle hand.

Then—what time was it anyway? Nearly eleven?—she woke to the sound of voices downstairs, Jo's deep, musical voice and Daisy's. For a moment Laura thought she couldn't possibly see Jo, not yet.

"She's awfully sick, Aunt Jo," she heard Daisy say. Then they must have closed a door.

Laura pulled a pillow up from the foot of the bed and stuffed it behind her. She sat up straight, suddenly in a sweat, feeling around for a comb in the drawer of the night table, but it wasn't there. I've got to get used to being helpless, she told herself. It is what I have to learn, that—and other things. I don't want to see them, she thought, as though Jo and everyone else close to her, family, were flying down out of the sky like predatory birds. Only Aunt Minna and Mary O'Brien and Dr. Goodwin could come because they did not ask her full attention, she supposed. Or perhaps each of them had a niche, and everything fitted into their comings and goings. Jo's arrival today when Laura knew she was close to exhaustion was a trial. Would Daisy be able to shield her—if only Daphne were the one, Laura thought. But why do I need shielding from my sister? And then she heard Jo's firm step on the stairs.

"I haven't been able to get here till today," Jo said. "It's a week of trustees' meetings. Darling, why didn't you tell us?"

"Jo—when I was so ill in Switzerland, I became the prisoner of other people—I need to do this alone. Can't you understand?"

Jo was standing by the bed. She looked handsome in a dark-green tweed suit and white ruffled blouse, her dark eyes set wide apart in her head, and something impassive in her white marblelike skin. She looked young for her age, though her hair was white, cut short and curled. She's my sister, Laura thought, this handsome, powerful person, but I don't know her. She's a stranger.

"Sit down, Jo, you make me nervous standing there."

"Don't be cross," Jo said, pulling up a low chair so that she could sit at the foot of the bed and lean on its end. "It wouldn't be quite human if I couldn't see my own sister . . . when . . ."

"I'm dying, but it isn't bad," Laura said gently.

Jo swallowed nervously.

"I have a very good nurse-housekeeper and Jim Goodwin comes to drain the lungs—that relieves the pressure. Gosh, Jo, you wouldn't believe the huge quantities of a dark-orange fluid he gets out, and it doesn't hurt." Laura felt that discussing symptoms and the purely physical aspect of things was the only way to handle this unexpected visitation.

When they had talked about all that, Jo asked about Ben, and Laura explained he was finishing a big painting.

"What is the point of his coming here to agonize?"

"He is your son," Jo said.

"But that's just what I can't handle, the burden of what other people are feeling, don't you see? I want to be left in peace to feel my own feelings."

"I don't understand you at all," said Jo.

"No, I guess not. After all, Jo, you have managed to close off personal feelings as irrelevant."

"I don't have time to think a great deal about myself. One of the good things about a college is that it provides young women with something other than feelings to deal with. And for someone nearly sixty-five, I must say, yes, I do believe one should have outgrown what is commonly called love. But family is different," she added.

"In what way? Besides, Jo, you haven't been much of a family person, have you?"

Jo smiled. "For someone very ill you can still pack a powerful punch." Jo always had liked the colloquial, but her usages were often slightly antiquated and made Laura smile. We are smiling antagonists, she thought, watching Jo absent-mindedly pluck the tufts on the white bedspread. Having said what she had said, Laura realized that Jo's presence was quite simply irrelevant.

"I'm tired today. It makes me irritable." And she laughed. "Why should families stick together anyway?"

But Jo was perturbed and did not respond. "Laura," she said, "I'm eaten up by my job, and I honestly don't think it's a stupid or ungiving life. The problems we face in any liberal arts college today are simply stunning—I mean there is money, for one thing. The pressure is on to take in less than qualified students, and that's especially true in a young college. Oh, well," she looked up at Laura, "why plague you with my problems?"

"You appear to thrive on them. You look awfully well I must say. Not a wrinkle!"

"Don't be absurd. I'm a fat old woman."

They had just escaped a passage of some bitterness, and Laura lay back on her pillow and waited.

"I mustn't tire you."

"The person who is dying is really very young. Have you ever thought how little, deep down inside, one is aware of aging? Only the body knows it, and God knows it is there to remind us. The things that happened to me long ago are what seem most real to me now. It's strange," Laura said, looking up at the ceiling. She was thinking aloud and had almost forgotten that Jo was there. "I think a great deal about Ella—you remember, my English friend?"

"Vaguely—she married a don, didn't she? You met her in Paris."

"Yes. I'll tell you something, Jo. I loved my husband. Sometimes I think we had an almost perfect marriage. But what haunts me now is Ella, and it is to Ella I talk in my dreams. Why is that, I wonder?" Laura turned her head so she could catch Jo's eye. "Do you ever dream about Alicia?"

There was not a tremor. "Good heavens, no!"

"You have been able to forgive Mamma for what she did?" This was the question that Laura had wanted forever to ask.

"I never think about it," Jo said.

"Oublieuse mémoire," Laura murmured. "But I have not forgotten, strangely enough. I guess it was the first time I had ever dared to admit that Mamma was not perfect. It was so cruel, Jo! You went around looking ill for months. I felt it was a murder, and I still do."

"I appear to have survived," Jo said ironically, "unless you think I am a ghost!"

"You survived but as a somehow mutilated person. Oh, dear, that sounds awful. But Jo, you have to admit that it has a grain of truth in it."

Jo half-closed her eyes. Laura now had her real attention for the first time since Jo had come into the room. And that was visible in her face, for Laura caught the tremor in her cheek.

"Mutilated? That's a strong word. I decided that loving a woman was more than I could handle ever again, too intense, and too painful," and she added with a sigh, "and in my world too dangerous." But having said so much she quickly closed the door. "Besides, I don't really like all that."

" 'All that,' meaning loving someone?"

"Oh, I suppose so. And I suppose I mean sex. I feel it muddies everything. In that respect perhaps you are right that I have shut out a lot deliberately. Were you and Ella lovers?"

"No, but I wish we had been. For me, sex has been a form of communion. I suppose we are both old-fashioned, each in our own way. For that is not the way it is looked at now—now it is a game in which the body in all its intricacy is simply used as a mechanism to be cleverly handled." But this, Laura felt, was a digression, and she could not afford to digress. "I've been thinking a lot about it because the last book I worked on for my publisher was by a lesbian. She is so much more honest and aware and responsible than we were, or could be, perhaps. The book has to do in part with telling her parents of her life-style and their violent reaction to it. She has come here twice close to despair. You see, if she publishes, she will probably lose her lover, a teacher who fears exposure."

"And quite rightly, my girl. Surely you advised this person not to publish?"

"I didn't advise, I listened."

"And if she goes ahead and publishes, what is so different from me with Alicia? I could have run away and followed her, I suppose. Instead I went to college and did brilliantly. I do not consider that contemptible. If your young writer gives up her love for her work, isn't that the same thing, and won't she too be 'mutilated,' to use your word?"

Laura sat up, crossing her arms around her knees.

"I don't know," she said after a pause. "But self-revelation in the cause of truth, or of art if you prefer, does seem in a different category to the pursuit of power."

"That's not fair, Laura. I did not want power. I wanted to do something in the world of education."

Without ever coming to terms with what drove you to it, Laura thought, but she did not speak the words. Harriet Moors would suffer but she *was* coming to terms with her own life, and fundamentally so.

"I have so much to think about," Laura murmured. "I would so much like to get it all clear in my mind."

"I wonder if we ever do."

"For me that is what dying is all about. Jo, I went to see Sybille after Jim Goodwin told me what I could expect. I told her I was dying—I wonder why. Of course there was no reaction."

"None?"

"None. She looks quite beautiful, but she is not there."

"I haven't seen her for months."

"The strange thing is I did not feel liberated. Shall we ever be liberated from that devastating influence, I wonder?"

Jo got up and walked to the bureau where she picked up and set down various small objects.

"What was it, really?" she asked after a moment.

"Control, the need to control everything, and that meant also herself. Because if she could not control, chaos would take place—the dam would break, if you will—and that was too terrifying."

"Nothing was very relaxed, as I remember. It was all rather tense, wasn't it? Is that why we were ill so much, I have sometimes wondered? I mean then Mamma exerted all her charm and concentrated on one, for a change. It was lovely to lie in bed and be brought junket and eggnogs."

"Being a nurse was one of her best roles," Laura said, and sighed. "But years of that kind of attention—by the time it was over and I was well, after Davos, I felt quite unreal to myself, and to everyone else."

"I remember your smile," Jo said, "as though you smiled all the time at something no one else knew about. What was it?"

"Oh, I expect I learned to smile in order not to scream." After all, to whom except Jo could she say such things? Jo and Daphne, her fellow cripples? "Ella saved my reason then, and of course Mamma was frightfully jealous of her. While we talked and Ella held my hand, Mamma always had to come in for one reason or another and supervise as it were. And just when we had got to the point of any real exchange, Ella would be reminded that I must not be tired. She came only four times in the two years, but each visit managed to reanimate the emotional idiot I was becoming. Has it ever occurred to you," Laura said, hunching herself up so she could look at Jo again, "that people can become emotionally stupid? Infants, for instance, who are never fondled do not develop. For a long time, for months I existed by shutting most things out."

"I suppose you think I am emotionally stupid." Jo had evidently been thinking her own thoughts.

"Oh, I don't know," Laura said. "How can I know?"

"Marriage and children aren't the only possible fulfillment for a woman, after all."

"Indeed not. That's not what I am talking about."

"Laura, I ought to go downstairs. I didn't come here to take your last ounce of strength."

"You sound like Mamma. Why shouldn't I spend it?" Laura was suddenly cross. "Why shouldn't I, for God's sake?" Then she added, lying back on her pillows, "Jo, go down and see if there's a little champagne left in the bottle Daisy brought. I may be able to keep that down. Put a piece of ice in it and make yourself a drink or something and then come back. Meanwhile I'll breathe a little, quietly."

There were so many things she suddenly wanted to ask Jo—why, for instance, she didn't have an animal. I really know her so little, Laura thought. I read about her in the newspapers—she has just been given another honorary doctorate or is present at the investiture of a president somewhere in the academic world, or she is embattled (as she was some years ago) over quotas.

[175

Jo came back after a while—minutes or half-hours glided into each other for Laura—and Laura took several sips of champagne. It was not as flat as she had feared it might be. Jo had brought a cup of coffee for herself.

"Why did you come, Jo?"

"After all, you are ill."

" 'Families are different,' you said, earlier. And yet—forgive me for being blunt—you must have intimate friends who are far closer to you now than I. We haven't talked like this for years."

Jo took a swallow of coffee and put the cup down.

"Daisy told me you and Daff went down to the old house."

"Yes, I wanted to remember Mamma as she was during those happy summers. I really have to make up a reckoning about Mamma before I die, but," Laura smiled, "it appears to be very hard to do."

"Do you really think Daff's life—she is some sort of worker at an animal shelter, she told me—is less inhuman than mine, Laura? I must confess I feel attacked, and I don't understand why. Some people would say I'd made a valid contribution to society."

"In her peculiar way Daff has become rather a person," Laura said, seeing vividly Daphne's lined face, so much older-looking than Jo's, yet moving in a way that Jo's would never be.

"She looks a wreck," Jo said. "Of the three of us you're the one who has made a go of it as a human being."

"I've been a success at the commonplace, rather odd for a daughter of Sybille's. You at least have reached a little touch of glory—Mamma was apt to show me a clipping about your latest degree or something when she was still able to read."

"Did she?" Jo was visibly pleased. "Somehow when we were growing up we felt starved for praise, at least I did. She was always holding up some super example against whatever we achieved in school—Daff, you remember, wrote poems at one time. Mamma was quite patronizing about them. Of course she didn't mean to be. She didn't know what those words of relative praise could do to wither one."

"She wrote poems herself," Laura reminded Jo. I wonder why she never published, or only that one book she had privately printed for Pa. Let's face it, they just weren't that good."

"You say Daff has become 'rather a person.' But after all, you have to admit that Mamma was a far greater one than any of us. We are all dwarfs beside her."

"I don't believe that." Laura felt hot and prickly before this outrageous untruth.

"That we're dwarfs, or that she was a giant?"

"I don't know. Can destructive people be giants?"

"On your terms maybe not. But she did loom rather large—and I wonder whether she was really destructive, except to her own children. So many people of all ages, Laura—you have to admit that!—adored her. And she was a real beauty. My God, was she not!"

"Yes," Laura said meditatively, "she was."

"She was simply on a larger scale than most women are. It can't have been easy, can it? She needed a large stage, and Pa, dear man, never got onto the big stage, an ambassadorship, for instance. Think what Mamma would have done with the Paris ambassadorship!"

Here they burst into laughter—and for the first time since Jo had come into the room an hour ago, Laura recognized her as her sister.

"We would have rolled our hoops in the Luxembourg gardens, gone to lycées—"

"And you would have married a Frenchman, Laura."

"No one but Charles, thank you very much."

[177

"You and your Charles," Jo teased. Then she looked at her watch. "I have to get back, Laura!"

"Yes."

Jo was standing now. The sisters exchanged a long look that Laura held because she hoped for something, some sign perhaps. Who knows what the naked ask of the clothed?

Jo bent down and took one of Laura's hands in a firm clasp. *"Courage, mon enfant."* It had been a phrase of their father's. Laura pulled her hand away.

"It's not courage I need," she whispered, "not really. Good-by, Jo."

When the door had closed, the tears flowed down Laura's cheeks. Not courage, she thought, but communion. There had been so little. And now she was left to sink back into weakness, a gathering weakness, weakness like a tide. I must keep family away from now on, she told herself. I can't do it anymore.

Chapter XVII

Laura heard a faint scratching at her door which Jo had closed as she left. "Sasha!" I must have slept for an hour, she thought as she unwound herself from the sheet and went to let the cat in.

"Where is everyone, Sasha?" Daisy must have taken a long walk with Grindle. But then Laura noticed a little note on the floor and picked it up as Sasha wound round her legs, purring loudly. "Mother, I have gone over to Brooks and Ann. I didn't want to wake you. There is an eggnog in the frig if you get hungry. Just stir it up a little. Daisy."

"So we're alone, Sasha." But not for long, for Grindle was plunging up the stairs now at the sound of Laura's voice and licked her feet with great enthusiasm before she got back into bed. Then, with Grindle stretched out on the rug beside her and Sasha curled up against her side, Laura lay very still, wide-awake. The room was bathed in gentle morning light, the sun having risen, so it no longer touched Laura's cheek, but it all blossomed in a golden blur. Overnight the maple she could see against the window had burst into flower, small parasols wide open. So often she had wondered whether she would ever actually see it happening, like a soft explosion. Once more it had taken place at night. Grindle gave a groan in his sleep. There was no sound except, quite far off, the insistent, plaintive notes of a white-throated sparrow.

Birds, Laura was thinking, have such short lives, short and intense—that savage, ceaseless hunt for food, the constant motion. Were they ever still? Still as she was now, while in her head, in the mysterious infinity of the brain, great constellations of memories came into focus. She was walking up the rue de l'Odéon with Ella on their way to the Luxembourg gardens, books under their arms, for the idea was to study. The chestnuts were in flower, and at the pond children were sailing boats. They would walk first, up and down the wide, sandy allées, and then settle into deck chairs and read for an hour or two. There Laura had read Baudelaire for the first time. "Mon enfant, ma soeur/ Songe à la douceur/D'aller là-bas vivre ensemble!" She had known hundreds of lines by heart, but only a few floated back now. "Nous avons dit souvent d'impérissables choses/Les soirs illuminés par l'ardeur du charbon"; poems that would always have for her the background of chestnuts in flower, baby carriages, the sharp cries of children, and Ella looking up for a moment from her book to yawn, stretch out her arms, and smile one of her rare, beatific smiles that expressed everything she would not or could not say.

In those early days it was Laura who talked, endlessly about Sybille, and about life and death and why we are on earth, and was it possible not to get married and still lead a whole life? Then her fantasies were to hug trees, to feel rough bark against her palms, to swim, to ride furiously on a willing horse through green meadows, to gallop and smell the smell of horse. Now her fantasies were not fantasies but some great reality she could not even imagine, something working its will inside her body, something gathering her up in a struggle that was slowly involving her whole being to each tiny cell, and the blood itself. She was trying to make friends with it, for death must be met as a friend, welcomed even. It was something she was creating, her body creating, and she had to lie very still and let it happen. But not before—

Before what? Before some final gathering together and sorting out of her life. Jo had not helped in this. The more they talked, the farther away Jo seemed to go. Who could help? If Laura asked her, Ella would come. But how could she tell whether that would be the right thing? How take such a risk for both of them? Implant this dying into a past that had been so rich in living, at such depth and with such intensity? Yet it was Ella who returned after all these visits, the image of Ella. "Families are different," Jo had said, meaning simply, Laura surmised, that one should visit family when ill, and the ill member ought to wish to be visited. But that was quite absurd, as Laura could prove on her own pulse. Jim Goodwin and his quiet, expert care, his very presence, did more for her than any member of her family could—and Mary O'Brien! Daphne had come closest, but already the time when she could make a journey such as they had made together was past. Laura reminded herself that she wanted to be downstairs and if possible dressed when Daisy came back from Brooks and Ann's.

"Just a little longer, Sasha," she murmured, "just a little snooze—perfect peace—"

It was finally hunger that exerted enough pressure to get Laura up in a dressing gown. She combed her hair, washed her face and hands, and, accompanied by Grindle, went slowly downstairs, feeling quite dizzy, so

[181

she was afraid for a second that she might fall. She found the eggnog and took it into the library and lay there, looking into the cold hearth, which had not been laid. Someone, perhaps Jo, had brought an azalea of a lovely orange-pink, and Laura drank it in. Then she sipped at the eggnog through a straw. She felt sure it was chiefly lack of food that made her feel so weak. If she could keep a little nourishment down, she would feel able to face saying good-by to Daisy. And then in a few hours Mary O'Brien would come back.

Every now and then she felt for Grindle lying beside her. And when Daisy pushed open the front door and called, "Mother, I'm back!" she did feel ready and held out her arms for this only daughter.

"Are you all right?"

"I drank the whole eggnog."

"Good."

Daisy sat on the edge of the sofa and took one of her mother's hands in hers. "I have to pack now. Shall I put on a record?" But she was not asking that, she was visibly trying to say something else, and Laura saw the anxiety and pain clouding her eyes. "Mother, must you go through this alone? Is that what you *want?* Ann and Brooks feel you are warding them off."

Laura withdrew her hand and closed her eyes.

"I know," she murmured. "You'll just have to let me do this my way. I have to get ready for something huge and sometimes frightening."

"That's just it, Mother. You must let us help you."

"I have, haven't I?" Laura said quite sharply.

"Let me come back," Daisy said. "Please."

"We'll be in touch, darling. I can't foresee—I have to live each day as it comes." It was frightful not to have more to give, but Laura felt now as though a heavy stone had been placed on her chest and was bearing down.

"You'd better go now and pack, or you'll miss that plane." And, as Daisy slowly walked toward the stairs, Laura managed to say it: "Thank you, darling, for coming and for our good talk."

"I'm furious with Aunt Jo for coming like that unannounced," Daisy said from the stairs. "She brought the azalea, you know, and when she left she seemed very upset. For once, I could tell she was bowled over."

"Really?"

"Mother, you don't know how much people love you!" And Daisy ran up the stairs.

Yes, Laura thought, it's like a web. Whatever the secret, the real connections, we are inextricably woven into a huge web together, and detaching the threads, one by one, is hideously painful. As long as one still feels the tug, one is not ready to die. At this moment Laura realized, and it was like some explosion inside her, that she would never know whether Daisy would marry Saul, or what would happen to her. But, she reminded herself, the future is not my concern now. I have to shut it out. Only the present moment can have any real substance—so she looked again at the azalea and noted what unusually large single blossoms it had, and she felt that this looking, this still intense joy in a flower, was her way of praising God. Outside the human web there was another far more complex and yet not binding structure that included Grindle and the azalea and she herself, and in that she could rest.

Chapter XVIII

"You're all tuckered out," Mary O'Brien said after taking one look at Laura, lying on the sofa where she had been half-asleep since Daisy had left after promising to come back with her guitar and sing. "You can just be in bed upstairs" Daisy had said, "and I'll sing my songs down here," and the idea had clearly been of such comfort to Daisy herself that Laura had assented.

"Tomorrow you'll stay in bed all day," Mary O'Brien said. It was not hard to assent to that. "You'd better get to bed now, and I'll bring you some hot tea." Mary knew just how to lift Laura up, and they progressed slowly back to the bedroom, step by step, Laura leaning heavily on Mary's arm.

Halfway she began to giggle. It was absurd to feel as weak as she did. After all, she had managed to have long talks with both Daisy and Jo. "It was my sister Jo—she came unexpectedly."

"I'm going to stay next weekend," Mary said firmly.

"And be my dragon?"

"There now, just four more steps and we've made it."

It was wonderful beyond words to find herself in bed,

with Mary fluffing up the pillows and helping her sit high enough against them to be comfortable.

"Perfect peace with loved ones far away," she murmured and again was suffused with laughter.

"Would you like me to bring you your book?" Mary asked as she turned to go.

"No thanks, I'll just rest." It occurred to Laura that she didn't want to read, even Herbert. It seemed years ago when she had looked for him eagerly, when those poems were the food she needed most. Things are changing very fast, she thought. It's a metamorphosis. I wonder what I am being changed into, a person who does not want to read or see her own family, who wants—what? Silence. A little while when breathing could still be possible and that strange animal so alive inside her—for she could hear her heart's slow thud—could keep going. "Till spring," Jim Goodwin had said—and she must hold on for Ben. She could not say "it is finished" yet, not quite yet.

So when Mary brought the tea she swallowed it in small sips, making an effort to pay attention and so keep it down. And she must have fallen asleep with the empty cup still in her lap, for she had no memory of Mary's coming to take it. Unfortunately at two, long before light, she was wide-awake. Sasha had woken her by jumping onto the bed.

The discomfort was such that it took her some time— and these were the times when fear took over—before she achieved floating, but finally as the dawn came and she could distinguish the objects in the room, she rested her eyes on her blue wrapper flung over a chair. The way it lay in folds to the floor seemed quite beautiful. It reminded her of paintings of Piero della Francesca. Strange how it was always a clear, precise image that led her into the floating. From there, she found herself wondering why it was that during all this time of waiting and preparing, she had been haunted chiefly by women, that women inhabited her consciousness as even dear Charles did not—Sybille, Ella, Daphne, Daisy, even Ann and conflict-ridden Harriet. Was it that there was something unfinished here, not whole as her relation with Charles had been? That did not need probing; she could rest in it. But what really was involved? It was way outside her sexuality, this preoccupation. Perhaps indeed it had to do with herself as woman, woman in relation to herself, not to men.

Why did she think so rarely of Pa? Sometimes he came into her mind with great clarity, usually an image of summer in Maine, Pa getting a boat out, Pa looking immensely handsome in tennis flannels, Pa coming for brief visits to her bedside in Switzerland, smiling and teasing her gently, telling some small joke, embarrassed but so *warm*. Whereas she had only to evoke Sybille to find herself in a blur. Nothing was clear, not even that beauty Jo had spoken of with such feeling. For there had been too much strain in the beauty, the tendons in Sybille's neck so taut—no wonder she suffered from arthritis—and her eyes, never hooded, a naked blaze. In the hospital she had not wanted to be looked down at by those amazing eyes that, because she was flat on her back, she could not escape.

Laura turned her head from side to side on the pillow, trying to turn off the current she was floating on, the dangerous one that brought her to a kind of anguish when she faced the puzzling image of Sybille.

Perhaps it was that Sybille was so glorious—Laura could see her head bent over a book, sitting at the bedside, the marvelous, haunting voice reading Descartes and Pascal and Péguy—at one time those long cadences of Péguy were what Laura had most enjoyed. Sybille had wanted to read poetry, but Laura couldn't take it. For those two years she simply could not afford to feel very much. And her mother reading poems made her feel spiritually raped, there was no other word. She had somehow to keep a wall between herself and Sybille. If they had merged at that time, Laura knew she would have drowned, gone mad, actually lost *herself*. The ever-present presence, the guard—oh, it was not an angel who had guarded her! Any more than it was an angel who had cut Jo off from her passion for Alicia.

What really motivated Sybille? Why were they never supposed to have what they wanted? What was the taboo? Daphne when she was thirteen had wanted dreadfully to be allowed to go away to school—this had not been allowed. At the very center of Sybille, Laura suspected, there must have been a tight knot of conflict, conflict between her own passionate nature and something that held back at the very moment of giving out. Conscience? Or what? How would she ever, ever know? She and Sybille could never have talked as she and Daisy had, yet Daisy too had felt criticized, had viewed her mother as in some way a censor. Is it partly that mothers fear for their daughters more than for their sons? The risks of being a woman are so much greater, the danger of being caught in a life one did not altogether choose—Daisy and Saul. But that hardly explained the degree of control exerted when she, Daphne, and Jo were children.

Quite suddenly the room was flooded with light as the sun came up at last, and Laura, feeling it on her face, let go. Soon Mary would bring her a cup of tea and the day, the new day would begin.

That day brought flowers from Houghton Mifflin, from Dinah, and a warm, admiring letter from George, Laura's editor, to tell her that they had signed a contract with Harriet Moors and were very pleased with the book and grateful to Laura for working with Harriet. It ended, "Here we at the firm have depended greatly on your wisdom and flair. We are going to miss you more than I can say. I am very reluctant to believe that you will not be back, so we shall wait a while before sending someone over with the things from your desk. I personally believe in phoenixes."

Laura laid the letter aside. She didn't want to think about it, about that finality anyway. Letting work go at the moment seemed harder than letting people go, for she surmised the dissolution of the work was a dissolution at the center of her *self*, the immensely private self for whom she had undertaken it in the first place. "I have to do something of my own that is not bringing up children, Charles," she had explained. And of course Charles had understood.

But also she laid the letter down because the thought of Harriet Moors caused a pang. The contract signed. Good news. But she had some idea what it had cost. So she turned to the slim blue envelope from England and opened it, her hands shaking. It had come from so far and felt so near.

"Dearest Snab, you are never far from my thoughts these days. It's not exactly thinking, but rather some attentive being with you. Yet I find it hard to write.

"It is so strange to know that Sybille still lives—but not as herself. I wonder whether you will able to unravel or come to an end of your preoccupation with her. I feel sure that you think about her. It is awful not to know just what conclusions you are near to arriving at. Mother goes on in her usual compulsive way, expanding the gardens at Fernwood though there aren't enough gardeners, forgetting what plants she has ordered, amazed when some huge, terribly expensive azaleas arrived the other day. She pays absolutely no attention to anyone else and at the same time needles me subtly whenever I see her. I sometimes long for *all* my relatives to vanish. Do you suppose some people (they *must*) manage to operate pretty freely while a parent remains above ground? How *do* they do it?"

At this point Laura began to laugh with the sheer pleasure of being completely understood and of completely understanding. Ella, Ella, she wanted to cry out, come! Instead of finishing the letter, she lay and smiled, and it was after lunch when she resumed. "It is taking an enormous amount of strength not to fly over, but I shall await your word, dearest Snab."

After the day in bed, Laura felt restored enough to be downstairs when Aunt Minna arrived at four on the dot.

"It seems ages, darling—what a weekend!" Laura rested her eyes on Aunt Minna. The dark circles round her eyes only emphasized their brightness, bright as a bird's eyes and as impersonal. That is what made these visits so restful, Laura was thinking. Aunt Minna, unlike almost anyone else Laura saw these days except Mary, had a definite role, a role she enjoyed playing as anyone would who read aloud so well. "Pour your tea, will you? Mary was inspired to make those little cakes for you."

"Delicious," Aunt Minna said, eating one ravenously, and for a second Laura felt jealous of someone who could eat with pleasure, for whom eating had not become fraught with the risk of violent nausea.

"Jo descended on us. It really was a bit much with Daisy here as well."

"The dutiful sister?"

"It was clearly such a thing for her to extract herself from the college, the effort so great, that it never occurred to her that she might not be welcome."

"Imagination is hardly Jo's long suit, is it? Oh, well," Aunt Minna said, brushing Jo aside. "Here we are."

"You and Trollope are my best medicine," Laura said. "Let's read."

Laura did not actually listen some of the time. Some of the time Aunt Minna's clear, sweet voice simply flowed on like the murmur of turtle doves, but it was becoming increasingly important to have this companionable, undemanding hour in the day, when she could rest in the simple presence of this old woman who for some reason was able to be there in the room without displacing so much atmosphere that Laura was dragged out of herself, out of her own orbit, which was narrowing down. There is only Ben now, she thought—

Aunt Minna stopped to laugh aloud at something Laura in her reverie had missed. "Isn't that delicious?" she asked.

"It's you who are delicious." Laura smiled.

"Well, I've been called a lot of things, but 'delicious' is not one of them." And Aunt Minna chuckled.

"You know one thing about dying," Laura said, sitting up a little to relieve the weight in her chest, "is that one can say outrageous things—but to whom should one say them? Mary O'Brien seems to enjoy them, and you, dear Aunt Minna, for you are good at saying the outrageous yourself."

"Am I?" Aunt Minna held the book closed in her hands.

"Yes, you are. So tell me now why it is that the journey I am making is taking me deeper and deeper into what it is to be a woman? Strange, isn't it? I never thought much about it before."

"Laura, I know very little about that."

"Oh, yes, you do."

"I suppose I have lived my life outside what women's lives are meant to be."

Laura lay back, looking at the ceiling, feeling for some word that could link Aunt Minna and what had preoccupied her own mind for days. "I think that however original and powerful a woman may have been—and as you surely are—we have allowed ourselves to be caught in all sorts of stereotypes. What is a woman meant to be, anyway? We don't think of men as 'meant to be' primarily married and fathers, do we?"

"You know, I never thought of it quite like that before!"

"Well, neither did I," Laura said, surprised at herself. "But I've done some thinking lately. I wish I could get it all settled in my mind before . . ."

"Come to some final reckoning, eh? I wonder if that is possible. In my experience just when one has arrived at what appears to be, momentarily, a final judgment, life throws the whole thing out by some quirk or unexpected insight—like what you just said. I'm elated to have been given a clue just now to what the woman's movement is really all about. Such a little thing, yet it has really opened my eyes. I have, you see, always regarded myself as an eccentric, a stray fish in some side pool outside the great tides of life—oh, I quite enjoyed myself, you know."

"I know. You kicked up considerable waves in that pool!"

"But I did feel that a married woman was somehow more—"

"More what?"

Aunt Minna gave her short laugh, self-deprecatory, a little wry. "Is 'appropriate' the word?"

At this Laura laughed aloud, then leaned forward to

try to control the fit of coughing. Anything but shallow breathing was fatal now. "Oh, dear."

"Shall I read a little more?" Aunt Minna asked. It was just too bad, Laura thought, not to be able to catch her breath. And too bad to alarm Aunt Minna.

"Oh, damn" she murmured, sweat pouring down her forehead into her eyes. "Damn."

This time she did manage to achieve control. Finally she was able to lie back on the pillow. "I'm so sorry," she murmured.

"None of that," Aunt Minna said sharply. "The Alpine climber is often in an agony for breath—remember that—and we have talked of this as a kind of climb to wherever you are bound, Laura."

Amazing woman, Laura thought. She's really the only person I can bear. And why was that? Because Aunt Minna had her feelings under almost perfect control, though Laura could hear her blowing her nose.

"It's getting worse, of course," Laura murmured. "But I wanted to say something."

"Rest a little," Aunt Minna said, "and I'll read for a half-hour."

And so she did while Laura listened and half-listened with her eyes closed. Finally she was able to say what she had wanted to.

"You have given so much to life, Aunt Minna. Isn't that the thing? I mean not how a woman does it, but whether she does it at all. What I begin to see—Jo's visit somehow clinched it for me—is that women have been in a queer way locked away from one another in a man's world. The perspective has been from there. Jo thinks of herself as a man. All that is changing and perhaps women will be able to give one another a great deal more than ever before."

Aunt Minna was silent for a moment. Then she said, "You have reached quite a high cliff, haven't you?"

"All that tenderness held back out of fear—"

"You really do astonish me, Laura." Aunt Minna was sitting up straight in her chair and seemed a little tense suddenly. "Of course I wouldn't know," she added defensively. "I never could stand the whole emotional thing. When I was in college, a girl called Alice had quite a crush on me—that's what it was called in those days. I didn't like it at all," she said crisply. "It made me wildly uncomfortable. Sappy, I thought it."

Laura smiled. "I expect you did."

"All that is quite outside my sphere."

"But I'm not talking about 'all that,' " Laura said, amused now by the violence of Aunt Minna's rejection.

After Aunt Minna left, she had quite a think. Her mother, Jo, Daphne, Daisy—all women stopped somehow, somewhere—in some way, she supposed, "unfulfilled." But how to find the all-encompassing reason was quite beyond her power—when Mary O'Brien came in with an eggnog for supper, Laura was asleep.

Chapter XIX

The next days were a limbo. Jim Goodwin came and drained the lungs again, this time drawing out even more of the appalling fluid. For twenty-four hours or so that meant that Laura could lie down comfortably and sleep until four in the morning. Aunt Minna had caught a cold and so couldn't come to read. During those days there was no music in the house, and only Grindle's feet tumbling up and down the stairs interrupted a blessed silence. Laura felt sure she had heard Ann's voice murmuring with Mary O'Brien, in the hall. The phone rang several times, but Laura let it be answered for her. She was not in pain, but she felt obscured, as though a light inside her were being dimmed, as though sleep were her only real climate, and she sank down into it as into deep water, hardly breathing.

Meanwhile spring had come, for Mary set a glass with three daffodils in it beside her bed, and the shadow on the wall danced with maple flowers. Once just at dawn Laura heard an oriole. The oriole had always set its seal, that thrilling song, on the coming of spring, marking a rebirth not only of a season but of Laura herself. This time she murmured, "You'll come back, but this is my last chance to hear you, bird."

She looked forward to Mary's presence, so quiet and protective, but she had no wish to see anyone else at all. It was no surprise when Jim Goodwin came back to sit on her bed, holding her hand with a warm, comforting clasp, and announced that he would feel better if she could have a few days in the hospital.

What for? In her subdued state Laura did not ask. She supposed that he himself needed some reassurance, that X-rays would give him some idea where things were at, that he might change the medicines he had prescribed to see that she was not in pain. It was somehow understood that people fight for life, and she wondered why. She was now halfway or more down the long tunnel—turning back, learning to live again, seemed next to impossible. What was possible, even acceptable, was dying.

"All right, Jim, if you say so."

"You were doing so well, it's a little surprise that we have had a sudden drop. Mary thinks it's because you had too many visits, so I think we'll allow no visitors in the hospital."

"Ben," Laura said, sitting up a little. "When Ben comes, I must see him."

"Maybe he won't get here till you are home again."

"You won't let me die in the hospital, will you?"

"I promised you the spring, didn't I?" Jim said with a return of his smiling, bantering way. Until now he had appeared too anxious to smile.

When he let her hand go she felt as though a transfusion of blood, some life-giving fluid, were leaving her.

"I'm going to see if there is a room, and if there is, we'll have an ambulance here early this afternoon."

"Can you go with me?"

[195

Jim frowned. "I don't see how I can. I have appointments at the office. Do you think Ann and Brooks might be able to take you in?"

Laura's resistance to this possibility was so great that she couldn't answer. Now it was coming, what she had feared most all along, what she had to learn to accept, total dependence. Anger at the slide of a tear down her cheek, at her weakness, made her sit up.

"Laura," Jim said quietly and firmly, "I think you have to let the family in now." But before she could react, he sat down again and held her hand. "I'll come in on my way home around seven and see that you are comfortable. And we'll set up X-rays for tomorrow. O.K.?"

But without Mary, without Jim, in that strange world, how could she manage? Would she be able to "float" there? It was Mary who saved her from these fears. She came in, took one look at Laura, and said, "You'll be home in three days, dearie. It won't be long."

"Oh, Mary, I don't want to go."

Mary lifted Laura so she could pull the pillows up behind her, and at that familiar, expert touch Laura closed her eyes and sank back.

"There, that's better, isn't it?"

"Thank you. You're the only one who really knows."

"I don't know about that," Mary said with one of her shy smiles. "But I'm here, so I notice."

Laura opened her eyes and met Mary's. Neither of them had intended that open look to take place, but Laura could not avoid the depth of compassion flowing out like an angelic balm. She had closed herself off from feeling for days now. To have it come back was hard to handle.

"Why am I so much worse, Mary?"

"You're not coughing as much, that's one good thing."

"Yes, but—I feel so weak."

"I'm going to bring you some consommé and see if maybe you could take a few swallows. Brooks is coming to go with you, Brooks and Ann. You'll need strength."

"I don't want them to see me like this," Laura swallowed to try to stop the tears she felt rising. "My hair—"

"Now, now," Mary said briskly, "you look fine considering you're starved. Your skin's like a baby's. If you ask me, you're a beautiful woman."

"Hardly," Laura said with a wan smile. "But then I never wanted to be one, strangely enough. My mother— she was the real beauty."

"I noticed the photograph. She looks like a queen."

"I didn't want that, that glittering kind of beauty."

"Now don't you tire yourself out with talking. Tell me what you want me to pack for the hospital."

"Oh, whatever you think—my blue wrapper, slippers, a clean nightgown, brush and comb, toothbrush. There's a small suitcase on the shelf in the closet."

Laura watched Mary pack in silence. It was a restful sight, as she did it so quietly, folding things with care.

"Now then," she said, "you'll want a photograph or two from the dresser maybe."

Laura shook her head. No photographs.

"A book? That little transistor radio by your bed?"

"Yes—and George Herbert's poems, though I doubt if I can read, but the idea of Herbert is a help."

Mary found the book on the bedside table and held it for a moment in her hands. "He's a poet, is he?"

"A religious poet," Laura said.

"Oh, well," Mary laid it on top of the suitcase. Then she asked something that had perhaps been on her mind for some time. "Your minister hasn't come to see you—I wondered."

"Yes." Laura lay back looking up at the ceiling as though, she thought, smiling to herself, a divine message might be written there. "But I don't really believe, you know. For me God has always been absence."

"I don't see how you can be so brave without Him," Mary said, then she closed the suitcase and stood looking out the window. "I'm sure I couldn't."

"I try to feel part of something—something greater than myself, to go with it, Mary."

"If that's not believing!" Mary said as she left. "I'll come back in a little while. You sleep."

Laura did not sleep, but without the slightest change in her position—she was still looking at the ceiling—she found herself floating, and that had not happened lately. What she heard very distinctly in her head was the fourth part of Brahms's Requiem, which they had used to sing in school before she became ill. "How lovely is thy dwelling place, O Lord of hosts." She remembered how at that time it had seemed the most beautiful music she had ever sung, though her mother, when she said so, had of course put it down. "Brahms," she had said, "never quite first-rate, is he?" But it had to be admitted that it was Sybille's reading of Herbert when they were quite small that had created such reverberations lately. How does one extricate one thread from such a complicated web?

For the moment Laura let it rest and remembered singing, remembered being lifted up on such sweet music. It had smitten her like love, with a poignant ache in all her being. She turned her head so she could see the light shining through the daffodils and watched it turning the petal's flesh to a transparency, more alive than stained glass. Brahms and the daffodils—life—life.

First, life as pure contemplation, and then life in the shape of a cup of consommé, something she had to throw up!

"Oh, dear, Mary."

"Here, hold this against your forehead," Mary was saying as Laura retched over the basin in her bathroom. "You're all upset over going away," she murmured. "Don't worry. The spring will be waiting when you come back."

At last, after retching, the sheer relief of being back in bed was such that Laura fell asleep, and when she woke there was just time for Mary to help her into a clean nightgown and a light wool dressing gown and slippers. She had meant to be downstairs when the ambulance came, but Mary was adamant.

Brooks and Ann were at the door.

"Hi," Brooks said. He gave her a quick, hunted look. Ann came right in and kissed her and then the men were there with the stretcher, and she was being lifted into it like a baby and strapped down.

"Is that comfortable, ma'am, not too tight?" Laura looked up at a very young, serious face, dark eyes.

"Thank you, yes, I'm fine." Then she added, teasing, "I guess I won't be able to escape, will I?"

"I guess not," he said solemnly. The joke, if it had been a joke, fell flat.

"All right, let's go," the older man said. Laura couldn't see him very well as he had his back to her, lifting the other end. And it was really amazing how cleverly they maneuvered her round the banister and down the stairs, the descent just slightly vertiginous for a few seconds, then straight out the open door into delicious spring air.

"Oh, please wait a second," Laura said impulsively, "The apple tree's in flower!"

She saw it fleetingly, a rosy mass, a bower of pink and white, and then she was being gently slid into the ambulance.

"Shall I come with you, and Brooks follow us in the car?"

"All right."

Mary was standing in the doorway and gave a brief wave. And there Laura was with Ann on a low chair at her feet, and the shades left up so she could see out of this curious conveyance, gliding along like a flying gondola.

"Everything's so beautiful," she said as they passed an apple orchard, then flowering cherry, then woods, the greens still so fresh and brilliant; it all seemed like a stained-glass world. "This is fun," she murmured.

"Look, the crews are out!" Ann said, as they swung out along the river, and sure enough, there were two shells, their long oars sweeping them up the river.

"Why does it always seem so Greek?" Laura asked. "I don't suppose the Greeks had shells?"

" 'The young men, all so beautiful,' is that it?"

"If only we could turn back now and go home," Laura said with a smile. "This has been quite a treat so far."

Then they were silent as the ambulance turned off the drive, proceeded through dirty city streets, and drew up at the Massachusetts Memorial Hospital. Laura closed her eyes. The very look of it was appalling, cold, a jail for the sick. "Ann, stay with me," she said.

"Of course. That's why we're here. We're not going to abandon you, dear Laura."

With the knife thrust of fear Laura realized that she wanted their help. She had to admit that. In this dreadful impersonal place. She hated the thought that the young man would leave her now. Already she was being lifted from the ambulance stretcher to a hospital one on wheels. "Good-by," she called, and the young man turned and waved. "Good luck," he said with a smile. As he went through the door Brooks came in.

"Take it easy, Mother. You know what hospitals are like. It may be a while before we know where you're going." Ann was standing by the stretcher holding Laura's hand.

"It's good of you to do this," Laura said. Then she closed her eyes. A voice came over the public address system, "Dr. Warner. Dr. Warner." Feet shuffled past, subdued voices, the sound of a typewriter. Laura felt she was in the middle of a huge, empty world, a center of loneliness among strange, busy sounds. And she was terribly tired.

"Ann, is my suitcase there?"

"Right here, Laura."

"Mother, we'll need your Blue Cross number." Brooks had returned from somewhere, very businesslike and calm.

"Look in my purse, Ann. I think it must be there, somewhere among the credit cards."

Laura had broken out into a sweat—papers, things one had to have! She had not put her mind on all this. She had let herself be bundled away to a hospital without even thinking of these necessary preparations.

"Here, I've got it," Ann said in triumph.

"Thanks. I'll be right back."

"And indeed in a very short time Brooks was there with an orderly to wheel the stretcher to room 103 on the fifth floor. She was wheeled into a huge elevator, Brooks and Ann on either side of her. Brooks had the suitcase now.

There were two nurses and an intern in the elevator. They talked in loud voices and laughed about the food in the cafeteria. It was as though Laura on her stretcher simply did not exist. The voices hurt her ears. "After all," she thought, "I might be dying."

"Can't you be quiet," Brooks whispered furiously. "My mother is very ill."

"Oh, sorry," said the intern. Laura opened her eyes

[201

and caught his lifted eyebrow and a muffled giggle from one of the nurses, and she hated them.

The elevator crept from floor to floor, an interminable progress, now made in complete silence, a self-conscious silence, exposing Laura, she felt, to incurious resentment. What do they care? She thought. I'm just another body to be carted around and done things to. Why did I ever allow Jim to persuade me? To be trapped like this. Very far away down an interminable tunnel she evoked the apple tree in flower in her garden, Mary waving at the door. Would she ever see them again?

"There, at last!" Ann breathed, as Laura was wheeled out on the floor and into her room. "And it's a single room, thank God."

"And you can look out on some pretty dreary roofs," Brooks added. "But at least there's some sky."

Ann meanwhile was unpacking the suitcase. She took the transistor out, set it at the station with classical music, and laid it beside Laura under her pillow.

"Now I have some hiding place down here I'll be all right," Laura said. "It was just that awful feeling when we were dumped in the hall!"

"Of course," Ann said.

"Wouldn't you like us to stay until they have been in to check on you?" Brooks asked. He managed, Laura noticed, never to look at her and was now staring out of the window at the pigeons wheeling over the roofs. "Carrier pigeons, I shouldn't wonder," he said.

"What about your supper? Do you suppose Dr. Goodwin will have seen to that?" Ann asked. Under the spell of the hospital they all felt stiff and ill at ease.

"I doubt it. But I can't eat anything much anyway. It doesn't matter."

A young nurse in starched white bustled in with a thermometer and took Laura's pulse while she waited.

Laura was grateful that this one didn't chatter. "Some-
one will be in in a little while to ask you a few questions.
Can I do anything to make you more comfortable,
Laura?"

Laura winced at the first name when she did not even
know who this person was but caught Ann's eye, and
they smiled, for Ann, she suspected, knew exactly what
she was thinking. When the nurse had left, Ann said,
"This first-name business! I suppose they want to make
patients feel they are all one big family."

"Well," Laura thought it over. "I noticed that Jim
Goodwin began to call me Laura when I became rather
ill—people in hospitals return to infancy, I suppose."
Laura closed her eyes, afraid a coughing fit was about to
seize her. "Maybe you'd better go now," she managed to
say.

"Will you be all right?" Ann asked at the door. "Try to
rest."

"I'll be all right. Jim promised to look in at seven."

"Well then, I guess we'd better be getting home,"
Brooks said.

"Just one thing," Laura suddenly remembered. "If
Ben comes, I want to see him."

"Jim Goodwin told us no visitors," Brooks said firmly.

"I told him—Ben."

"It's all right," Ann intervened. "Don't worry."

"Why hasn't Ben come? We called him weeks ago."
Brooks sounded cross.

"He's finishing a painting. I asked him to finish it
first," Laura explained.

"Oh, my God," Brooks said between clenched teeth.

"Come on, Brooks." Ann took his arm.

"All *right*," he said crossly.

"You rest now, dear Laura." And then at last they were
gone.

One way of handling what Brooks was finding it hard to handle was anger, of course. But Laura knew more than ever that her instinct to keep the family at a distance had some reason in it. Their anguish could only ricochet against her, and she had no wall to protect her from it now.

She was exhausted and tense. No possibility of dozing off. There was too much noise, and the transistor when she tried it for a moment only provided some soupy music, so she lay wide-awake, waiting, and was quite glad to see the intern come in with his pad and pen and sit down in the armchair across the room.

"How old are you, Laura?"

"Sixty."

While he asked the routine questions, and she answered, Laura took him in: a thin, self-conscious young man with a quaintly long neck and protruding Adam's apple. There was something seedy about him that Laura found attractive—his tufted eyebrows and small gray eyes behind huge, round glasses made him look a little like a ruffled owl.

Of course the questions had to do only with illness. By the time he was through this young man would know all about her years in the sanatorium, about her hysterectomy, and about her damaged lungs—and that is all he would know. Laura was amazed to discover that she was struggling to make a connection on another level. In a hospital one is reduced to being a body, one's history is the body's history, and perhaps that is why something deep inside a person reaches out, a little like a spider trying desperately to find a corner on which to begin to hang a web, the web of personal relations. Yet she had imagined she was through with that, that personal relations had become irrelevant.

"You look as though you could do with a good night's sleep, doctor."

"Do I?" He shot her a shy smile. "The thing is, I'm on duty for thirty-six hours, and this is the last hour. It's been rather busy here." Then she caught his glance, a personal glance for the first time.

"You're Dr. Goodwin's patient."

"He's an old family friend. His father was my mother's doctor."

"That's great," said the young man. "You're in good hands."

"I didn't want to come in here at all, but he persuaded me. I'm dying, of course." And then as Laura saw the man wince, she asked quickly, "What's your name?"

"Dr. Edwards. John Edwards."

"Don't people often say they're dying, Dr. Edwards?"

Now a faint smile appeared. "Yes, but that doesn't mean they are, you know. I've seen patients pull through when there didn't appear to be the slightest hope."

"The will to live." Laura gave a deep sigh. "It's so strange."

"Built in," John Edwards said. He got up. "I'm sorry but I must go. I have three more patients to interview."

Of course to do their work they couldn't afford to come in contact with a patient's soul. There was always that out. Laura looked at her watch. Only four, and Jim wouldn't be here for hours. Better try to settle down. But that was just what she was not going to be permitted to do. A different nurse came in to take a blood sample, and Laura reacted violently to the puncture. She felt outraged that her body, weak as it was, should be attacked in this brutal way.

"Come on, Laura, it's not that bad," the nurse said crisply.

"I'm so tired," Laura said, ashamed of behaving like a child. Tears started in her eyes.

"There—see, it's all over."

Laura tried to turn away onto her side and had a violent fit of coughing, the first since she had entered the hospital. In a second the nurse was holding her with evident expertise. Sweat poured down Laura's cheeks. And then finally it was over.

"I've rung for another nurse," the nurse said as she left.

But no nurse came, and Laura was just as glad. She lay still, feeling her heart thud on inside her. I'm really so ill, she thought, why did Jim have to do this to me?

Then in a few minutes a contraption with two bottles suspended from it was wheeled in.

"What's that thing?" Laura whispered.

"I.V."

"Oh." Laura withdrew deep inside herself while the tube was inserted and the tape taped. This she would have to have out with Jim when he came. But for now, she was not about to watch life seeped into her drop by drop. she turned her head away.

"Perhaps you'd like to be a little lower? Shall I try rolling the bed down?"

"No, thanks. I'm afraid of coughing."

"Anything else I can do?"

"Move the orange juice so I can reach it."

It was this lack of imagination that made hospitals such engines of torture, she was thinking. You have orange juice all right, but it is set just out of reach by someone in a hurry who never really puts herself in a patient's place. A patient is simply a small cog in the machine. Laura had dreaded coming here, but she was amazed at how quickly all the horrors began. Someone across the hall had a soap opera going on TV. She

couldn't catch words, but the continuous intense mur-
murs prevented rest. Then there were voices, too, people visiting patients in nearby rooms. Why did people
always appear to raise their voices when saying good-
bys?

Laura turned her head from side to side trying to find a
comfortable position. She took a sip of orange juice, and
it stayed down.

After that she must have dozed off, for, sensing that
someone was looking down at her, she opened her eyes
and there was Jim Goodwin.

"Oh," she breathed. "Jim."

"You've had a little sleep," he smiled. "That's quite a
feat in this noisy place."

He pulled up a chair and sat close to the bed. Laura
was so glad to see him that she almost forgot about the
I.V., but then she saw the transparent tube and the bottles.

"It took some doing to get a private room," he went on.
"You know you can close the door. There's no law
against that."

"Good," she murmured. "Close it when you go."

"Tomorrow you are set for X-rays at nine. We'll know a
little better what is going on when that has been done.
And while you're here we'll get the lungs drained—that
should ease things. I can see you're having rather a time
breathing."

While Jim talked gently about these factual things,
Laura felt something less tangible, a kind of transfusion
of compassionate interest, but even as she felt this balm,
she resisted its effect, which was to make her weep.

"I'm so tired, Jim," she said.

"I'm going to prescribe something to give you a long
night's rest. The I.V. will begin to have an effect by tomorrow, too."

"I wish—" but the words stuck in her throat and came out as a humiliating sob. She turned her head away.

"You've had a hard day," Jim was saying, holding her hand in his warm clasp. "Don't try to talk."

But she must manage to utter what had to do with her integrity as a person. "Jim, you promised."

"What did I promise? I know I promised you'd see the spring, and I bet you enjoyed seeing the trees in flower on your way here, didn't you?"

"Yes," Laura smiled. "I did."

"I bet Mary will find a way to have you lying outdoors when you get home. Don't you have a chaise lounge somewhere?"

He was cajoling her now, but Laura was not going to allow herself to rest in his kindness and imagination—not yet. It took an immense effort, but she lifted herself up a little to look him in the eyes.

"I want those bottles taken away," she said.

She saw the pupils widen in Jim's clear eyes. Then he bowed his head, looking down at his hand clasping hers.

"Laura, I don't think I can do that."

"You promised to let me die in my way."

"All I am doing is trying to make you a little more comfortable. The I.V. will not arrest what is going on in your lungs, Laura. It's mostly water, with a little glucose. You'll feel a little less exhausted, that's all, and your mouth won't feel so dry. You're dehydrated."

Laura lay back to consider this. "Maybe you're right. I have to see Ben—he may come while I'm here. But I hope not," she added.

"He can wait a few days surely. I have given orders that you are not to have visitors, not even family."

"But it's so lonely here," she said to her own astonishment. "If Ben comes, please let him see me."

208]

"Hospitals," Jim sighed. "We do the best we can, but—"

"I'm losing myself, my identity. It scares me."

"Just hold out for two days, Laura. Then you'll be home again, I promise."

"I'll try."

"If you want to see Ben, I'll leave word that he can come in for a half-hour."

"Thank you," Laura whispered. Her throat was tight from trying to keep back tears.

"They'll bring you an eggnog and something to help it stay down. Try to rest. Think spring," Jim said with an anxious smile. He gave her hand a squeeze and then let it go.

"The apple tree," she murmured. She saw it very clearly, an apparition behind her closed eyes. When she opened them, Jim had gone and the door was closed.

Panic. She had thought she wanted the door closed, but now she was terrified. *I might die and no one would know. I might cough myself to death*—quickly she felt for the bell and pressed it as hard as she could.

Chapter XX

Twice in the night Laura waked and did not know where she was for a moment. There seemed no way to get comfortable in the hard hospital bed with only one pillow behind her head. A neon light on a building opposite shone with nightmarish intensity, yet Laura didn't want the shade pulled. The room was too much like a cell, and at least she could see the sky as the dawn slowly, slowly dimmed artificial lights and bathed the sleeping city in a wan real light hours before the sun rose.

She had finally dozed off into a deep sleep when she was roused by feet in the corridor, and a nurse coming to take her temperature, a different nurse of course. They were never the same, so there was no way to make contact, and Laura settled for being completely passive, hardly responding to a good morning, turning her head away.

Eventually they would come with a stretcher, she supposed, to wheel her down to X-ray, but before that she must try to get to the bathroom, brush her teeth, go to the john. It was now half-past six, so there was infinite time, and before making the effort of getting up Laura gave herself an hour. It was strange how the hospital atmosphere had anesthetized her capacity for thought—or feeling, for that matter. She felt absolutely naked in a glare of light, frozen there in a complete suspension of being. She tried floating, but always just as she had almost achieved that blessed state someone came in, or she was interrupted by the repeated call for a doctor. She tried the transistor and for a little while caught the end of a Mozart quartet. Breakfast trays were being distributed, but she supposed she would not get one. Instead the empty bottles on the contraption at her side were exchanged for filled ones.

How was she to get to the bathroom anyway? But that at last was a real challenge, something to occupy her mind, and she found that she could wheel the contraption with her into the bathroom, and in fact it gave her some support. Even sitting up, let alone standing, made her feel terribly dizzy and weak. She was just emerging from the bathroom feeling quite triumphant when a nurse caught sight of her and rushed to her side.

"Laura, for heaven's sake, what are you doing?"

"Going to the bathroom. Is that not permitted?"

"You're supposed to ring for a nurse."

"Oh, well, you're all so busy, I thought I'd invent a way."

"Let me help you. At least you didn't wrench the tube out," the nurse said, as one might tell a small child who had done something naughty that at least there was no damage.

"I thought I had been quite clever." Laura sank back into the bed. The nurse was reading her chart. "No breakfast," she said.

"I wonder whether you could find a small bottle of lavender somewhere. I know it was packed."

"Here you are."

"Thank you."

Laura poured a little in her hand and put it behind her ears, as Sybille used to do in Switzerland. "That's better," she said and closed her eyes. She must try now to leap as gracefully as possible from one small moment of respite to another. And soon enough she was being helped to slide from her bed to a stretcher and wheeled away down endless corridors, stared at by people in ordinary human clothes on their way to make visits, in and out of the elevator, a bundle of nothingness being taken nowhere. She was left in a brilliantly lit waiting room, with nothing to shield her eyes, flat on her back as she was, a room filled with people in wheelchairs and one old man on a stretcher like hers. Complete suspense, this state of absolute waiting, created a stupid amount of tension, and she wondered why. She was in their hands, the bright, efficient young women who called out a name and disappeared into the X-ray room, but they were not hands one could rest in. There was no handclasp here like Jim Goodwin's to pump reassurance into her. Identity reached zero. Soon, she thought, I shall forget my name.

But when at long last she heard "Laura Spelman," she responded foolishly by trying to get up.

"Oh, no, Laura, don't you move. We'll wheel you in." And it proved surprisingly easy to slide from the stretcher onto the table. What was not easy was to remain sitting up while the machine was rolled down against her back, and to stay still. The first try was a disaster as Laura bent over wracked by a coughing spell.

"It's all right, Laura, you just lie down and rest."

"I'm sorry," she murmured, but lying down was no good, and once more a stranger had to lift her and hold her and wipe her sweating face with a kleenex.

"Brother Ass is not behaving very well," she managed to utter.

"Brother Ass?" This nurse, Laura noted, had a pleasant voice. That was a help.

"My body—it's on some wild caper."

"Oh, I see." The nurse gently stroked Laura's back.

After a while she tried again and was confident that all was well. Then there were more X-rays taken from the front this time—and finally Laura was wheeled out into the bright lights to wait what seemed an eternity until the nurse said the X-rays had developed well. But I can't ask—I can't know, Laura thought. That nurse with the kind voice knows how bad things are, but I don't.

Laura closed her eyes and pretended to be dead, so that she couldn't take in anything more around her. She slid into a cocoon of total passivity, down the interminable corridors, feeling slightly nauseated, and into the elevator where again people talked as though she were not there.

Finally she was back in her room, back where she could see the pigeons whirling up from the roof below, and one tree in leaf. And sky.

They came with the bottles and she was attached to that lifeline again, but she didn't mind. She would do everything asked, and she would not complain as long as Jim allowed her to go home soon. She even managed to swallow a little orange juice through a straw; her mouth had felt so dry.

A new nurse came and washed her and brought the bedpan, which was excruciatingly uncomfortable. Laura felt now completely detached from her body. It was, she considered, simply a piece of machinery that was running down. But how could the separation be made? How could she find herself without this machine that labored for breath and rejected food and sent her into misery with the coughing? It could not be tamed. It could not be cajoled. It had, she felt, to be quite simply rejected as ir-relevant.

When Jim finally came in and held her hand, she was able to say quite calmly, "I'm getting through with my carcass, Jim. It's not much use anymore, is it?"

"The X-rays do show some deterioration. I expected that," he said in his firm, gentle voice, the voice she recognized as one that had been trained not to show emotion and to be wary of frightening a patient.

"I'm going to need help," she then heard herself say-ing. "I see that some part of this journey I can't do alone, after all."

Tears slid down her cheeks. Things were out of con-trol. "I want to go home. Don't let me die here, Jim, please."

"Just try to trust me, Laura. The only thing we still have to do is drain the lungs. You'll feel more comfort-able and cough less then. I think we'll be able to get you home late this afternoon."

"Mary—" she said with a sob. "She'll help."

"She's the best medicine you could have," Jim said with a smile. He was holding her hand very tight, and after a moment she could feel it. She had been too upset before.

"Sorry I'm such a baby," she murmured. "It's the hos-pital."

"I know. We're going to get you out of here."

Laura had closed her eyes. When she opened them she saw the naked compassion and grief on his face. He really cares, she thought. How strange. I'm leaving car-ing now—but this doctor, almost a stranger, he cares. She felt bathed in the radiance of it. It was an intimation of something larger, something she could not think about yet. But even the rejected body felt the power of it like an injection. Laura smiled.

"Laura," Jim said quietly, "Ben is downstairs. If you would like to see him, he could come up, but he can perfectly well wait till you're home again, and come tomorrow to the house—so—"

"I don't know," Laura said after a moment of taking in the news. "He'll be upset, seeing me with these bottles."

"You look beautiful," Jim Goodwin said and coughed as he did when he was embarrassed, Laura remembered. "You've changed."

"Have I?"

"In the last few minutes."

He didn't know what had happened, but Laura did.

"Thanks, Jim. I never knew what it meant before that we are all members of each other."

And as Jim looked slightly bewildered, Laura added, "Yes, send Ben up."

She rang for a nurse and for once someone came imediately. Laura asked her to roll the bed up so she was sitting suddenly quite high up in the air.

"My son's coming, and he hasn't seen me since—since—could you help me comb my hair? I must look pretty awful."

This nurse looked very Irish, and fresh as a daisy. She was quick to see what was needed, even found the bottle of lavender and put some behind Laura's ears.

"That's what my mother used to do," Laura said. "How did you guess?"

"It feels good behind the ears, doesn't it?"

"Thanks. I guess I'll have to settle for myself as is—do you think it will be an awful shock?"

"Oh, no—why he'll be so glad to see his mum he won't notice nothing."

The trouble was that in this upright position Laura felt a little dizzy. Her head felt like a flower on a long, frail stem.

"Just one more thing. Could you put a pillow behind my head?"

"There, now you just take it easy."

Laura's heart was beating in an absurd way. She realized that some deep part of her had been waiting for Ben for weeks. Something had been held taut by his coming, and now the suspense was hard. But by some miracle she found herself floating. She had not until now been able to achieve it in the hospital. She was this time floating down a river in a canoe with Ben, about ten years old, trailing his fingers in the water ahead of her in the bow while she steered with a paddle. Summer stillness . . .

And then he was there, standing in the door, smiling. "I'm here," he said.

"So I see," said Laura, smiling too. There he was with his long El Greco face, the dark eyes darting a tender look at her then away, as he came in and kissed her on the cheek, then pulled up the armchair so he could be quite near the bed.

"Oh, Ben," she sighed, "I'm glad to see you. It's been rather a long journey, this illness, long and exhausting." Then, as she saw the shadow cross his face and the familiar frown, she added, "long but interesting."

"Can you tell me about it?" he asked. It was so much the right question, and no one had asked it before.

"I'll try to tell you, but first, did you finish the painting?"

"I did. You'll find it in your bedroom when you go home." He clasped his hands tightly together as he had always done when he was trying to say something important. "I think it's good—it's a sequence. It's anemones, the way they appear almost to be dancing at first, and then the way the petals change color, and finally fall. I wanted it to be like music—oh, I don't know! You'll probably think it's awfully abstract. I couldn't do it straight—to get the motion, you see, the way they die, so beautifully."

"Dear Ben," Laura murmured. "You're just the same. I'm so glad to see you, you can't imagine."

"Oh, Mother." He lifted his head and looked out the window away from her, then got up, walked over, and stood there looking out.

"The pigeons," she said, "the only thing I could look at in this machine of a hospital."

"Tell me about the journey," he said quietly, still standing.

"Come back. If I talk too loudly I'll cough."

"Of course." He sat down, one hand palm down on the sheet as though he were really caressing her, smoothing it, back and forth, his head bowed.

For a moment there was silence. Laura lifted her head and lay back on the pillow. Very rarely had anyone except Jim permitted silence, she realized. People hurried in to fill it with words, because they were afraid, perhaps, of being overwhelmed by emotion.

"Thanks," she said.

"For what, Mother?" He gave her a startled look.

"For the silence. Most people have to talk so they won't hear, so they won't have to face whatever it is I am doing."

"I know," Ben said gently. "You don't have to tell me."

"You see, I wanted to do it alone," she began. It felt as though she were about to unroll a long Chinese scroll such as one sees under glass in museums, with one scene after another painted, women playing a game, men hunting, a party, falconers on horseback, but as she prepared to unroll the scroll, she realized that it would take strength she did not have. "Oh, Ben, I'm not sure I can. Dying is turning out to be harder than I supposed, and longer. I do not believe that we wish to leave our bodies, perhaps it is that. Mine is of very little use to me now, but—"

"Absent thee from felicity awhile." In school Ben had played Hamlet.

"What a good Hamlet you were," she said.

"I felt I was in my own skin—nearly twenty years ago. Sometimes I get there when I'm painting. But not often, that feeling that I'm wholly myself, that everything is functioning together." He sighed.

"And sometimes in love?" Laura asked. She had never asked Ben things like this before, but now it was possible. Dying opened doors.

"Very rarely," he said, biting his lower lip. "My love affairs have been disasters on the whole. I want too much, I suppose."

"I had imagined that dying might be like that—coming into a wholeness, but the trouble is one has no strength. It leaks away."

"I don't want to tire you."

"Oh, well," Laura smiled to reassure him, "everything tires me so I might as well enjoy all I can. I decided that weeks ago, to spend what I have. Besides, you are the one I wanted to see most." Then she turned her head away. "You and Ella," she whispered.

"Ella? Who's that?"

"My English friend. She goes back almost to childhood with me. We were at the Sorbonne together that winter in Paris—surely you know who she is."

"Vaguely."

Ben seemed uncomfortable, and Laura wondered whether he was longing for a cigarette.

"Ben, when they told me—when I knew I had a limited time ahead—the strange thing was that I didn't want to see family at all, not even you. I wanted to disappear into my shell like a snail and close the door. Dying seemed such a huge adventure—for a time I was lifted up by the very idea. I wanted to do it alone, you see."

"Yes, I can understand that."

"People disturb the deep current. But then I hadn't reckoned with the weakness, the nausea, the poor old body that keeps getting in the way."

"I suppose that is the journey you spoke of. Do you feel it is a journey toward something, Mother, or only away?"

"Toward," she said, "but I don't know toward what." There he sat, her son, thirty-five years old now, a man, not looking at her, his hand absent-mindedly stroking the sheet, and with him she was experiencing a continuation of the radiance she had found with Jim Goodwin an hour or so earlier. Ben had always had an exceptional capacity to feel with others, especially animals, when he was a boy. A dead cat in the road caused him real pain. But he was giving himself, his full attention, to her, so quietly, with such control now, that he had apparently been able to shut out or keep at bay whatever her dying meant to him—he was truly with *her*.

"At first it was easy to detach myself—a kind of freedom, I suppose. But—" she swallowed and found it hard to go on.

"Take it easy, Mother. Maybe I should go away for a half an hour and let you rest?"

"Not unless you want to—a cigarette?"

"Good Christ, mother! I'm not thinking of cigarettes!" This time he got up and went to the window. His hands were clenched in his pockets, Laura could see, in the tight jeans he insisted on wearing. She resisted the impulse to beg him to stand straighter. He was quite stooped, she noticed.

[219

There was a long silence because Laura was unable to say what she wanted to say. It would, she feared, bring on an unstoppable flood of tears. It was Ben who broke it finally.

"I tried to detach myself. I felt the only salvation for me was to move right away from people. It didn't work. Somehow we are *in* our bodies."

"Brother Ass," Laura said, feeling better.

"Brother Ass and Brother Angel, who knows which. Both, I guess."

"As I got weaker, I learned that I couldn't do it alone, Ben."

"I should have come sooner."

"I didn't want you. Aunt Minna, and the wonderful woman Jim Goodwin got to live in, Jim himself— Daphne came, Daisy came, Jo came, but they exhausted me. Only those three—Aunt Minna, Mary O'Brien, and Jim. The hardest thing for me, Ben, has been to become dependent, but I am." A short, dry sob could not be quelled.

"Oh, Mother—"

"It's all right," she said in a queer, high voice, for she was not going to weep. This was too important. "It's been a kind of revelation. When I gave up trying to do it alone, a lot of light flowed in."

"I don't understand, but I'm glad," Ben said.

"Now maybe let's have a little rest," Laura said. "Go and get a cup of coffee and have a cigarette. In half an hour I'll be rested. There's so much I want to hear about you."

Ben bent down and kissed the top of her head. It had great sweetness in it, that gesture, fatherly in a way and protective. Then she was alone again in her cell with the pigeons circling outside.

When Ben came back, Laura was surrounded by Jim,

an intern, and a nurse and they were busy draining the lungs and making the cheerful noises of experts involved in a delicate task.

"I'm sorry, Ben." Laura managed to say, between clamped teeth, for this time the operation seemed unbearably long, and she was entirely absorbed in trying to stay in position, sitting up, and leaning forward with her head down, trying to hold out. Heaven, for the moment, would be being allowed to lie down.

"You can stay, Ben," Jim was saying. "The worst is getting the needle in, and that's done now."

"Easy there," the intern said as Laura began to pant from sheer nervous strain. The nurse bent over to wipe her forehead with a damp cloth.

"Just a few minutes more, Laura." That was Jim's reassuring voice. Laura couldn't tell whether Ben was still in the room. In a way she hoped he had fled. It would be an awful shock for him to see those bottles filling up with the dark-orange fluid—she dreaded it herself, the visible sign of corruption.

"As soon as you've had a rest, an hour or two, we'll get you home. Ben and I will go with you, Laura, so don't be anxious about anything. Now take it easy," for he must have seen that she was trembling uncontrollably. "There—there—"and at last Laura could lie down, her eyes closed. At last she could rest.

Somewhere very far off, perhaps in the corridor outside, she could hear the murmur of Jim's and Ben's voices. But she didn't want to hear the words, or to be conscious of anything, except a greater ease in breathing, and to rest in that ease.

Chapter XXI

Laura had longed to be home, but now that she was safely in her own bed with a bunch of daffodils and poeticus in a glass by her bed (Ann's thought, that), and Ben's big painting leaning against the bureau, and the afternoon light making the walls glow softly, and Grindle lying on the floor beside her, she recognized that in the hospital a subtle change in her whole chemistry must have taken place. With her eyes open she saw all this, recognized it, and listened to Grindle's little groans of pleasure as he slept, but the outer world no longer held her attention as it had. With her inner self she observed it all as if from very far away, through the wrong end of a telescope. "It has become irrelevant, all this," she thought.

Yet she still wanted to feel Grindle's ears, so silky soft, and leaned down, but she felt so dizzy that she had to give up trying to reach him.

"You're just tuckered out," Mary said, coming in then with something on a tray. "Maybe a sip of this, it's eggnog with a teaspoonful of brandy in it—doctor's orders."

"I don't want it," Laura said.

"Just a sip, dear. It'll do your heart good, after all you've been through."

And like an obedient child, Laura lifted herself a little and took a sip. And then another.

A third would have been to tempt fate and a coughing spell. And she shook her head. She wanted to tell Mary that what did her heart good was to look up into those kind, calm eyes, but she found it impossible to utter the words. Instead she smiled and closed her eyes. "Thanks."

She heard the door closing softly, and the last thing she remembered for a long time was Grindle licking her hand, which must have dropped down within his reach as she went off into a doze.

When she awakened it was dark, and she didn't know where she was. She fumbled for the light and managed finally to turn it on, wincing at the brightness and for a moment closing her eyes against it, trying to rest in the crimson place behind her lids.

"Are you all right, Mother?" asked Ben's voice in a whisper.

Where had he come from? Laura felt bewildered. "Ben," she said in quite a loud voice that surprised her.

"I'm across the hall. When I saw your light go on, I thought you might need help to the bathroom."

The whole scene was so bizarre, Ben suddenly appearing in the middle of the night and that wild jumble of purple and red and white anemones blazing out at her from the painting near the floor, that Laura began to giggle. "Oh, dear," she said, "I'm in a whirl of your colors."

"It's too violent, isn't it?" he said anxiously. "It's a kind of dance, you see—the petals are so still, but they are really falling, falling already. Can you see what I mean?"

"I do see."

"It's awfully crude."

"No—" Laura had hesitated to turn to where Ben was

standing, to see his face. When she did she saw his tousled hair, and that elongated face, those deep-set eyes staring at his painting with such intensity that she had ceased to exist. It was a moment of acute awareness for Laura, one of the few she had experienced lately. "I do see, Ben," but what she was seeing was not the painting, but her son coming into his own. Being himself.

"If you can lift me up," she said, "maybe it's not a bad idea to go to the bathroom."

He took her hand in a firm grip and with his other arm around and under her shoulder lifted her so easily that Laura, without an effort, found herself standing, while Grindle, in an ecstasy at all these goings on, was busily licking one foot.

At this she and Ben exchanged a smile.

"Now, Grindle," Ben said, "get out of the way."

The few steps to the bathroom were more like floating than walking because she was actually being carried. "Just call, when you're ready," he said, closing the door.

And in a short time Laura was back in her bed and had not coughed even once, although the effort made it hard to catch her breath.

"Now will you and Grindle sleep peacefully?" Ben leaned over and kissed her softly on the cheek.

"Yes, we will," she breathed. "Thanks, Ben."

Laura did not wake again until the dawn. She felt rested, and when she turned toward Ben's painting in the subdued light she was able to look at it for a long time, and not with just her eyes. She began to float with it, the colors merging, and to sense what was happening in it and in Ben's mind while he painted it, not the shock, the explosion she had thought she saw when she was too exhausted to take it in. This was not motion, but the poise just before motion, a kind of perfection that could not stay, the moment before dissolution. If only the body were as simple as a flower, opening and fading in an hour or two. For the body it seemed such a long, intricate process by comparison, whole galaxies of molecules slowly transforming themselves into what? Going where?

This time it was Mary who stood in the doorway, in her wrapper, her hair in two plaits.

"Mary," Laura said, "I'm afraid."

Without a word Mary came and sat on the bed and held Laura's hand.

"I don't know how to let go," Laura said. "I don't know what is happening to me. I'm scared, scared," she repeated, "scared of the dark."

"It's all right," Mary said. "The sun's just rising." It was not an answer, but in a way it was. For the moment the words held a true promise: whatever happened the sun would rise.

"There now, I'm going to bring you a cup of tea." Mary got up to go, but Laura tugged gently at her skirt.

"Stay a little while," she begged. "What time is it?"

"It's just after six," Mary said, settling down again, this time rather formally, sitting up straight.

I must only ask what can be given, Laura told herself, trying to read Mary's face which seemed now gently withdrawn. Was she thinking? Praying perhaps?

"Is your family getting on all right without you?" Laura asked.

"Oh, yes! I went home for a day while you were in the hospital." Mary gave a low chuckle, "Found the frigidaire filled up with TV dinners and beer. I guess they'll survive!"

"It's awfully kind of you to stay."

"I wouldn't leave you now," Mary said firmly then added with a smile, "except to go and get dressed. I expect that son of yours will want an early breakfast." And this time she did get up to go. "Shall I leave the door open?"

"Yes, please."

"There's a bell right there beside you if you need me."

Being home, Laura thought, was to hear friendly sounds again, a dog's bark, someone clattering dishes in the kitchen, a bird singing, for just then she heard a robin and the twittering of goldfinches. And where was Sasha, she wondered? The cat had not been on her bed all night.

For a few moments she could stay aware, then she felt herself sinking into a kind of nothingness, not asleep, not awake, taking shallow breaths, waiting in a strange calm for whatever would happen next. The panic of the early morning had seeped away into weakness, and she must have dozed, for there was Mary with a cup of tea on a tray.

Mary held her up, and Laura held the cup in her two hands because she was too shaky to do it with one. She swallowed the tea greedily, aching for a little strength, just enough for one more day, she told herself. But that proved to be a mistake, and before she could stop its happening the tea was all over the bed. "Oh, Mary," she groaned, "I'm sorry—such a mess!"

"Now don't you worry. I was going to change the sheets anyway. It'll only take a minute."

Mary tactfully closed the door, then gathered Laura up into her arms like a baby and set her down gently on the chaise longue by the window. She fetched a face cloth from the bathroom and wiped Laura's face.

"That feels good," Laura murmured. Tears slid down her cheek. She felt trapped like a baby who can't control itself. She was now at the mercy of this cage of her body—for how long? The struggle was so awful that she was close to despair. How to let go? How to stay in this abject state?

But after what seemed hours, she was back in her bed, safe, her eyes closed, and glad to be absolutely alone, glad even that Grindle had been put out.

It would not be hard in the end to give everything up, even the faint sound of leaves in the light wind . . . everything.

She woke to a light scratching at the door, then a gentle tap.

"Sasha wants to come in, Mother."

"Oh, Ben, yes, let her in."

"May I come in too?"

"Of course, dear."

"I'll only stay a little while," he said, bending to kiss her cheek.

Sasha jumped onto the bed and proceeded to give her own face a very thorough wash, the paw going up and down and round the ears. Laura watched her with a smile. But the constant motion was enervating, and she was glad when the cat wound herself into a perfect round ball and lay purring against Laura's thigh.

"We don't have to talk," Ben said. He was sitting on the end of the chaise longue, his hands clasped round his knees, rocking himself slowly and not looking at Laura.

"I *am* a little dim today," Laura said, closing her eyes, wondering whether it would be possible to rest in Ben's presence, whether he could bear the silence because— because—she couldn't formulate why. Perhaps words kept the truth at bay, and the truth was hard. There was very little time left now.

The silence grew and grew until it contained too much tension, and Laura murmured, "I wish you would talk to me, talk about yourself—we had so little time in the hospital."

"Oh, Mother, I can't!" She heard the sob held back, a queer break in his voice. "I can't," he said, and she heard him running down the staris, running away from her dying. But could she have listened? She heard the front door open and close. Now Ben was safe outside with trees and grass and could fling himself down on the earth and weep. It was all right. It was the way things were. Only up to a point can the living help the dying. Laura closed herself in, just touching Sasha's head for a moment, resting there as though all life for the moment had flowed into her fingertips against the soft fur, all life in that touch. And she remembered a poem—but whose?

> His kind velvet bonnet
> And on it
> My tears run.

But she was not crying now. She was in an absurd state of tension and had a cramp in her foot.

Later that morning Jim came to take her pulse, to hold her hand, to say that he and Brooks and Ann had cooked up a way to give her the spring "as I promised," he said, smiling so eagerly at Laura that she had to respond.

"How will you do that?" she asked.

"We're going to carry you downstairs and out onto a chaise in the garden. Then you can look up at the sky through the leaves. It's a perfect day, not too hot, clear air."

"Jim—" she was going to say that she didn't think she had the strength to move, but then she saw his face, lit up by his own hopes. Could she deny that hope? "It sounds impossible, but I know you keep your promises."

"I want you to see those red tulips."

"Aunt Minna will be coming to read to me."

"Mary can bring tea out to the garden." Jim was holding her hand now. "I wish I hadn't had to get you to the hospital."

Laura knew that he was trying to make up somehow for the hell he had put her through. He had invented this plan as a reward. "You were a trump about that."

"I was helpless," Laura said with a smile. "Could I have said no?"

"Probably not," he gave her hand a squeeze and let it go. He was on his way, but suddenly Laura reached for his hand and pulled him back to sit on the bed. She did it violently, and Jim registered his surprise.

"Wow, you've got a lot of strength in that hand," he said, smiling at her.

"At first all those weeks I wanted to be alone," she said quickly—she was so afraid there was no time and he would leave—"now I need help, Jim. Ben came to sit beside me but he couldn't stay—you know."

"Yes, perhaps he can't. Would you like Ann to come and just be here for the rest of the day, until we take you down to the garden?"

Laura frowned. "I don't know."

"Aunt Minna, maybe?"

"She's so old—and afraid of death—I wonder whether I could ask that."

Jim gave a sigh. Laura read his troubled face. He would have liked to stay with her, she knew that. But of course he couldn't. Other people needed him. Hundreds of sick people, frightened people. And now he looked at his watch.

"Yes, you have to go," Laura said.

"I think Mary is the person you really need. I'll send her up." Jim stood there, looking down at her with his kind, aloof expression, and Laura closed her eyes. She felt abandoned, cold and abandoned.

"Thanks," she said.

For the rest of the morning Mary sat on the chaise mending socks and a torn sweater of Laura's and it was—

[229

Jim had been right after all—just what Laura needed. It was strange how supportive this busy silence of Mary's was. Laura found herself floating—processions of people passed before her closed eyes, she saw her mother in a blue dress with a square lace collar, bending to kiss her good night in the hospital in Switzerland—a kiss on the forehead that Laura resented, but she no doubt, had been then, as now too frail for the strong, warm hug she had longed for. She saw her mother walking across a field in Maine with a bunch of wildflowers in her hands, her face rosy with the pleasure, scattering a diamond smile as she moved. Charles then came toward her, looking unexpectedly grand in tails—was there a wedding going on? Brooks and Ann maybe—yes, there they were now, fleeing down the road toward their new Buick, laughing and waving to the wedding guests assembled in the doorway. Then it was Ben, such a queer, elongated baby, reaching out toward a red toy on his crib with an eager starfish hand, clutching it then and sucking it as though color were something to eat.

"Ben was such a funny little boy," Laura said aloud. "He was passionate about flowers, used to pick the tulips off by their heads when he was two or three."

"He's the eldest?" Mary asked.

"Yes, Brooks came two years later—and finally Daisy. We did so want a little girl. Charles, my husband, did. It's all gone like a dream—a whole life—" but it was said with no regret, for Laura was floating somewhere above it all, watching it go by. Even her anguish about her mother, the unresolved rage and conflict, was being diffused into this luminous bubble of memories which she could watch for an instant before it was dissolved. It was, after all, not going to be hard to let go.

Yet it was at least in part Mary's quiet presence, asking nothing, that made this all possible. Something about her hands moving in and out of a sock with the darning needle kept panic away. And even when Laura had her eyes closed, she felt Mary's presence, a benign effluence that enveloped her and held her safe in its spell.

So the morning slipped away, and then Laura slept. She was awakened by voices in the hall, Brooks and Ben whispering about something, Ann then saying, "But should we wake her?"

"I'm awake," Laura said, but they didn't hear her, so she leaned over and rang the little bell Mary had left on the night table.

"You go, Brooks," she heard Ann say.

And there he was in the doorway, hesitating, smiling, looking so much like Charles that for a second Laura thought it was Charles.

"I've come to take you downstairs, Mother, for tea in the garden."

"Oh," Laura breathed. "I don't think I can."

"I'll carry you," Brooks said reassuringly. "And then you can lie outdoors for a while instead of in bed. Jim Goodwin told us he thought it would be a good change— under the trees."

"A tree house on the ground," Laura smiled. But downstairs seemed a terribly long and perilous journey, and she didn't really want to make the effort. They couldn't know what an effort it would be, of course, nor how much she needed to stay safely in her own bed. They were so terribly strong and alive, how could they know?

"Are you ready?" Brooks was saying. "I'm going to lift you up."

But Mary was there explaining that Laura would need a dressing gown. "You stay still," she admonished Laura.

"My blue one," Laura said.

[231

The effort of getting her arms into it properly was so great that Laura sank back onto the bed, trembling.

"Let her rest a minute," Mary whispered. She was frowning and shaking her head, and for the first time Laura saw anxiety in Mary's calm face.

But Brooks did not see it, perhaps. Anyway he was determined to do what had been asked, and in a very few seconds he lifted Laura up in his arms, her head leaning over one shoulder, like a baby, she thought ironically. She had carried Brooks around on her hip not so long ago, and he had been heavy.

"Am I too heavy, Brooks?"

"Light as a feather," he said cheerfully, managing the stairs on careful feet, quickly and easily.

Ben held the door for them and Ann followed, and soon enough Laura was being set down on the chaise longue while Mary knelt down to slip her bedroom slippers on her feet. Brooks was not even out of breath, Laura noticed, but she herself was panting those hard, short breaths that sounded harshly in her chest, and hurt.

"I'll be all right in a minute," she offered, for she found herself in a circle of anxious faces.

"I think she should be left alone for a little while," Ann whispered. "Mary will get the tea, and you just lie here and rest, Laura. Aunt Minna won't be here for a half-hour—what Jim Goodwin wanted was for you to be able to look at the garden, those glorious red tulips."

"Oh, yes," Laura said, turning her head toward the tulip bed. But she didn't really want to see them. She wanted only to be back in her bed, in the shelter of walls. It's all a mistake, she thought, Jim's mistake. So she lay there, and after a while Grindle must have come out, for she heard a short, questioning bark at her side.

"Hello, Grindle," she murmured. And this time she was able to stroke his ears before he lay down.

After a while she opened her eyes again. Look up at sky through the leaves, Jim had said. But looking up made her dizzy. What she could do was listen to a wood pigeon cooing; the monotonous, repeated, half-swallowed coo was soothing. Then she began to see the trees, one by one. The white birch Charles had planted for their twentieth wedding anniversary was covered with small, shining leaves. The ash too was in leaf, she saw, troublesome tree that shed and made a mess on the lawn. Charles had wanted to cut it down. Now it was outliving both of them, and Laura felt glad for the strength of the tree. Only she was not able to look at anything for long, and soon she closed her eyes, resting in the thought of trees, the cypresses of Italy leading the eye down long perspectives to a stone fountain or statue, the marvelous beech trees in that forest near Brussels where she had walked with Ella in the autumn through the endless choirs of immensely tall silver trunks, with a carpet of bronze leaves at their feet and the light trickling through. They had got lost and finally became quite frightened—"Ella, Ella!" Laura felt such an ache as the name came to her lips, they were dry with it, with the absence of Ella.

Had Ella written lately? Laura could not remember. Mostly she let the letters lie unopened—Ella, where are you? So far away. Laura opened her eyes, feeling like a stranger in her own garden. But if she was a stranger here, where was home? And who was she herself now? The real panic was a loss of identity, for she seemed inextricably woven into her body's weakness and discomfort, into her struggling sick lungs. What essence was there to be separated from her hand, her flesh, her bones? Laura lifted her hand, so thin it had become transparent. Is this I? This leaflike thing, falling away, falling away, this universe of molecules disintegrating, this miracle about to be transformed into nothingness.

"Your aunt will be here in a moment," Mary was saying as she carried the tea tray across the lawn, followed by Brooks with a table to set it on.

"Oh, yes," Laura murmured. She felt trapped suddenly and shook her head from side to side.

"Are you all right, Mother?"

"Oh, I suppose so," she said irritably. "I'm awfully tired."

Brooks and Mary exchanged a glance.

"I'll be right here to take you up when you want to go. We thought you and Aunt Minna might have a little read out here."

It didn't matter, one way or another, and Laura closed her eyes. People came and went, but nobody mattered anymore.

"Well, dear," Aunt Minna said in her bright, cool voice, "It's good to see you out of doors on such a fine day!"

Laura felt unable to respond. She opened her eyes and took in Aunt Minna, the dear wrinkled face, the bright eyes looking out so shyly, but she couldn't speak. "Shall I pour our tea?"

"Yes, dear." Summoning the heavy word "dear" was difficult. I don't want to feel anything, Laura thought. Trees, not people. Eventually this ordeal would be over, and she would be back in her bed again. Just hang on, she admonished herself. "Myself? Who is that?"

"I didn't catch what you said. I'm getting awfully deaf," Aunt Minna said as she poured the tea. "What was that?"

"Nothing," Laura said.

"Ben is here, Mary told me."

"Yes, he finished his painting and brought it."

Aunt Minna hesitated before offering Laura her cup, and for a second their eyes met. Laura's were pleading, but she did not know for what, and Aunt Minna's filled suddenly with tears.

"Do you want your tea?" she asked then, quite matter-of-factly.

"I don't know." Laura managed to sit up a little. "I'll have a sip. Perhaps you could hold it for me? My hand shakes so."

"Of course, dear." They were each grateful, Laura recognized, for some small gesture such as lifting a cup of tea, for now there are no disguises. I'm absolutely helpless and naked.

Laura drank two sips and lay back.

"Would you like me to read a little?"

"Nothing seems relevant," Laura said.

"Yes—well—shall we just sit here a little while together?" The tone was anxious, not comforting.

"Yes."

But Aunt Minna fidgeted in her chair, and out of the corner of an eye Laura took in her wild look about her, as though sitting still was the one thing this wondrously alive, active, imperious old woman could not bring herself to do. She drank her tea in loud swallows, then set the cup down.

"Such a beautiful day. Do you remember, 'Look thy last on all things lovely, every hour'?"

"It's hard to look now," Laura said. She had gone beyond protecting Aunt Minna. She closed her eyes. It was better not seeing. In that enclosed state, she confronted the fact that she had somehow to try to meet Aunt Minna for the last time, not pretend any longer. But how to speak? It seemed so hard to do that Laura imagined that perhaps she had lost her voice.

[235

Aunt Minna was getting hold of silence; she was no longer shifting around in her chair. That made it easier, and Laura rested on the silence, waiting.

"It's been a long journey," she said finally, "and you have helped me make it. Dear old Trollope too."

"What was that?" Aunt Minna said. "I didn't catch the last thing you said, Laura."

"Dear old Trollope," Laura repeated as loudly as she dared, but that extra effort was fatal, and she was suddenly seized by such a fit of coughing, she couldn't stop. The cough wrenched and wrenched at her. She could hear Aunt Minna getting up and calling frantically, "Mary! Brooks! Please come!" Then muttering to herself, "Damn my deaf ears! This is my fault."

It seemed minutes, but at last Laura felt Mary's arm around her shoulders, that strong arm supporting her. "Oh, thank you," she said. She was panting now, and the terrible cough had quieted. She leaned her head against Mary's breast. "Hold me, Mary."

"It's all right, Laura. It's over," Mary whispered, and Laura's cheek rested on the gentle breathing against which she found herself like a drowning man upon a calm shore. There were so many people now—Ben, Brooks, Ann, Aunt Minna. She was exposed to such a crowd, all standing there to witness the tears sliding down her cheeks.

"Please take me back to my room," she managed to utter.

"I'm here, Mother." Brooks was instantly at her side.

"Hadn't you better wait a moment?" Ben's voice.

"I think she wants to go." Ann's controlled voice.

"Yes," Laura whispered, "please."

Ben and Brooks lifted her very gently until she was again carried on her son's shoulder and slowly taken across the lawn and up the stairs, but she couldn't stop crying, and poor Brook's shoulder was wet when she was laid down on her bed at last.

"I'm so sorry, Mother," Brooks was saying, "it was all a mistake, but we didn't know, and Jim thought—"

"It's all right," Laura managed a smile. "Lovely to be back here. It's just I'm so weak—I mean, the tears. So stupid, but . . ."

"Here's one of Dad's handkerchiefs I found for you," Ben said, and Laura blew her nose on the soft linen, gratefully.

"I think she'd better have a rest," Mary said. "You all come down and have a good cup of tea with Miss Hornaday. I'm afraid she's upset."

"Thanks, Mary."

Then they were all gone, all except Grindle who was lying by the bed, his nose on his paws, his eyes not leaving Laura's face. He had a rather absurd and saintly look. Laura took it in, then turned her face away. I can't take the love, she thought. It's too much for me. I can't give or take it anymore. Poor Grindle.

It was getting easier to let go. What she felt was an immense pity for the living with the journey still before them. But it was not a pity she could communicate. Only, strangely enough, she didn't want to be left alone. When would somebody come?

Downstairs she could hear the murmur of voices, Aunt Minna's so pure, so young, clearer than the blur of the others. It was good to know they were there, not far away after all. She could lie and listen to them and after a while someone would come.

Chapter XXII

When Laura came back to consciousness, it was late afternoon, she guessed, because the room, flooded with sunlight in the morning, felt dark. Dark and empty. Grindle was not by her bed, nor Sasha on it. And she did not hear a sound downstairs. She lay there wide-awake and listening, not for outside sounds but for the sensation of being inside a dying body, for the minute stirring in her chest, the breath still holding her alive, in and out, in and out, a slight, wheezy sound.

When Mary came in on tiptoe to smooth her pillow and put some lavender water behind her ears, Laura whispered, "I really don't want to go on . . . breathing."

Mary didn't answer, just laid her hand on Laura's forehead. It felt wonderfully cool, that smooth hand.

"What can I do to make you more comfortable?" she asked after a moment, sitting on the edge of the bed.

"Nothing, thank you."

I'm beginning to lose the way to make a connection, Laura thought. She felt remote, too remote for words.

"It's nice and peaceful anyway," Mary said gently. "Ben has gone over to Brooks and Ann for supper. So you rest awhile."

"I've been resting," Laura whispered. "Maybe you would stay with me, Mary."

"I'll get a bit of sewing and be right back."

In the interval before Mary came back, Laura found herself floating. She was floating along with Brother Ass, thinking that soon they would be parted, and she smiled at the impossible thought, for how could one be separated? Where, without breath, would Laura be? There were so many people she would never see again, but this caused no grief. She felt ready to leave them all.

What then was she waiting for? What still held her in the empty house, in the empty world, what tiny, delicate thread still held her back from what she had imagined as an adventure when she still felt well but was only some trailing away, some letting go into nowhere. All flesh is grass, Brother Ass.

When Mary had come back and had settled on the chaise with her sewing basket, Laura breathed a deep sigh.

"What am I still waiting for, Mary?"

"The blessed dark, maybe, and another dawn."

"I don't know."

When Laura opened her eyes, she asked Mary to turn Ben's painting to the wall. "It's too much now," she said, "too alive for me now."

And a little later, "My mother, she's still alive. It seems so strange."

Then there was a long silence. Laura turned her head away as if to shut out those pictures of a floating world that the word "mother" had summoned beyond her will to keep away. No one had ever loomed so large, no one so to be reckoned with, beautiful and terrible. Terrible as Medusa, she had frozen her children into people somehow diminished themselves by her extraordinary power. "Oh, let me be," Laura murmured. "Let me go."

But there were those blazing blue eyes looking down on little Laura in her sick bed in Switzerland, totally possessing her, making her unable to escape.

"Now don't you fret," Mary said soothingly. She had come to the bedside, because Laura was restlessly turning her head one way and another in a torment of memory. Again she laid her quiet hand on Laura's forehead.

"No, Mother, don't touch me," Laura said, frowning.

"It's Mary."

"Oh." Laura opened her eyes. "Oh, I guess I was dreaming."

Ella had said it would never be solved, and she was right. If only—but, Laura reminded herself cruelly, the dying cannot indulge in such hopes. Ella was three thousand miles away. Yet it was not clear whether that single thread that still held Laura alive and waiting might be Ella. Some message from Ella.

"Was there a letter from England in that pile?" Laura asked quite loudly. She had been slipping away when her mother came into the room, and now she was coming back.

"I'll look through them." Mary picked the pile up from the bedside table. "No, I don't see an English stamp."

"Oh." The disappointment was acute. She felt it as an actual pain, she who had been quite beyond pain a moment before. "It's so dark, Mary. Please turn on a light."

Mary had long since said good night, leaving the door open so Laura could see the light in the hall, when she heard the front door open and close and Ben's footsteps creeping up the stairs.

"I'm awake, Ben," she said.

"Is there something I can bring you, Mother?"

"No—but maybe you could come and sit here for a while in the dark. If you're not too tired."

"I'd like to do that," he said, coming close to kiss her cheek. Then he felt his way to the chaise and stretched out.

A bird somewhere outside gave a tentative cheep, then subsided. The headlights of a passing car lit up the far wall for a second, and Ben must have seen that the painting had been turned to the wall. But Laura felt incapable of explaining. She was very busy coming back from a long tunnel, forcing herself back.

"Ben?"

"Yes, Mother."

"Talk to me about your friends, about your life—in the hospital we had only begun."

"It must all seem pretty irrelevant," he said.

"No, one of the strangest things about this journey—" Laura lifted herself up a few inches so she could talk. "I have understood some things about—your androgynous world. I tried to talk to you about Ella. It's she who has accompanied me all these months, the only person I wanted to see. Why?"

"I don't know, Mother. Something unfinished maybe?"

"No. Nothing unfinished."

"There is no one I would want to see," Ben said after a short silence.

"No one?"

"Well," she seemed to hear some inner door opening in Ben, "maybe Pierre."

"Tell me . . ."

Ben gave a deep sigh, then there was silence.

"He was older than I, and I treated him badly in the end."

"Some good things can't last," Laura offered.

"He was really too much for me, too much of a person. I was such an unlicked cub then, so violent, so full of myself, so insecure about the painting, having to justify what could hardly be called a successful career."

"What did Pierre do?"

"Stage designs, mostly for opera—and he is a genius at that. I suppose I was jealous of all that fame and money."

"Yes."

"But he taught me a lot about love in his own peculiar way. He really cared. But he pushed me too hard, you see. I felt finally like a prisoner of his will . . . as far as the painting was concerned." Then Ben said quite firmly, "Yes, if I were dying I would want to see Pierre."

"Do you suppose he would know and come?" Laura whispered. She was thinking of Ella.

"Who knows? There have been plenty of people for each of us in ten years."

"Yes, but time and other people don't really matter," Laura said. "After all, I married Charles."

"Mother!"

It was not going to be possible, after all. Mothers and sons. Mothers and daughters. Ben was shocked.

"There are so many kinds of love, Ben. Marrying Charles was the best thing I ever did. He broke the spell of my overwhelming mother. He bore me away into the natural world, and it was high time."

She could hear the intent breathing on the chaise longue. But Laura was beginning to feel the effort of bridging so much, of explanations beyond her strength.

"You mean your feeling for Ella was not natural?"

"Oh, heavens, no. I meant mother's world was not natural."

"I don't quite understand."

Laura fell silent. She wanted to go back into the tunnel and not try to connect. It was too difficult, too intricate to put into words now. But she had started something, and she was acutely aware of the strain on Ben lying there in the dark, being asked to take in things that were hard for a son to take in about his mother.

"One thing about this journey has been an entirely new understanding about what women can mean for one another, and men for one another. I don't know why, but I have thought a lot about it, how the world is opening up, how separated we have all been, by fear and by taboos. How deprived."

"I suppose," Ben said, "when a whole life gets reckoned up, strange truths may be clear, may become clear, a new awareness of where the strong threads in the pattern began to be woven in."

"Yes, yes, that's it. You've said it for me, Ben."

"You were young when you and Ella met. Did she marry too?"

"Oh, yes." And then in a last burst of vision and recognition, Laura managed to bring it all into focus. "We were very different, and yet whenever we met it was as though we became one person in two bodies—we were never lovers, Ben—but there was a kind of understanding, of shared response to everything from art to landscapes, to food, to people. Being with her I became fully myself."

That was all Laura had strength for, and now she felt herself sinking away.

When the dawn came, Ben was still there fast asleep on the chaise longue, his mouth slightly open, looking like a young boy. For a long moment Laura looked at him and then turned away, for people asleep are too exposed. She saw what a long way he still had to go to grow up. How vulnerable he was. But she saw it from a great distance. As though her son lay there in a painting.

The morning turned out to be clear, bright, cool, and for the first time in days Laura drank a cup of tea without nausea. After so long a time without nourishment she felt revived by its warmth, a true cordial, and from the chaise longue she watched Mary changing the sheets, her silent presence and the way she patted the pillows a cordial in itself.

"Where's Ben?"

"Downstairs having his breakfast."

"We had quite a talk in the middle of the night."

"Tired you out, I expect."

"No, I feel better."

"Dr. Goodwin will be looking in on his way to the hospital—and—" Laura felt Mary's hesitation, "perhaps I should tell you that your sister Daphne and Daisy are coming this afternoon. I explained that you were very tired and couldn't talk. It was Miss Daphne I talked to, and she said they would come and take turns sitting with you, or do whatever they could."

"It's good when someone sits here and doesn't talk." Laura sighed. "I didn't think I would ever need that but I do."

"Daisy told me she had promised to sing you some songs," said Mary with a fleeting ironic look in Laura's direction, "She's bringing her guitar."

"Oh." Laura closed her eyes. They mustn't ask her to respond to anything. "Downstairs," she said, "ask her to sing downstairs."

"Yes, dear." Laura was so weak that she nearly fell over while Mary was getting her into a clean nightgown, and the clumsiness of it made them both fall into a fit of laughter.

"Oh, Mary, thank you," Laura murmured as she sank back into bed.

"There's the doctor now." Mary ran down to answer the doorbell.

"Well," said Jim as he came in and looked around,

"everything is in apple-pie order here, I see." He sat on the bed and laid his hand on hers gently.

"I'm like a Venetian glass," Laura said, smiling at him. "Touch me and I might break."

"I'm so sorry my little scheme about getting you down yesterday was such a dismal failure, Laura. I came to apologize."

"You were keeping a promise."

"Sometimes that can be a stupid thing to do."

"But," Laura said. It was something she had been planning to say ever since the hospital. "But you kept the important promise."

"Did I? What was that?"

"To let me have my own death. We managed to keep science out of it as much as possible, didn't we, Jim? I was so afraid you would feel you had to try chemotherapy or—something."

His hand closed on hers and pressed it.

"You never thought you were God."

Jim laughed. "No, I never did, that's a fact."

"Well, some doctors do, don't they?"

Jim didn't answer because he was busy taking her pulse. When he laid her wrist down he said, "I've learned a lot from you, Laura."

"I can't imagine what!"

For a moment he was silent, and Laura saw that he looked tired. His face was drawn. For all she knew he had been up half the night. "It's hard to put into words. I really can't. But all I can say is that it seems you have been living your death, living instead of dying it, I mean. It has been a meaningful journey, hasn't it?"

"Yes." Then Laura smiled. "Jim, today I feel well, better than I have in ages. I wonder why."

"It's called a remission," Jim said quietly.

"It won't last?"

"It might." He was standing now. "I must run along, Laura."

"Thanks for coming—and Jim, for everything."

He gave her a quick, intent look. And somehow, though there was no reason since she felt so much better, Laura knew that this was good-bye. There was no struggle to breathe this morning, yet Laura sensed that she was being borne away, borne on some great tide, and she was not afraid anymore. She was happy to lie there alone, on the cool, clean pillow, in the morning light and let herself go on the tide.

There was only a slight thread that still held her to the shore, and no doubt that would break soon.

She was dozing when Ben came in to kiss her good morning.

"I'll just sleep a little, Ben."

"I'll be next door in my room if you need anything." Later Mary came with chicken broth, but Laura didn't want it.

"I'd like to rinse my mouth, it's so dry," she said, "but I'm not hungry."

She was not floating; no images rose up from the past. But she was in some obscure, distant place in herself, waiting for something, she did not know for what. Not, she knew, for Daphne, though when later on Daphne was there beside her when she opened her eyes after a long sleep, she smiled and held Daphne's hand for a moment.

"Don't talk, darling," Daphne said, bending to kiss her. "I'll just sit here quietly."

"Thank you," Laura whispered.

After a while Laura said, "I want to die." She realized that she had never uttered those words before.

"You're so tired," Daphne said.

"Yes." Why then couldn't she let go? The warm afternoon light flooded the room, but she kept her eyes closed. Laura felt relieved of any obligation to recognize people or to respond. A quiet, loving presence was all she needed.

"I feel so well, it's strange," she said after a long interval.

Chapter XXIII

Laura was alerted to some event happening downstairs by Grindle's excited barks and the sound of a car driving away. Mary must have been keeping the dog downstairs today, for Laura had not seen him. She opened her eyes. Daphne whispered, "I'll go down and see who it is, maybe Daisy took an earlier plane."

But Laura felt sure it was not Daisy. She was swept by a wave of agitation and wished she had the strength to get up. That she could not do, but she did manage to lift herself into a semisitting position as Daphne ran down the stairs. The front door opened and closed. She heard women's voices but could not distinguish them one from another.

Is this a dream, Laura wondered? I'm dreaming the end of a journey. It's not real. So many times in the last weeks she had heard the door open and wondered who was there, whose feet would come up the stairs in a moment—Mary's or Jim Goodwin's or Ben's in the middle of the night. She closed her eyes. Could it be death opening the door at last, death coming up the stairs? Whoever it was on the way, Laura felt an imminence and was seized by a tremor so deep she held the sheet tightly in her hands to keep them from shaking. This waiting was the longest of all, and she silently begged that it not be prolonged.

Then she heard quick, light feet on the stairs.

Laura opened her eyes, but she couldn't see very well—there was a dim figure standing in the doorway.

"Darling, it's Ella."

"Oh, Snab." And then Ella was holding her cold, trembling hands, locking them into her own warmth. "Oh, Snab," Laura whispered, "I never thought you would come."

"I had to. The day before yesterday I simply knew I had to and got on the first flight I could."

Laura felt the tears pricking her lids and sliding down her cheeks one by one. "Pay no attention, I'm so weak."

"Don't try to talk."

But Laura wanted to explain. She whispered, "It's been such a long journey, but I couldn't let go—and I didn't know what I was waiting for."

"I'm here."

"Yes." Ella found a kleenex and gently wiped Laura's wet cheeks. "Don't go."

"I won't."

Then she opened her eyes. At first Ella looked very far away—she had white hair and her brown face was wrinkled—so much older than imagined, for Laura realized that in these last months she had thought of Ella as young. At least the dark eyes had not changed. They were deep and shining.

"It's been such a long time," Laura said, looking down at her own wasted hands. "But I've thought of you, of Paris, of us nearly every day since—since Jim Goodwin told me."

"I wanted to come when you first wrote, but I didn't dare." And Ella smiled her wary, secret smile that Laura remembered perfectly.

"Perfect peace," Laura whispered.

She didn't want to talk yet, there was fulfillment, such fulfillment simply in Ella's being there, sitting on the bed, touchable, real, not thousands of miles away, to be conjured up for comfort during the interminable nights of waiting for the dawn to come. She didn't want to talk yet, but she knew that she must summon herself back one last time. There were things she needed to say.

"You must be tired," she whispered. "Why don't you stretch out on the chaise longue. Later we'll talk."

"We don't have to," Ella said, lifting one of Laura's hands and kissing it. "Rest now."

A quiet flood of happiness lifted Laura as she lay there, not that flowing tide bearing her away, but the tide at full, just before it turns. She rested there.

Was it moments or hours later when Laura opened her eyes, feeling rested, and began to talk? Her breath came in short spasms, but at least there was still breath.

"Ella, can you hear me, Snab?"

"Perfectly," said Ella from the chaise longue.

"Lately nothing has seemed very real—the children—my sisters—but Sybille still looms, holding me back. Then I thought always of you, and thinking of you—oh, sitting in a deck chair in the Luxembourg gardens—"

"Looking up at the marvelous clouds, everything so alive."

"I had to go very deep. It's hard to explain."

"Take your time."

Laura rubbed a hand back and forth across her forehead trying to make the elusive connection. "I think this whole journey towards death has been in a way joining myself up with women, with all women."

"Yet Sybille still looms, holds you back."

"I have to go beyond her."

"Beyond being possessed, yes. Snab, since I have known what you were facing, I too have thought a lot about Sybille."

"Tell me."

"She was really very much afraid."

"Mamma?" Laura smiled. In the legend Sybille was fearless.

"Afraid of things she couldn't face in herself, I mean. So she tried to protect you from all those dangers."

"What dangers?" Laura asked in a faint voice.

"She carried out a terrible, rending war against her own nature, against passion itself perhaps, and the only way she could do it, maybe, was to play a role, to act what she wanted to be and couldn't be, a sovereign person in perfect control."

"She deprived us."

"Yes, she did, but in such a lavish way that it was hard to detect the real deprivations under all that high talk, and all those noble acts."

"But what did she deprive us of?"

"Daring to love what you loved and to like what you liked. You had such bloody good taste, you know. It was killing." Laura heard Ella's adorable laugh, a kind of chortle in her throat.

"I dared love you," Laura answered.

"She tried to come between us, you remember. In Switzerland it was made clear to me that it would be kinder if I did not come to see you again, the second time I got through the barrage."

"Why was she afraid? We were not lovers."

"No, but what we had was real on a level of reality she couldn't take, that threatened her in some way. It has lasted our lifetime, Snab."

"Yes," Laura said, sighing and lying back on the pillows staring at the ceiling. "Real."

"What did you mean just now about joining with women?"

There was a pause. Words had begun to be elusive. Laura could not pin the right ones down. They floated around in her head. Finally she managed to say, "Communion. Something women are only beginning to tap, to understand, a kind of tenderness towards each other as women. Just as Sybille was, we have been afraid of it. Snab, you are the only person I wanted to see, no one else—even though I told you not to come." After a moment she added, "I did talk to Ben because he understands these things. Only for him it has been complicated, harder maybe, because he is living a life still strange to many people." Laura now felt lifted up on a wave of strength. She could breathe more easily. "He didn't really want to hear about you, though."

"I suppose not. Mothers are not supposed to have these feelings, after all."

A smile floated in the air between them. Out of it Laura said, "Strange that we were not lovers. Why not?"

"My God, Laura, surely you remember the atmosphere of scandal, worse, of sin, around any such relationship at that time! We had been poisoned by the whole ethos, taught to be mortally afraid of what our bodies tried to teach us. Besides we were the marrying kind. A passionate love would have created terrible conflict. Snab, I truly believe we had the best of it."

"The best?"

"All that we did share—the way we could talk about everything, no holds barred. It was friendship at a mystical intensity. Every leaf on the trees in spring, every fountain, even the damp pavements under our feet, the sickly sweet smell of the Métro. It's all there imprinted on the spirit."

"Mmmm," Laura assented, but she was listening now also to what Ella's presence had released inside her, and that was almost beyond her power to put into words. After a while she murmured, "Tenderness. Sybille did not understand it. In a letter sometimes, but never in the flesh could she give it to us."

"And that, you feel, is what women can give each other, but have held back, and are learning?"

"To share the experience of being a woman. It's almost undiscovered territory, Snab, do you agree?"

"Yes, but difficult—perhaps impossible—between mothers and daughters."

"All the years she was growing up, Daisy was my antagonist, you know."

"Maybe that's natural. But your mother could never have allowed it. In her inimitable way she tried to be everything for her children—lover, friend, governess, teacher, and above all goddess! No wonder you were snowed under and nearly died of her, every one of you."

Suddenly Laura was able to sit up, pulled up by revelation. "Yes," she said in her normal voice, "but she was to be all those things for her friends, both men and women, and that's why she was great in her strange way!" Laura felt light breaking inside her, reached her hand out toward Ella. "I think I begin to see her. At last."

The effort had been immense, and now she lay back panting.

"Rest, Snab, rest."

"I didn't cough," Laura whispered. "That's the miracle."

"Shhhh." Ella put a finger to her lips.

There was a long silence. And within it Laura knew the tide had turned and was beginning to ebb. Ella was there, not to be touched again, but strangely Laura did not want her to come closer. It was enough that she was there.

The doorbell rang. Again there were voices in the hall. Daphne, Laura thought she heard, then Daisy whispering, and a little later the guitar being softly strummed.

"It's Daisy," she murmured, "to play for me."

"Do you want her to come up?" Ella asked.

"No." Then, after a silence, "Only you."

There was nothing now, no silent thread to hold her back. She had only to let go, let the tide gently bear her away. She felt light, light as a leaf on a strong current.

Some time later—am I still here in my room?—she heard a young voice somewhere far off, singing, "Fais dodo, Colas, mon p'tit frère, Fais dodo." Sybille's song.

Daughter singing to a mother, mother singing to a daughter—she could barely hear it now. Then she was floating away. So strange, she could see Ella down there, holding her hand, but she could not feel it. She had let go.